Christmas Stories from Mississippi

Christmas Stories from Mississippi

EDITED BY

Judy H. Tucker and Charline R. McCord

ILLUSTRATIONS BY *Wyatt Waters*

UNIVERSITY PRESS OF MISSISSIPPI JACKSON

Publication of this book was made possible in part by the
SELBY AND RICHARD McRAE FOUNDATION

"A Worn Path"; the excerpt from *Light in August*; "Clara's Star"; "Christmas 1976"; "The Morning Stove"; "Sermon with Meath"; "Home for Christmas"; "Big Red"; "Presents"; "Land of the Giants"; "Christmas Lights"; and "Poets, Plumbers, and the Baby Jesus" are works of fiction. Names, characters, incidents, and places are fictitious or are used fictitiously. The characters are products of the authors' imaginations and do not represent any actual persons.

"A Worn Path" from *A Curtain of Green and Other Stories*, copyright © 1941 & renewed 1969 by Eudora Welty, reprinted by permission of Harcourt, Inc. Excerpt from *Light in August* by William Faulkner, copyright © 1932 & renewed 1960 by William Faulkner, reprinted by permission of Random House, Inc. "Surviving the Holiday Season: One Woman's Crusade Against Christmas" by Ellen Gilchrist, *Harper's Bazaar*, December 1994, reprinted by permission of the author. "Quilts: Kiver for My Children" reprinted from *The Last Train North* by Clifton L. Taulbert, copyright © 1992 by Clifton L. Taulbert; used by permission of Council Oak Books, 1290 Chestnut St., San Francisco, CA 94109. "Sermon with Meath" by Barry Hannah, *Oxford American*, January/February 1997, reprinted by permission of *Oxford American* and the author. "Presents" by Elizabeth Spencer from *The Stories of Elizabeth Spencer*, copyright © 1981, Doubleday & Co. Inc., reprinted by permission of the author. Excerpt from *The Peddler's Grandson: Growing Up Jewish in Mississippi*, copyright © 1999 by Edward Cohen, reprinted by permission of University Press of Mississippi. "Christmases Gone Revisited" from *Homecomings*, copyright © 1989 by Willie Morris, reprinted by permission of University Press of Mississippi. All other stories reprinted by permission of their respective authors.

Library of Congress Cataloging-in-Publication Data
Christmas stories from Mississippi / edited by Judy H. Tucker and Charline R. McCord ;
illustrations by Wyatt Waters.
    p. cm.
  ISBN 1-57806-381-7 (alk. paper)
    1. Christmas stories, American. 2. Mississippi—Social life and customs—Fiction. 3. Short stories, American—Mississippi. I. Tucker, Judy H. II. McCord, Charline R.

PS648.C45 C458 2001
813'.0108334—dc21   2001026041

British Library Cataloging-in-Publication Data available

Contents

CONTENTS

Christmas Stories from Mississippi

A Worn Path

Eudora Welty

It was December—a bright frozen day in the early morning. Far out in the country there was an old Negro woman with her head tied in a red rag, coming along a path through the pinewoods. Her name was Phoenix Jackson. She was very old and small and she walked slowly in the dark pine shadows, moving a little from side to side in her steps, with the balanced heaviness and lightness of a pendulum in a grandfather clock. She carried a thin, small cane made from an umbrella, and with this she kept tapping the frozen earth in front of her. This made a grave and persistent noise in the still air, that seemed meditative like the chirping of a solitary little bird.

She wore a dark striped dress reaching down to her shoe tops, and an equally long apron of bleached sugar sacks, with a full pocket: all neat and tidy, but every time she took a step she might have fallen over her shoelaces, which dragged from her unlaced shoes. She looked straight ahead. Her eyes were blue with age. Her skin had a pattern all its own of numberless branching wrinkles and as though a whole little tree stood in the middle of her forehead, but a golden color ran underneath, and the two knobs of her cheeks were illumined by a yellow burning under the dark. Under the red rag her hair came down on her neck in the frailest of ringlets, still black, and with an odor like copper.

Now and then there was a quivering in the thicket. Old Phoenix said, "Out of my way, all you foxes, owls, beetles, jack rabbits, coons and wild animals! . . . Keep out from under these feet, little bob-whites. . . . Keep the big wild hogs out of my path. Don't let none of those come running my direction. I got a long way." Under her small black-freckled hand her cane, limber as a buggy whip, would switch at the brush as if to rouse up any hiding things.

On she went. The woods were deep and still. The sun made the pine needles almost too bright to look at, up where the wind rocked. The cones dropped as light as feathers. Down in the hollow was the mourning dove—it was not too late for him.

The path ran up a hill. "Seem like there is chains about my feet, time I get this far," she said, in the voice of argument old people keep to use with themselves. "Something always take a hold of me on this hill—pleads I should stay."

After she got to the top she turned and gave a full, severe look behind her where she had come. "Up through pines," she said at length. "Now down through oaks."

Her eyes opened their widest, and she started down gently. But before she got to the bottom of the hill a bush caught her dress.

Her fingers were busy and intent, but her skirts were full and long, so that before she could pull them free in one place they were caught in another. It was not possible to allow the dress to tear. "I in the thorny bush," she said. "Thorns, you doing your appointed work. Never want to let folks pass, no sir. Old eyes thought you was a pretty little *green* bush."

Finally, trembling all over, she stood free, and after a moment dared to stoop for her cane.

"Sun so high!" she cried, leaning back and looking, while the thick tears went over her eyes. "The time getting all gone here."

At the foot of this hill was a place where a log was laid across the creek.

"Now comes the trial," said Phoenix.

Putting her right foot out, she mounted the log and shut her eyes. Lifting her skirt, leveling her cane fiercely before her, like a festival figure in some parade, she began to march across. Then she opened her eyes and she was safe on the other side.

"I wasn't as old as I thought," she said.

But she sat down to rest. She spread her skirts on the bank around her and folded her hands over her knees. Up above her was a tree in a pearly cloud of mistletoe. She did not dare to close her eyes, and when a little boy brought her a plate with a slice of marble-cake on it she spoke to him. "That would be acceptable," she said. But when she went to take it there was just her own hand in the air.

So she left that tree and had to go through a barbed-wire fence. There she had to creep and crawl, spreading her knees and stretching her fingers like a baby trying to climb the steps. But she talked loudly to herself: she could not let her dress be torn now, so late in the day, and she could not pay for having her arm or her leg sawed off if she got caught fast where she was.

At last she was safe through the fence and risen up out in the clearing. Big dead trees, like black men with one arm, were standing in the purple stalks of the withered cotton field. There sat a buzzard.

"Who you watching?"

In the furrow she made her way along.

"Glad this not the season for bulls," she said, looking sideways, "and the good Lord made his snakes to curl up and sleep in the winter. A pleasure I don't see no two-headed snake coming around that tree, where it come once. It took a while to get by him, back in the summer."

She passed through the old cotton and went into a field of dead corn. It whispered and shook and was taller than her head. "Through the maze now," she said, for there was no path.

Then there was something tall, black, and skinny there, moving before her.

At first she took it for a man. It could have been a man dancing in the field. But she stood still and listened, and it did not make a sound. It was as silent as a ghost.

"Ghost," she said sharply, "who be you the ghost of? For I have heard of nary death close by."

But there was no answer—only the ragged dancing in the wind.

She shut her eyes, reached out her hand, and touched a sleeve. She found a coat and inside that an emptiness, cold as ice.

"You scarecrow," she said. Her face lighted. "I ought to be shut up for good," she said with laughter. "My senses is gone. I too old. I the oldest people I ever know. Dance, old scarecrow," she said, "while I dancing with you."

She kicked her foot over the furrow, and with mouth drawn down, shook her head once or twice in a little strutting way. Some husks blew down and whirled in streamers about her skirts.

Then she went on, parting her way from side to side with the cane, through the whispering field. At last she came to the end, to a wagon track where the silver grass blew between the red ruts. The quail were walking around like pullets, seeming all dainty and unseen.

"Walk pretty," she said. "This the easy place. This the easy going."

She followed the track, swaying through the quiet bare fields, through the little strings of trees silver in their dead leaves, past cabins silver from weather, with the doors and windows boarded shut, all like old women under a spell sitting there. "I walking in their sleep," she said, nodding her head vigorously.

In a ravine she went where a spring was silently flowing through a hollow log. Old Phoenix bent and drank. "Sweet-gum makes the water sweet," she said, and drank more. "Nobody know who made this well, for it was here when I was born."

The track crossed a swampy part where the moss hung as white as lace from every limb. "Sleep on, alligators, and blow your bubbles." Then the track went into the road.

Deep, deep the road went down between the high green-colored banks. Overhead the live-oaks met, and it was as dark as a cave.

A black dog with a lolling tongue came up out of the weeds by the ditch. She was meditating, and not ready, and when he came at her she only hit him a little with her cane. Over she went in the ditch, like a little puff of milkweed.

Down there, her senses drifted away. A dream visited her, and she reached her hand up, but nothing reached down and gave her a pull. So she lay there and presently went to talking. "Old woman," she said to herself, "that black dog come up out of the weeds to stall you off, and now there he sitting on his fine tail, smiling at you."

A white man finally came along and found her—a hunter, a young man, with his dog on a chain.

"Well, Granny!" he laughed. "What are you doing there?"

"Lying on my back like a June-bug waiting to be turned over, mister," she said, reaching up her hand.

He lifted her up, gave her a swing in the air, and set her down. "Anything broken, Granny?"

"No sir, them old dead weeds is springy enough," said Phoenix, when she had got her breath. "I thank you for your trouble."

"Where do you live, Granny?" he asked, while the two dogs were growling at each other.

"Away back yonder, sir, behind the ridge. You can't even see it from here."

"On your way home?"

"No sir, I going to town."

"Why, that's too far! That's as far as I walk when I come out myself, and I get something for my trouble." He patted the stuffed bag he carried, and there hung down a little closed claw. It was one of the bob-whites, with its beak hooked bitterly to show it was dead. "Now you go on home, Granny!"

"I bound to go to town, mister," said Phoenix. "The time come around."

He gave another laugh, filling the whole landscape. "I know you old colored people! Wouldn't miss going to town to see Santa Claus!"

But something held old Phoenix very still. The deep lines in her face went into a fierce and different radiation. Without warning, she had seen with her own eyes a flashing nickel fall out of the man's pocket onto the ground.

"How old are you, Granny?" he was saying.

"There is no telling, mister," she said, "no telling."

Then she gave a little cry and clapped her hands and said, "Git on away from here, dog! Look! Look at that dog!" She laughed as if in admiration. "He ain't scared of nobody. He a big black dog." She whispered, "Sic him!"

"Watch me get rid of that cur," said the man. "Sic him, Pete! Sic him!"

Phoenix heard the dogs fighting and heard the man running and throwing sticks. She even heard a gunshot. But she was slowly bending forward by that time, further and further forward, the lids stretched down over her eyes, as if she were doing this in her sleep. Her chin was lowered almost to her knees. The yellow palm of her hand came out from the fold of her apron. Her fingers slid down and along the ground under the piece of money with the grace and care they would have in lifting an egg from under a setting hen. Then she slowly straightened up, she stood erect, and the nickel was in her apron pocket. A bird flew by. Her lips moved. "God watching me the whole time. I come to stealing."

The man came back, and his own dog panted about them. "Well, I scared him off that time," he said, and then he laughed and lifted his gun and pointed it at Phoenix.

She stood straight and faced him.

"Doesn't the gun scare you?" he said, still pointing it.

"No sir, I seen plenty go off closer by, in my day, and for less than what I done," she said, holding utterly still.

He smiled, and shouldered the gun. "Well, Granny," he said, "you must be a hundred years old, and scared of nothing. I'd give you a dime if I had any money with me. But you take my advice and stay home, and nothing will happen to you."

"I bound to go on my way, mister," said Phoenix. She inclined her head in the red rag. Then they went in different directions, but she could hear the gun shooting again and again over the hill.

She walked on. The shadows hung from the oak trees to the road like curtains. Then she smelled wood-smoke, and smelled the river, and she saw a steeple and the cabins on their steep steps. Dozens of little black children whirled around her. There ahead was Natchez shining. Bells were ringing. She walked on.

In the paved city it was Christmas time. There were red and green electric lights strung and crisscrossed everywhere, and all turned on in the daytime. Old Phoenix would have been lost if she had not distrusted her eyesight and depended on her feet to know where to take her.

She paused quietly on the sidewalk where people were passing by. A lady came along in the crowd, carrying an armful of red-, green- and silver-wrapped presents; she gave off perfume like the red roses in hot summer, and Phoenix stopped her.

"Please, missy, will you lace up my shoe?" She held up her foot.

"What do you want, Grandma?"

"See my shoe," said Phoenix. "Do all right for out in the country, but wouldn't look right to go in a big building."

"Stand still then, Grandma," said the lady. She put her packages down on the sidewalk beside her and laced and tied both shoes tightly.

"Can't lace 'em with a cane," said Phoenix. "Thank you, missy. I doesn't mind asking a nice lady to tie up my shoe, when I gets out on the street."

Moving slowly and from side to side, she went into the big building, and into a tower of steps, where she walked up and around and around until her feet knew to stop.

She entered a door, and there she saw nailed up on the wall the document that had been stamped with the gold seal and framed in the gold frame, which matched the dream that was hung up in her head.

"Here I be," she said. There was a fixed and ceremonial stiffness over her body.

"A charity case, I suppose," said an attendant who sat at the desk before her.

But Phoenix only looked above her head. There was sweat on her face, the wrinkles in her skin shone like a bright net.

"Speak up, Grandma," the woman said. "What's your name? We must have your history, you know. Have you been here before? What seems to be the trouble with you?"

Old Phoenix only gave a twitch to her face as if a fly were bothering her.

"Are you deaf?" cried the attendant.

But then the nurse came in.

"Oh, that's just old Aunt Phoenix," she said. "She doesn't come for herself—she has a little grandson. She makes these trips just as regular as clockwork. She lives away back off the Old Natchez Trace." She bent down. "Well, Aunt Phoenix, why don't you just take a seat? We won't keep you standing after your long trip." She pointed.

The old woman sat down, bolt upright in the chair.

"Now, how is the boy?" asked the nurse.

Old Phoenix did not speak.

"I said, how is the boy?"

But Phoenix only waited and stared straight ahead, her face very solemn and withdrawn into rigidity.

"Is his throat any better?" asked the nurse. "Aunt Phoenix, don't you hear me? Is your grandson's throat any better since the last time you came for the medicine?"

With her hands on her knees, the old woman waited, silent, erect and motionless, just as if she were in armor.

"You mustn't take up our time this way, Aunt Phoenix," the nurse said. "Tell us quickly about your grandson, and get it over. He isn't dead, is he?"

At last there came a flicker and then a flame of comprehension across her face, and she spoke.

"My grandson. It was my memory had left me. There I sat and forgot why I made my long trip."

"Forgot?" The nurse frowned. "After you came so far?"

Then Phoenix was like an old woman begging a dignified forgiveness for waking up frightened in the night. "I never did go to school, I was too old at the Surrender," she said in a soft voice. "I'm an old woman without an education. It was my memory fail me. My little grandson, he is just the same, and I forgot it in the coming."

"Throat never heals, does it?" said the nurse, speaking in a loud, sure voice to old Phoenix. By now she had a card with something written on it, a little list. "Yes. Swallowed lye. When was it?—January—two, three years ago—"

Phoenix spoke unasked now. "No, missy, he not dead, he just the same. Every little while his throat begin to close up again, and he not able to swallow. He not get his breath. He not able to help himself. So the time come around, and I go on another trip for the soothing medicine."

"All right. The doctor said as long as you came to get it, you could have it," said the nurse. "But it's an obstinate case."

"My little grandson, he sit up there in the house all wrapped up, waiting by himself," Phoenix went on. "We is the only two left in the world. He suffer and it don't seem to put him back at all. He got a sweet look. He going to last. He wear a little patch quilt and peep out holding his mouth open like a little bird. I remembers so plain now. I not going to forget him again, no, the whole enduring time. I could tell him from all the others in creation."

"All right." The nurse was trying to hush her now. She brought her a bottle of medicine. "Charity," she said, making a check mark in a book.

Old Phoenix held the bottle close to her eyes, and then carefully put it into her pocket.

"I thank you," she said.

"It's Christmas time, Grandma," said the attendant. "Could I give you a few pennies out of my purse?"

"Five pennies is a nickel," said Phoenix stiffly.

"Here's a nickel," said the attendant.

Phoenix rose carefully and held out her hand. She received the nickel and then fished the other nickel out of her pocket and laid it beside the new one. She stared at her palm closely, with her head on one side.

Then she gave a tap with her cane on the floor.

"This is what come to me to do," she said. "I going to the store and buy my child a little windmill they sells, made out of paper. He going to find it hard to believe there such a thing in the world. I'll march myself back where he waiting, holding it straight up in this hand."

She lifted her free hand, gave a little nod, turned around, and walked out of the doctor's office. Then her slow step began on the stairs, going down.

Light in August

William Faulkner

One evening they came to the schoolroom and got him. It was two weeks before Christmas. Two of the young women—the dietitian was not one—took him to the bathroom and washed him and combed his damp hair and dressed him in clean overalls and fetched him to the matron's office. In the office sat a man, a stranger. And he looked at the man and he knew before the matron even spoke. Perhaps memory knowing, knowing beginning to remember; perhaps even desire, since five is still too young to have learned enough despair to hope. Perhaps he remembered suddenly the train ride and the food, since even memory did not go much further back than that. "Joseph," the matron said, "how would you like to go and live with some nice people in the country?"

He stood there, his ears and face red and burning with harsh soap and harsh towelling, in the stiff new overalls, listening to the stranger. He had looked once and saw a thickish man with a close brown beard and hair cut close though not recently. Hair and beard both had a hard, vigorous quality, unsilvered, as though the pigmentation were impervious to the forty and more years which the face revealed. The eyes were lightcolored, cold. He wore a suit of hard, decent black. On his knee rested a black hat held in a blunt clean hand shut, even on the soft felt of the hat, into a fist. Across his vest ran a heavy silver watch chain. His thick black shoes were planted side by side; they had been polished by hand. Even the child of five years, looking at him, knew that he did not use tobacco himself and would not tolerate it in others. But he did not look at the man because of his eyes.

He could feel the man looking at him though, with a stare cold and intent and yet not deliberately harsh. It was the same stare with which he might have examined a horse or a second hand plow, convinced beforehand that he would see flaws, convinced beforehand that he would buy. His voice was deliberate, infrequent, ponderous; the voice of a man who demanded that he be listened to not so much with attention but in silence. "And you either cannot or will not tell me anything more about his parentage."

The matron did not look at him. Behind her glasses her eyes apparently had jellied, for the time at least. She said immediately, almost a little too immediately: "We make no effort to ascertain their parentage. As I told you before, he was left on the doorstep here on Christmas eve will be five years this two weeks. If the child's parentage is important to you, you had better not adopt one at all."

"I would not mean just that," the stranger said. His tone now was a little placative. He contrived at once to apologize without surrendering one jot of his conviction. "I would have thought to talk with Miss Atkins (this was the dietitian's name) since it was with her I have been in correspondence."

Again the matron's voice was cold and immediate, speaking almost before his had ceased: "I can perhaps give you as much information about this or any other of our children as Miss Atkins can, since her official connection here is only with the diningroom and kitchen. It just happened that in this case she was kind enough to act as secretary in our correspondence with you."

"It's no matter," the stranger said. "It's no matter. I had just thought . . ."

"Just thought what? We force no one to take our children, nor do we force the children to go against their wishes, if their reasons are sound ones. That is a matter for the two parties to settle between themselves. We only advise."

"Ay," the stranger said. "It's no matter, as I just said to you. I've no doubt the tyke will do. He will find a good home with Mrs. McEachern and me. We are not young now, and we like quiet ways. And he'll find no fancy food and no idleness. Nor neither more work than will be good for him. I make no doubt that with us he will grow up to fear God and abhor idleness and vanity despite his origin."

Thus the promissory note which he had signed with a tube of toothpaste on that afternoon two months ago was recalled, the yet oblivious executor of it sitting wrapped in a clean horse blanket, small, shapeless, immobile, on the seat of a light buggy jolting through the December twilight up a frozen and rutted lane. They had driven all that day. At noon the man had fed him, taking from beneath the seat a cardboard box containing country food cooked three days ago. But only now did the man speak to him. He spoke a single word, pointing up the lane with a mittened fist which clutched the whip, toward a single light which shown in the dusk. "Home," he said. The child said nothing. The man looked down at him. The man was bundled too against the cold, squat, big, shapeless, somehow rocklike, indomitable, not so much ungentle as ruthless. "I said, there is your home." Still the child didn't answer. He had never seen a home, so there was nothing for him to say about it. And he was not old enough to talk and say nothing at the same time. "You will find food and shelter and the care of Christian people," the man said. "And the work within your strength that will keep you out of mischief. For I will have you learn soon that the two abominations are sloth and idle thinking, the two virtues are work and the fear of God." Still the child said nothing. He had neither ever worked nor feared God. He knew less about God than about work. He had seen work going on in the person of men with rakes and shovels about the playground six days each week, but God had only occurred on Sunday. And then—save for the concomitant ordeal of cleanliness—it was music that pleased the ear and words that did not trouble the ear at all—on the whole, pleasant, even if a little tiresome. He said nothing at all. The buggy jolted on, the stout, wellkept team eagering, homing, barning.

There was one other thing which he was not to remember until later, when memory no longer accepted his face, accepted the surface of remembering. They were in the matron's office; he standing motionless, not looking at the stranger's eyes which he could feel upon him, waiting for the stranger to say what his eyes were thinking. Then it came: "Christmas. A heathenish name. Sacrilege. I will change that."

"That will be your legal right," the matron said. "We are not interested in what they are called, but in how they are treated."

But the stranger was not listening to anyone anymore than he was talking to anyone. "From now on his name will be McEachern."

"That will be suitable," the matron said. "To give him your name."

"He will eat my bread and he will observe my religion," the stranger said. "Why should he not bear my name?"

The child was not listening. He was not bothered. He did not especially care, anymore than if the man had said the day was hot when it was not hot. He didn't even bother to say to himself *My name aint McEachern. My name is Christmas.* There was no need to bother about that yet. There was plenty of time.

"Why not, indeed?" the matron said.

Clara's Star

Judy H. Tucker

It was bitterly cold the day Myriah left. The relentless wind swept down out of the Billy Hills and through the hickory and the oak trees that grew in The Other Place. Snow had just begun to fall early on that Sunday afternoon. There was only a light dusting of powder covering the ground, and I stood for a long time watching her footprints disappear under the snow. Not that I had a premonition of what was to follow, and if I had, what could I have done? Chased after her, caught her and held her, locked her in the cellar? How long can you stay the will of one so strong-headed as that? Once her mind was made up, she would not have been dissuaded. I stood there and looked at the world covered in the fresh snow because it was so beautiful and because it was a way of measuring my time left on this earth, another snowfall, another Christmas, another year. Eighty Decembers I have seen, and the future is unknown, which is all for the best. One does not need to see the future; it would be too much to bear, for as surely as there are Christmas trees and candy canes and little girls laughing, there will also be tears and mourning.

This was to be a Christmas of bitter cold and bitter lessons learned.

When first Annabelle asked "Where's Mama?" I said she'll be right back, feeling full confidence in my words. I'd seen her dressing for the cold, putting on a sweater and then over that a red woolen coat that flared out from her slim waist, then the boots, black leather they were, lined with fur. Fancy boots but warm. Over her arm she carried the little velvet bag with the drawstring that I had sewn up from scraps as my present to her on her birthday just one month previous. She kissed her girls but I did not notice that she tarried over-long in her goodbyes. She held their faces in her gloved hands and kissed their foreheads and their cheeks. Three kisses each she gave them, but that was normal. She was given to much display of affection. She slipped a little on the step as she was leaving, turned her ankle, but it did not stop her. Wherever it was she was going, she had her mind made up and there was no stopping her. I did not ask, for that was not my nature, as it was not hers to have tolerated such questions.

It had been obvious that morning that a storm was brewing. The sky was leaden and the air was heavy, still and cold. "It smells like snow," I said.

"You can smell snow, Aunt Maude?" Clara asked, raising her eyebrows at me just like her mother did. In the next instance Annabelle rushed at her sister and they were off again, racing through the house.

"You're as wild as a bunch of Indians," I said.

Clara stopped, cocked her head, looked at me and said, "Wild Indians, Aunt Maude? Are all the Indians wild?"

"All the ones I ever knew were wild," I said.

"Wild as March hares?" asked Clara.

"Wild as March hares," I agreed, "but they couldn't hold a candle to you girls."

"It's snowing! It's snowing!" Annabelle cried and indeed it was.

Later that afternoon, Myriah and the two girls turned away from the window where they had been watching the snowflakes drift down, and we, foregoing our Sunday afternoon nap, went about our business of preparing the house for Christmas. We lit the first candle of Advent. A bright fire leapt and crackled in the fireplace. Annabelle, the little one, clamored about my knees, asking how many days 'til Christmas. I assured them Christmas would come, and that Saint Nick would be watching them, "But first," I said, "before trees and wreaths and toys and presents, we must think of the Christ Child born so far away and long ago."

We took out the crèche that was stored in the attic and we put out baby

Jesus in his manger on the table in front of the parlor window and we placed Mary beside him.

"Where's the father?" cried the little one, Annabelle, who looks so much like Myriah.

"The father," said Myriah, "where indeed?"

"God's the father," said the older girl, Clara. She took the figure of Joseph and placed him behind Mary where he stood looking over her shoulder at the babe lying on the hay. "Joseph stands in for the father," Clara said.

"And aren't you so clever, learning your catechism so well," said her mother Myriah.

"Here's hot apple cider with cinnamon sticks," I said, bringing in a tray of steaming cups.

The crèche along with the painted glass balls and the silver tinsel came out of an old steamer trunk Myriah brought with her when she married my great-nephew Rob. The old trunk held many things, but only Myriah knew what they were. Once, when Rob gave a party for his business friends and a ladle was needed for the punch, Myriah dashed out of the room and raced up to the attic to her trunk and brought back a ladle black with tarnish. We rubbed and we polished until at last it lay there on the table—heavy, ornate silver of the finest sort. There was an initial on the handle but in the way of that Florentine script, it was impossible to tell if it was a T or an L or even a C, though I tried to decipher it. Myriah sat back and beamed, so proud she was of her contribution. I have to confess, I tried once to look in that trunk but it was locked and the key was hidden away on Myriah's person. I'm glad I did not break that seal.

This house was my father's house and before that his father's, and back like that since 1834. This land has been my family's land since the last Indian left for the Reservation. This house that's seen so much—hooped skirts, music and frolic; war, depression, and yellow fever—the pendulum has swung between the good times and the bad—but never has this old house suffered the way it did the day Myriah walked down those steps out into the snow on the first day of Advent in the year of our Lord 1939.

I can remember back many Christmases in this house. Before electricity even, when the only light came from candles and fires in the hearth. My, it could be cold, especially when taking a bath. Papa would bring up a zinc tub from the kitchen to the family parlor and heat the water over the open fire so we could bathe without catching our deaths. I can remember when the kitchen was set apart, off the back porch across a breezeway to keep down the danger of a grease-fire burning the whole house up. Papa was the one who first moved the kitchen into the house. But Rob, when he brought Myriah home, he turned this old house upside down making it modern for his bride, putting that fancy bath in what used to be Big Mama's sewing room, taking in the sleeping porch for her sitting room. To pay for all that, he sold the timber off the New Ground (it was new in 1885). Everything changed in this old house when Myriah came. And by the same token, it changed again, oh! how it changed when she left. I thought I would never hear a laugh again inside these walls, or see a Christmas tree lit to a fare-thee-well, ceiling-high and smelling of the forest.

Myriah and the girls had gone to look for a Christmas tree on the previous Thursday. They would tag the chosen tree and leave it in the forest. Zan, the college boy who helped around the place, would go back and cut it and bring it home. That morning Myriah, Clara, and Annabelle took off early when the smoke from the chimney made a flat line across the morning sky, a sure sign of coming cold. Just that morning we'd seen the geese fly over, with a great honking, in a vee that stretched from horizon to horizon. Zan had called us out to see this sight and it was something to behold against that clear blue sky.

That morning, as Myriah and the girls prepared to make their pilgrimage to The Other Place to choose their tree, I heard Clara warn Annabelle, "Now you mustn't wear your good coat. Put on this old one because you know the briar patch around Hopaki will rip it to shreds."

"Hopaki?" I said to her. "Where did you come up with that gibberish?"

"Oh, you call it The Other Place, Aunt Maude," Clara said, "we call it Hopaki." And she skipped away.

The air was so clear that the laughter of Myriah and the girls carried all the way across the hay field now lying fallow in the winter. I heard their shouts as they disappeared into the edge of the woods at The Other Place which lay on a rise at the foot of the Billy Hills. Myriah especially loved The Other Place and would often go there, fight her way past the bramble, and wander about in the woods for hours at a time, lost it seemed to the present, lost to some world beyond Fairhope.

The best Christmas trees grew in The Other Place and a Christmas tree was the only tree that was allowed to be cut from that piece of land. The Other Place is special, a place where the wind blows without stopping, making a low moaning sound among the ancient trees, a sound that spooks me still. It is a plot of virgin timber that my great grandfather gave to his bride, the first Clara, on their wedding day with the promise that the trees would not be cut for as long as she did not cut her hair. Black Irish she was, and her mane of hair was her pride and joy and his also. Now our Clara, Rob and Myriah's Clara, has that kind of hair, thick and heavy, though she could as well have gotten it from her mother. Myriah's hair is so long and dark and thick that I was called upon to come to her bedroom and comb out the tangles after her shampoo. Who will comb her hair, I wondered, now that she is gone?

I called Rob at 3:30 at the bank where he had gone to take care of some personal business after church and Sunday dinner. "I don't want to alarm you," I said, "but Myriah left the house on foot over two hours ago and we have not heard from her since. The weather has turned bad out there." Out the window, I watched the snow fall, settle on the cedars that line the lane, already bending them down toward the ground. I heard a sharp snap, like the shot of a rifle, but it was only the sound of a tree limb breaking under the weight of the snow. The world that had been so bright and sunny yesterday was now all of a color, shades of shadow. "No," I said, "she did not say where she was going. She dressed warm and took her coin purse and wore her boots and left out the front door." Her footprints had long disappeared under the snowfall.

Rob was quiet. Finally he said, "Thank you, Aunt Maude. Thank you for everything. I will be home directly."

I had begun to worry almost as soon as Myriah disappeared around the curve in the lane. If I am honest with myself, I was worried because I had heard her quarrel with Rob on the evening past. They were in their bedroom and I was lighting the fire in the girls' room when I heard their voices rise in anger. I rushed out, and down the stairs so I would not hear, for it hurt me to hear them quarrel, which they so rarely did.

The girls had been quiet through that Sunday afternoon, the day their mother left, going to the windows and staring out at the snow for long periods of time, poking at the fire, playing with the kitten. They tucked their heads down and hardly spoke a word even when a limb from a pine tree cracked and fell on the power line and the house went dark. Ordinarily this would have been a cause of gaiety, getting out the candles and stoking the fire, but they did not rise to the occasion. There was no talk about Santa Claus or whispers about the presents they were making, nor teasing each other, not once asking, as they normally would have, to be allowed to play in the snow. Those poor little girls, they knew. They felt, far sooner than they knew, that something was terribly wrong that day.

About dusk, the girls heard their father come in the front door and they rushed out of the warm kitchen where we were making cookies and raced through the cold parlor and down the frigid hall. Because the expense of fuel was so great, we did not heat the entire house except on holidays when we laid fires in all the rooms and lit them as needed. When I was a girl, we had as many as a dozen fireplaces going at once, all ablaze, but then there came a time when all the help was down with the fever, and none of us left standing was able to use a cross-cut saw, so we were pushed to tear down the corn crib for wood to heat the cookstove in the kitchen.

"Annabelle!" I heard my nephew cry. "Clara!" He kicked the front door closed behind him. He came into the kitchen carrying one girl in each arm. For a little while there, we seemed to forget the awful truth that stared us in the face—Myriah's empty chair. Clara set the table for supper and lit the candles.

"Candles!" cried Annabelle, thinking it was a special party.

"They used them every night in the olden days," said Clara, who at seven was smarter than some adults that I could name, but will not out of respect. "There were no electric lights," Clara explained to her sister, "when Aunt Maude was a little girl."

The children ate their supper which was meager, as Myriah was the one in the house who loved to cook. What concoctions she came up with! Her *blanc mange* was without parallel. I, on the other hand, have never learned how to do much more than make tea and boil an egg. Why, Clara is a better cook than I am. Clara, the wise one, reminded me of my sister Hannah who has been gone now, lo these many years.

At eight, Rob took the girls up to bed. Not much had changed in their bedroom since I slept there beside Hannah. We'd slept, as Clara and Annabelle do now, in a huge spool bed under great piles of cover. Zan had laid a fire and I had gone up earlier to strike a match to it. Usually, the fire was more for atmosphere than anything else because by now the house had a central furnace, part of Rob's remodeling. Except, of course, that night there was no electricity and the fire was the sole source of our heat.

When Rob came downstairs from tucking in the girls, I asked him if he'd called the sheriff.

"The sheriff said it is not a matter for the law. She went of her own accord. She's no doubt with her family." Rob dropped his head.

Ha! I thought. Suddenly she has a family? It was the first I'd heard of it.

"What happened here, Aunt Maude? Was there anything unusual about the day?"

"No," I said. "After you left to go to the bank, we lit the first candle of Advent and by then the snow had begun to fall. Myriah excused herself and went upstairs and when she came down a little later, she was dressed to go out. Had on her woolen coat and her boots."

"She took no baggage with her?"

"No, none at all. Only the little velvet coin purse." And then I remembered. "Yesterday," I said, "yesterday, she got a letter."

"A letter?" Rob asked. "Did you see it?"

"No, Zan went to the mailbox. He put the mail on the highboy there by the pantry, but he handed Myriah an envelope."

"And?" Rob hunched forward waiting.

"And she looked at the letter and got up and left the room."

We called for Zan who came out of his room which used to be the butler's pantry, but he could tell us nothing. Except that the letter was handwritten, addressed to Mrs. Myriah Thornton. Written in a spidery hand-writing in ink. "And no, before you ask, I did not look at the postmark."

The candles flickered, and we grew quiet. I could not help but think of Myriah, how beautiful she was, how candlelight became her, darkened the shadows in her deep-set eyes, how it made her cheeks glow, and her hair shine.

And so, with everything said and nothing solved, we all went out to the back porch to bring in some firewood for the night. The wind whipped at my skirts and it tore my hair out of its pins and blew it about my face. I could hear it moaning like a wild thing in the grove at The Other Place.

Rob cautioned, "Be careful Aunt Maude, the floor is slippery with ice."

"We don't want a broken hip here, Miss Maudie," Zan said, trying to be lighthearted, I'm sure. But when you are eighty, you prefer not to hear mention of such as that, even in jest.

All of the ghosts of past Christmases visited me that night as I slept rest-lessly in Aunt Eugenie's bed in the room at the front of the house at the end of the hall. In my dreams I saw Papa pulling a Christmas tree across the field from The Other Place, and I saw Mama grating coconut for the ambrosia for Christmas dinner. I felt Hannah's warm breath on my face as I slept and I saw faces and heard voices belonging to those who had died long before I could have known them. I got up at midnight and put a log on the fire and, pulling a quilt around my shoulders, I went to the window and looked out. The storm had passed, the moon was out and the snow glistened. But even when the wind had stopped, I still heard an other-worldly whispering coming from The Other Place. As I stood there at the window, I saw one giant cedar begin to tremble, and then lean, and then bow, and then break with a great shudder and a keen, tearing sound and then a swoosh as it fell. Grandma Clara's cedar.

I know the story of Grandma Clara's Christmas tree very well, for it was told around the fire each Christmas of my life. It goes like this: When Clara was a little thing about the age Annabelle is now, she pleaded with her father not to cut the red cedar that she favored for her Christmas tree. "Let me deco-rate it right out here in The Other Place," she had begged. "What good would it do you here?" asked Great Grandpa. "Out here where no one can see it."

"But the birds and the deer and the rabbits will see it, and I will come out here every day," said Clara. "No. I'll go you one better," said Grandpa. "You stay away from The Other Place and I will dig it up and bring it home to you, roots and all." And that is when the cedar was planted there beside the lane in full view from Clara's room which was then Eugenie's before it became mine when my nieces were born and needed the room closer to their parents. For many years Clara's tree by the lane was decorated for Christmas until the year that Henry, the hired man hurt his back. He, having a touch of epilepsy, fell off the ladder as he reached up to take the star down from the tree. And so the sterling star, with Clara's name and the date of her birth—April 21, 1826—engraved upon it, was left atop the tree. That night, the night of Myriah's leaving, Grandma Clara's tree, under the blanket of heavy snow, fell across the lane. As I lay in my bed, I thought I heard a whispering running through the old house, "Hopaki, Hopaki." It's only the wind, I told myself. "Hopaki, Hopaki." Now I wonder if I dreamed it.

It is funny, it was a letter that took Myriah away from Fairhope, and it was a letter that brought her here in the first place. I thought of this the following morning as I, wrapped from my ears to my toes in flannel, stirred the fire to warm up the kitchen and start a pot of coffee over the open flame, for we still had no electricity. A summer's day, not ten years ago, the letter came. Postmarked Boston. I knew the handwriting. I tore it open, anxious to hear from my closest friend Edna, professor emeritus in the Sociology Department of Boston College. "Dear Maudie," she wrote, her beloved hand shaking from the Parkinson's that would take her life not two years thence. "How are things at Fairhope? How I miss the rolling Billy Hills and misty hollows in between; how I miss you!" I can still weep just thinking those words. "Maudie," she said, "I am about to ask a favor of you and I know that you will not refuse me. In the end, the favor for me will be a blessing for you. I have a young graduate student that I would like for you to meet and talk to. She is a most truly delightful girl. She is doing her thesis on the rise of the New South from ashes of the conquered South, and you of all people are uniquely qualified to tell her about both." Edna went on to say, "You may find she has a peculiarity or two

27

but they only add to her charm. She cannot drive a motorcar, for instance, and this causes no problems in Boston with its trolleys, but it may make problems at Fairhope. I know that you will help her."

So you see, Myriah came to *me*. I loved her first. She was my foundling. I met the train in Vicksburg and brought her here to Fairhope and I insisted that there was no need to get a hotel room, that I had all these rooms, all these empty rooms and no one to share them. Rob was away at school and, except for the widow Eunice Staten, to whom I gave board in exchange for a little help, I was alone. Seven bedrooms, empty. A music room, silent. Twin parlors, wrapped in sheeting. Myriah's young face was so welcome. Her demeanor was quiet, respectful, but there were times when she thought she was alone that I came upon her laughing and singing in the sweetest voice. Truth was, I was in love with this sprite, this slip of a girl who, as Edna had promised, turned out to be a blessing.

Myriah wanted to know all about Fairhope, for as Edna had explained, she was writing a thesis about the South. She carried a pad and pencil in her pocket and when I'd start to reminisce, she'd pull it out. She asked gentle questions about the olden days and I was more than glad to oblige with all the family lore that I remembered. We scoured the attic looking for letters and documents and pictures, artifacts, clothes. Whenever I turned the tables on her and asked about her background, she'd say, "I'm not the one we're studying. I'm not interesting at all." I respected that, which is not to say that I was not madly curious about her. There were no clues about her origins. I could not detect it from her speech though now and then a word had an accent foreign to my ear, and occasionally she used a word in an odd context, a French expression here and there, but I marked that up to being young and impressionable. In others, I would have called it pretentious, but Myriah—in Myriah I found it endearing. She'd brought next to nothing with her. One suitcase filled with threadbare sweaters, a gypsy-type skirt or two, a Mexican serape, a shabby sheep-skin coat.

It kept going through my mind—what will Rob think of her? And I concocted various daydreams in which he came home and fell in love with her and they married and lived happily ever after at Fairhope. "He put her in a pumpkin shell, and there he kept her very well," those foolish words ran around and around in my head. Of course that was farfetched, for Rob had never shown any interest in coming back to Fairhope to live. He was getting his degree at Harvard. He would wind up on Wall Street, that's what I thought. But still— but still I could not wait for him to come home at Christmas and see what I had found. I wanted to wrap her up, tie on a bow of ribbon and put her under the Christmas tree and mark the package, "For Rob, with all my love, Aunt Maude."

But I remember, the second week of December, Myriah coming downstairs carrying her shabby little suitcase and saying, "Would you be so kind as to ask Mrs. Staten to drive me to the station?"

"But you can't go!" I cried in dismay.

"But I must," she said firmly.

"It's Christmas!" I said. "You cannot leave at Christmas."

She came to me and put her arms around me and said, "Oh, Maude. Oh, darling. I'm so sorry. But I have obligations, too."

"You never told me about your—obligations. You never told me anything." I knew I had lost my dignity and I was ashamed when the tears spilled over.

"Oh, my sweet thing. *Ma chèrie*. I'll come back. I promise you that."

And she was gone.

And now she was gone again. The week after she walked down those steps into the snow was pure disaster and I am not given to exaggeration. Not only was our bright light, our Myriah, missing, but the electricity did not come back on and the cold was unrelenting. The moaning sound from The Other Place seemed so fitting, I was almost grateful for it, for it enunciated without effort on my part just how the whole of Fairhope was feeling. Bereft and cold beyond measure.

We began to conserve firewood and only warmed the kitchen until bedtime when we lit a small fire in the girls' room. We rolled up towels and put them around the cracks under the doors to keep out the wind. We brought down all the quilts and blankets from the attic, and we brought a stray dog into the kitchen out of the cold. I had Zan move a small daybed into the girls' bedroom where I slept for the duration, for my room at the front of the house was the coldest of the lot, with the exception, perhaps, of Zan's. He put a cot in the kitchen and took to sleeping there. Only Rob, out of some sense of martyrdom, stayed put in his bedroom and waited out the cold and lonely nights.

On Monday, Rob walked all the way into town and bought a new battery (the last one on the shelf) for the old tractor and cranked it up and pulled Grandma Clara's tree out of the lane into the ditch and then used the tractor to crunch down the ice so he could get the car out and on the road. When the snow melts, I thought, I will come and look for Clara's star. Surely it is still here, somewhere, buried in the snow.

While Rob and Zan and I scurried around trying to keep the household as well as the bank running and habitable, the little girls went about planning Christmas, as if the Christmas spirit could visit a house so miserable as Fairhope. At every juncture Myriah's absence was felt like the blast of cold that greeted an opened door. Only the business of taking care of the two girls and keeping the old house livable in the frigid dark gave me any relief from the fear and sorrow that gripped me like the deep cold that froze the world outside our walls. I watched Rob's face when he came home in the evening from the bank. It grew sadder and sadder. There was no use asking if he'd heard from Myriah. I thought it best not to mention her name.

"I will make the *blanc mange*," Clara said. She was planning the Christmas dinner. "And you, Aunt Maude, can make the ambrosia because it does not require cooking. We can order out a cake. What shall it be?"

"Mama wants caramel," said Annabelle.

"How do you know that?" asked Clara.

"Because she told me," declared Annabelle.

"Told you?" said Clara. "How can she tell you? The telephone is out."

"She told me at Thanksgiving. She said 'We will have coconut for Thanksgiving because that's what Daddy likes, but for Christmas we shall have caramel.'"

"Then we shall have caramel," I said with a lightheartedness that I did not feel. "And you girls must make your Christmas list, for how else will Santa know what you want?"

"Mama has our list," said Clara with finality.

"I will kill a squirrel for Christmas dinner," Zan announced. "That's what the Pilgrims had." He had come into the kitchen to warm his hands by rubbing them together over the fire.

Annabelle made gagging noises and Clara blanched. "The Pilgrims were at Thanksgiving," she said, "and they had turkey."

"And they had no Christmas?" mocked Zan. "Of course they had Christmas, and they had squirrel for Christmas dinner. I'll go to The Other Place and shoot a squirrel."

I could hardly breathe. Take a gun to The Other Place!

"There'll be no animal killing," Clara said. "I won't have you leave this house with a gun, Zan."

I heaved a sigh of relief. Clara, my sensible Clara, she knew better than I how to handle such a notion as that. Sometimes Clara scared me, she was so precocious.

"You have the makings of a good little general," Zan laughed, then pitched another log on the fire and stood back to admire the shower of sparks that shot up the blackened chimney.

"And we must watch the woodpile," Clara said, "for if this weather keeps up, we'll come up short before spring."

I scolded her, for she was much too bossy, and Zan was not a servant to be ordered about. When she was embarrassed, the freckle on her cheek seemed to stand out as it did then. I added to tone down the reprimand, "When I was a girl, one year it was so cold, we had to tear down the corn crib for firewood."

"We've heard it before, Aunt Maude," the girls chorused.

"Tell me, Miss Maudie," Zan said. "I've never heard it."

"Yes," said Clara softening, feeling sorry for me. "I'd like to hear that story again, Aunt Maude. Do tell us."

I retold the story, but in abbreviated form, understanding how well-mannered young people indulged their elders. I did not want to try their patience with over-long reminiscences.

We could not have done without Zan. Not only was he cheerful, he also kept the fires stoked, he brought the sleds down from the attic, he put up the huge Christmas tree that Myriah and the girls had chosen from The Other Place. He had rigged up a kerosene stove so we were able to cook a bite. And then he cut a small cedar tree from the fence row and installed it in the kitchen because the front hall where the big tree stood was too cold for us to go in there and decorate. So the big tree in the hall stood bare of trimming, but the kitchen tree was soon over-burdened with decorations. While Clara made hot chocolate, Annabelle and I strung popcorn and cranberries. We hung candy canes, we put on Myriah's pretty balls and tinsel which she had taken out of her trunk in the attic in preparation for decorating the tree.

We stood around and admired our creation. The girls shifted the ornaments and rearranged them. "There's a bald spot over here," cried Annabelle. And they flew to that side and loaded on more balls, more popcorn, more tinsel.

"All that's needed is a star," said Zan.

"I'll get it," Clara said and she ran out of the kitchen and up the stairs and was gone only long enough for her hot chocolate, left unattended on the stove, to scorch a little. "Here," she cried happily coming back into the kitchen, showing off a silver star. Then, like the good little homemaker she was, she turned and stirred the chocolate on the stove. "Where's the silver polish, Aunt Maude?" she asked.

I went to the pantry and brought her the polish and a cloth. She took the items and set about cleaning the star. "Annabelle," she directed even as she polished, "get the mugs and pour up the chocolate. Here, now, isn't this pretty." She showed off the gleaming star. "Get a stool," she said to Zan, "and put the star on the tree."

Zan saluted, then took the star from Clara and stepped up on the kitchen stool.

"Let me see it," I said holding out my hand.

Zan handed me the star. I turned it over. When I saw the engraving on the back of the star, I went as white as a sheet. "Where did you get this?" I asked of Clara.

"From Mama's trunk," said Clara.

It was all too much for me. I clutched the star so tight that its points dug into the palm of my hand. I was silent so long that dear sweet Annabelle came over and climbed up into my lap and snuggled against my bosom. Then putting aside the shock of seeing the silver star, I asked, "How did you get the key to your mother's trunk?"

"She gave it to me," Clara said.

"When?" I asked, for suddenly that was most important. If Myriah had given it to her right before she left, that did not bode well.

"Long ago," said Clara. And I breathed a deep sigh of relief, but at the same time I was stung. She had given Clara the key to the trunk that I was never allowed so much as a peep into. "The star," I said handing it back to Clara, "has your name on it." And indeed it did. Engraved on the back of the silver star were these words: "Clara April 21, 1826."

It is impossible, I thought. Impossible. No thing can be in two places at once. No star can lie buried under the snow and be locked in a trunk at the same time.

When the chocolate was drunk and the pan scoured and Grandma Clara's silver star firmly attached to the tip-top of the tree, I announced that I would take a walk. I might as well have set off a fire alarm.

"You can't walk on that ice, Miss Maudie," Zan warned.

"Can't never could," I said reaching for my coat.

"Aunt Maude, what if you should fall?" inquired Clara.

And Annabelle set up a howl as if I were leaving and not coming back. As if she did not have precedent for that fear. Poor child.

"I have good grips on my boots," I said. "And I suggest that you girls put on your coats and boots and go sledding while I stomp about in the snow. It's going to melt soon and then you'll miss it." And indeed the temperature was above freezing for the first time since Myriah left. The ice on the roof had begun to melt and the drip, drip, drip was constant. Each falling drop, like the ticking of a clock, was a reminder to me of how long Myriah had been gone. We three girls bundled up and went outside to brave the elements while Zan,

heeding Clara's warning, went to measure the woodpile on the porch and the
back-up pile out by the smokehouse.

Annabelle ran ahead, spinning and twirling, her arms waving, her hair
falling wild from under her cap. "Mali hila," Clara called after her, the wind
whipping the nonsense syllables from her mouth. "She's a wind-dancer, for
sure," Clara said to me as she watched her little sister play in the snow. Then,
calling to Annabelle, she dragged the sleds out beyond the gate to the rise that
fell away to the copse of trees bordering the hay field and they lay on their
sleds and flew down to the farm road at the bottom of the hill.

I went directly to the place in the front of the house where the cedar tree
had fallen across the lane. According to all the old stories, Clara's star had
remained in the top branches of the cedar tree. And yet, there was no way
around it, Myriah had had that star hidden away in her trunk. How could that
be? My head was spinning with the mystery of it. As I approached the fallen
tree, a covey of cardinals burst out of the branches and flew away. The sound
of them was as startling as their brilliant color was against the blue sky. I
watched them wing their way across the yard and settle in the holly by the corner of the smokehouse. I stared at the fallen tree, shorn now of all its
grandeur—broken, mangled. There was no sign of its past glory, of the days
when it was Clara's tree, no evidence of its silver star. I remembered Papa's
words clearly: "That star's still up there. You can't see it anymore because it's
tarnished by the elements. I last saw it when I was a lad and climbed up that
tree, but the star was out of my reach, the top of the tree too slender to carry
my weight. But I saw it, secured by a wire wound around the tree." Those were
Papa's words. I stomped around in the slush where I thought the star might
have fallen off the tree when it crashed under the weight of the snow. I poked
with my walking cane and prodded with the toe of my boot. I saw nothing,
not a single strand of tinsel, no ornament of any kind. But on the tree trunk,
half way up, I found a twisted piece of rusted wire cut deep into the bark of
the cedar tree where once Clara's star had hung.

I stared down the lane expecting to see Myriah's red coat, her black hair
flying, expecting to hear her call, "Maude! Clara! Annabelle!" But all I saw was
the snow melting, falling off the tree limbs. I saw the branches of the pine trees

suddenly released of their burden, shudder, shake themselves, and spring back. All I saw was the empty road. All I heard was the roar of the wind as it came down out of the Billy Hills and changed to a moan as it swept through The Other Place.

Five days—five long days—Myriah had been gone. I no longer asked Rob if he had news of her. The phones were on at the bank and he might have made inquiries, but I kept my own counsel and so did he. We were all harboring fears and anxieties, but we did not share them. We tried to protect each other and above all we tried to protect Clara and Annabelle who seemed fully confident that their mother would return home for Christmas. We were all harboring secrets, I knew that by then. Clara had the key to the trunk in the attic. She must know what treasures the trunk held. She was, after all, Myriah's eldest daughter, I reasoned, and it then followed that she should be the one to hold the key to the trunk in her mother's absence. But knowing that did not stay the awful jealousy that I felt. And Rob was her husband. He and Myriah must have had secrets that they kept only unto themselves. That is ordained by God. I kept my own secret—the silver ladle that Myriah had produced out of that mysterious trunk. Could the monogram have been a T? Could it, like the star, have somehow come from this house? What was I imagining? Just that suspicion opened a wound deep in my heart. The silver ladle, when we had finished with it at the party, Myriah did not hide it away again in her trunk in the attic, instead she had put it in the family silver cabinet. I did not dare look to confirm my suspicions that it might be Thornton family silver by examining it again, more carefully this time. I was too ashamed of my own dark thoughts to give action to them.

I did give Rob a list that I had been making. "Rob, you must take care of Santa for the girls. Annabelle says her mother has their Christmas list, but we must make sure that Santa doesn't skip this house on Christmas Eve. You do this shopping, or have Zan go into Vicksburg or Jackson and do it for you." I'd put on the list all the things that I could think of that might ease a little girl's heart at Christmas: velvet dresses, dolls and doll carriages, tea sets, roller skates, books, and painting sets. Such as that. I hovered and listened to their conver-

35

sations, hoping to catch some inkling of what they themselves had put on their lists. We talked endlessly of what to get Rob and their mother. They wanted to buy her a fur muff, and some ice skates. They'd got the idea of ice skates because the pond was frozen over and they did not realize that it might be ten years before it froze again. It had frozen only half a dozen times in my lifetime. And then they reasoned, their mother and father would want to skate together, so they put skates on the list for Rob and new leather gloves and a scarf. Myriah and Rob should have matching scarves, they decided. And we all sat still and imagined the two of them skimming over the pond holding each other, their breaths coming out in a blue cloud, Myriah's dark hair blowing about her face, her one dark freckle standing out on her pale cheek, her feet flying, her happy laughter ringing. In my mind's eye, I saw her turn to Rob and I saw them kiss and glide over the ice face to face; they looked like skaters in a snow globe, caught there, forever young, forever in love.

So, we put ice skates on the list that Zan would take to Jackson with him when he went to shop. The girls huddled and giggled and jumped apart when I approached and I knew they were plotting for me, so I dropped thinly veiled hints. "I've always wanted some lavender stationery." "I have always wished for a red sweater," or some such, I'd say. And I could hear the girls giggle and run off to pencil in "stationery" and "sweater" on their list.

The days passed and cruelly Christmas came on. We lit the second candle of Advent.

From the first time she set foot inside the front door at Fairhope, I wanted her for my own, the child, the daughter that I had been denied. When she left the first time, I was sure that I would never see her again and I grieved. I knew that I was grieving for the loss of a dream that I had no right to dream. What a foolish old woman I felt, grieving over a girl, a total stranger. Just because she laughed. Just because she showed a warm and generous spirit. Just because she talked about books we both had read and loved. Just because she wanted to know every jot and tittle about Fairhope.

When finally I had reconciled myself to the loss and had given up hope that she would ever come back, here she was again on my doorstep. I had to get Rob home. If he laid eyes on her, he would love her. He was in New York by then working at a big firm on Wall Street. So I did a very dishonest deed. I manipulated. I played sick. I'm not proud of it and considering what happened here at Christmas ten years later, perhaps I have gotten my just desserts.

Dr. Willis sent for Rob, and the day he came home, I lay on my bed pretending that I had the vapors. Dr. Willis was puzzled, but didn't dare suggest to me or Rob that I was malingering. It would have never crossed his mind, it was so unlike the Maude Thornton I'd always been. Myriah was a sweet and attentive nurse, and I recovered quickly under her loving care. I was back on my feet in no time but I was warned to take it slow and easy which was exactly what I had in mind. Rob and Myriah were left to entertain each other. Oh, I felt so clever watching them at the dinner table, their eyes locking over the pot roast, their fingers touching on the salt cellar, their voices bantering, their body language speaking volumes. Funny thing, I remember now that Myriah never mentioned her thesis on the new South versus the old. Now, now in light of what has happened, I cannot help but wonder, was there ever a thesis at all? What really brought her to Fairhope in the first place?

It was the third Sunday of Advent. We had wrapped the presents and piled them under the tree. Zan was gone now to his home in Montana "where they have *real* winter. Twenty below is nothing in Montana," he'd said. We all shivered at the mention of the cold. We sent him off with presents of gloves and a scarf and thick wooly socks. By the time he left the snow had melted at Fairhope, except for shady spots, and the electricity was back on and we could see the workmen from the telephone company down the road, which meant that any day now, we would have our service restored. That evening the family, shrunken as it was, gathered in the kitchen around the hearth where a small fire burned down low. The Christmas lights twinkled in the corner. Annabelle was snuggled up on the couch fast asleep. I was working on a piece of cross stitch, finishing up the red throat of a bluebird, about to nod off to sleep myself, when Clara said, "Daddy, did you see the star?"

"What? What star?" he asked, looking up from his book.

"The star I found in the ice," said Clara.

Suddenly my heart froze. I pricked my finger with my needle. A little bubble of blood rose up and stained the tablecloth I was working on. I stammered, "You mean the star on top of the Christmas tree, don't you?"

"No, no Aunt Maude." Clara was impatient with me. "That star was in Mama's trunk. I found this star in the ice, in the lane where the tractor crunched it into a little wad when Daddy ran over it."

"Let me see it," I demanded.

Clara reached into her pocket. "I straightened it out the best I could." She handed me the star with its wrinkled points. It was a pitiful thing, a tarnished copper star, nothing to compare to the elegant sterling silver one on top of our Christmas tree.

I handed it around to Rob. "What do you make of it, Rob?" I asked.

He put his reading glasses on and examined the crumpled copper. "I don't know," he said. "It appears to be very old. Where exactly did you find it, Clara?"

"Right where you pulled Grandma Clara's tree out of the lane," said Clara. "May I have it back? I want to give it to Mama for Christmas. She likes old things."

Annabelle struggled to wake up. "Mama?" she said. "Where's Mama?"

"Oh," Clara said, "You know Mama's with *Grand-mère*. She hasn't come home yet."

Grand-mère! For the second time that evening, my heart stopped in my chest. I gasped and put my hand over my heart as if I could shelter it from hurt.

"Aunt Maude," said Rob, moving to my side. "Are you all right, Aunt Maude?"

My voice would not come out. My throat was closed. I felt that I could not breathe.

"You know *Grand-mère* needed her *petite-fille*," Clara said.

Annabelle got up and came to me and snuggled up against me in the rocking chair. I could feel her heat through my sweater. Automatically, I put my hand to her forehead. "This child has a fever!" I exclaimed.

• • •

Have you ever been in a hospital at Christmas time? They try so hard to make it up to you. The nurses in their starched whites truly are angels. Carols play softly in the halls, and the waiting rooms are decked out with Christmas trees and the meal trays always have a sprig of holly, but that does not mitigate the awful gravity of a child under a croup tent. Annabelle's fever was 103 and Dr. Willis had called in Dr. Jenkins, a specialist from Jackson, who explained that Annabelle had a bad croup and that it would subside as quickly as it came on.

"We just have to be vigilant until it passes," he said. "We've pulled out all the stops. Now watch her fingernails carefully. When they turn blue, we have to stop the sulfa."

Dr. Willis was not so glib, nor so cheerful. He simply patted me on the shoulder and managed a weary smile.

Rob kept a lonely vigil at her bedside, hunched over, praying.

I don't think Fairhope has ever been so lonely as it was that night. We didn't bother to turn on the lights on the Christmas tree. Clara stared out the window into the dark night toward The Other Place. "They're restless tonight," she said.

I did not ask who? what? of Clara. By then I knew that she has an old soul and she has clairvoyance and she sees and hears and knows and understands more than I ever will.

We ate a bite in front of the fire. Later, as we prepared for bed, Clara said, "Annabelle will be all right, Aunt Maude." And I believed her. Children need their mother at a time like this, I thought, as Clara knelt to say her prayers. As if she'd read my thoughts, she said, "And God, send Mama home. Annabelle needs her. In Jesus' name we pray. Amen."

Ah, I thought, Clara thinks she can command even The Almighty.

It was a restless night I spent. Clara and I alone, the house creaking and popping, thawing out from the cold, the winds soughing, sighing as only the wind at Fairhope can. I dreamed, and though I cannot recall those dreams, they haunted me, nagged at me as I got Clara up to take her with me to the hospital to see her sister.

We returned to the hospital that morning. Clara lingered by a Christmas tree in the hall, replacing some icicles that had fallen on the floor. I opened the door to Annabelle's room. Lo and behold, Myriah sat at the bedside. God had answered Clara posthaste. Myriah slept, sitting up straight in the chair beside the bed, her head leaning to one side. She held on to one of Annabelle's hands that extended from under the croup tent. I could see that Annabelle slept with her sweet face turned toward us, her dark lashes long on her flushed cheeks, her forehead damp from sweating off the fever, her breathing no longer labored.

Myriah jerked awake at the sound of my footfall. She smiled at me and extended her other hand. She drew me down to her and kissed me on the cheek.

"God is good," she smiled. "Annabelle's fever broke at midnight."

I nodded. It was evident that Annabelle had passed the crisis point. "How is your grandmother?" I asked of Myriah, somewhat stiffly, I confess, for I was holding in so many conflicting emotions.

"She is better now, thank you. She sends her regards to you."

"Do I know her?" I asked. Cold. I am afraid my voice was cold.

"I don't imagine so." Myriah reached under the tent and pulled the blankets up around Annabelle's chin. "My grandmother has never been to Fairhope although her mother came back once, but she did not find so warm a welcome as I did. Your people thought she'd come to lay a claim."

"Who is she?" My voice rose. "Lay claim to what?"

"They thought she'd come to claim Hopaki."

Hopaki! That word! It made me tremble!

Clara came into the room. She ran to her mother, buried her face in Myriah's chest, held on to her for a long time and then she got up and went to her sister's bedside. "Mali Hila," she whispered. "You better get up, little Wind Dancer. Santa Claus won't know where to find you."

"I've wanted to tell you this story ever since I first met you, Maudie, but *Grand-mère* warned me that if you knew who I was, you would not accept me.

I tell you now with trembling." She paused, reached under the croup tent and felt Annabelle's forehead. Sighing deeply, she began her story, *"Grand-mère's* grandmother was a Choctaw, native born on the land you call Fairhope. Her name was Mali Hila which means Wind Dancer in our native tongue. She married a Frenchman, a trapper, as did her daughter," said Myriah. *"Grand-mère's* child, my mother, married an anglo, as did I. This," she pointed to the freckle on her face, "this is all the Indian that is left in me, but it is very powerful. It drew me here the first time. I hold it dear."

"I have one too, Mama," said Clara, crowding into the chair by her mother.

"Yes, you do, my sweet. Just like Mama." Myriah gathered Clara in her arms.

"What about me?" cried Annabelle, who had awakened under the tent. "Do I have the freckle?"

Clara bent toward the window of the croup tent. "Yes, you do. I can see it."

Myriah leaned over the bed. "I do think I see it. It is faint, but it is there, Mali Hila. And you have the spirit strong."

I couldn't see a thing, her little face was as pale and unblemished as the surface of a South sea pearl.

"You see it, don't you, Aunt Maude?" Clara nudged me with her elbow.

"Yes, indeed I do. A perfect little freckle," I lied.

An old Christmas carol drifted softly into the room from down the hall. *"O little town of Bethlehem, how still we see thee lie! Above thy deep and dreamless sleep the silent stars go by."* Myriah sank back into her chair and Clara snuggled tight against her. *"Yet in thy dark streets shineth the everlasting Light; The hopes and fears of all the years are met in thee tonight."* Annabelle closed her eyes and slept. I sat in the rocking chair the nurses had provided for me and picked up my cross stitch and counted over to the bluebird and pierced the linen.

Later, sitting down in the cafeteria for lunch with Myriah and Rob, I worked up my courage and asked, "Rob knew where you were? And Clara and Annabelle knew? Everyone knew but me." My pain must have shown.

"I am so sorry, *chérie*." Myriah poked at her salad. "They thought you knew where I had gone. I left in anger, it is true," she sighed. "But it is also true that *Grand-mère* was sick and she needed me. I did tell Annabelle and Clara that I had gone to look after *Grand-mère* and after my anger cooled, I called Rob."

"It was all my fault," said Rob. "I shouldn't have—"

I held up my hand. "Hush," I said. "That is between the two of you. I do not need to know. I'm just so glad that you are back, Myriah."

"Oh, dear Maudie. Did you think I wasn't coming back?" Her face was stricken.

"I suppose I have a thing or two to learn about faith," I said.

Annabelle came home from the hospital on the fourth Sunday of Advent.

Myriah cut out the gingerbread men and the girls decorated them with sprinkles of every color. "And so," said Myriah, finishing her story, "when it was time for your great-great-great grandmother Mali Hila to move to the Reservation, she and her best friend Clara, who is also your grandmother, exchanged their stars. Clara took Mali Hila's copper star and Mali Hila took the silver one engraved with Clara's name. Clara's star was handed down to me by my *grand-mère* after *ma mère* died when I was young. Clara put Mali Hila's copper star on the cedar tree, and there it stayed until the tree was toppled by the snow and the star fell off and our Clara found it."

"Hopaki?" I whispered, almost afraid to say the word out loud.

"Hopaki," Clara cried, "you call it The Other Place, Aunt Maude."

"In Choctaw it means 'it will last a long time.' It is hallowed ground, the burial place of my ancestors," said Myriah.

On the fourth Sunday of Advent, we said prayers of thanksgiving, and never were they more heartfelt. After we lit the Advent candle, Rob excused himself from the dinner table saying, "I have to run down to the bank for a little while. You girls mind your manners and help Mama with the dishes because, remember, Santa is watching you."

"Oh, Daddy!" Clara and Annabelle answered in unison.

He kissed my cheek and then he turned to Myriah and kissed her and looked deep into her eyes and I blushed to see the passion that burned between them.

Not an hour later, while Myriah measured sugar for the Christmas cake and I sifted the flour, we heard car doors slamming. "Who could that be?" I asked.

"Maybe the Pastor's come to call," Myriah said as she poured a mound of sugar into the mixing bowl. The girls, who had been playing school in the corner of the kitchen, jumped up to run out to see who'd come.

Presently, Rob came bursting through the door. "I have a surprise for you, Aunt Maudie. Close your eyes and hold out your hands."

I did as I was told. In the darkness, I heard Myriah suck in her breath; I heard the wind whistle around the corners of the house; I heard a tapping on the floor; I felt electricity in the air. I smelled a spicy odor, pleasant, not unlike the gingerbread cooling on the table. And then I felt the coolest flutter, fingertips on my own.

"Open your eyes, Aunt Maude," the girls cried.

I opened my eyes to see the tiniest little old woman standing before me, her face as brown and as round as an acorn, her gray hair like a halo around it, her eyes bright, her cheeks withered. She was wrapped in layers of clothing of many colors down to her tiny feet shod in fine leather.

The room was silent for ever so long, then the girls could not stand it another moment. They literally jumped in the air and shrieked, "It's *Grand-mère*, Aunt Maude! It's *Grand-mère!*"

I took her in with my eyes and then I opened my heart and said, "Welcome home, Mali Hila."

I listened and I did not hear it. I went to the door and still, while the winds rustled the dead leaves and blew them up against the smokehouse, I did not hear it. I did not hear the weeping from The Other Place. All I heard was the chimes that hung from the eaves of the porch as they danced in the sunlight and tinkled out a melody of Christmas carols. And all I know is that for as many Christmases as I have left on this earth, I will spend them here at

Fairhope with my family all about me, and two stars will adorn our tree and all the spirits in Hopaki will be at peace, as will our own, for that is the promise made in Bethlehem so many years ago.

Surviving the Holiday Season

One Woman's Crusade Against Christmas

Ellen Gilchrist

I n October of 1705, when he was 20 years old, Bach traveled 300 miles across Germany, much of it on foot, to hear Dietrich Buxtehude play the magnificent organ at the Marienkirche in Lübeck. There were Christmas concerts and a grand concert in memory of Emperor Leopold I. I like to think of the young man walking so many days to hear the aging composer whose work he had studied and played. Perhaps he stopped at inns along the way. Perhaps he slept on the ground, his pack for a pillow, his cloak around him against the cold. October turned into November. The fields and towns, which were covered in gold when he left his home in Arnstadt, became covered with snow. Perhaps he saw such scenes as Monet would later paint in masterpieces like *The Magpie*.

This year I am going to think of Bach's journey as the days lead up to Christmas. I am going to listen to great music as the nights grow longer and colder and the dangerous holidays draw near. Every time I want to turn on the television I am going to listen to Bach and Beethoven and Mozart instead. Instead of concerning myself with riots and earthquakes and plagues I am going to listen to Mozart's *Jupiter* Symphony, or Beethoven's Sixth Symphony, or a Bach Prelude and Fugue No. 1 in C from the *Well-Tempered Clavier*, or the Mass in B minor. Instead of being preoccupied with the chaos of the world, I am going to concentrate on the things that make the world worth saving.

Actually, this is just my latest strategy in a lifelong attempt to escape the celebrations our culture has created to lighten up the winter solstice. I was a

47

loved and indulged child with two parents who were married to each other. Still, my main memories of the holidays are unpleasant ones. If I think of Thanksgiving I think of disgusting amounts of fattening foods. I think of the refrigerator stuffed with leftovers and of stacks of dirty dishes. The only Thanksgiving I remember with any real pleasure was when I was in the second grade and had a role in the school pageant. I was a pilgrim and got to sing, "We are little Pilgrim maidens, in our caps of snowy white. We came over on the Mayflower, on a dark and stormy night." Although I liked the pageant, I really wanted to rewrite it. I would have much preferred to be an Indian maiden and get to recite *Hiawatha*.

My memories of Christmas always begin with the trauma of having to keep secrets and the worse trauma of having secrets kept from me. Because of this terrible secret-keeping, there is always a letdown after the presents are opened. "That's all there is?" any child worth his salt will ask. "We've opened everything?" "That's all I got?" Cause and effect, tension and release, simple physics.

The best defense against the holidays is to remember what it is we are really doing: We are trying to lighten up the darkness of winter. That is why I am going to spend the next two months listening to music—to remind myself that the idea is to cheer people up. I no longer need to cheer myself up during the holidays; I have already tried every conceivable way to keep from being depressed, so I have those strategies to fall back on, plus this new one of music.

The main thing I have learned is to stay flexible. I don't have to cook a turkey and make cornbread dressing. I can take everyone out to dinner or go to someone else's house. I can have a simple, elegant meal of vichyssoise and a soufflé. I can fast all day or go for a 20-mile walk or buy everyone watches that are little automobiles that can be taken off and raced across the table.

By the time my sons were teenagers I had begun to experiment with ways to make Christmas more bearable. My first efforts were feeble and fragmented. I fixated on the tree. I decided it was ridiculous to cut down millions of trees and haul them around the United States and install them in living rooms at a cost of $25 to $100 per household. Millions of dead trees festooned with cheap lights and decorations, sitting forlornly in their plastic holders full of stagnant water.

48

The first Christmas I rebelled I got a ladder out of the garage and painted it silver and hung it with lights and laid presents on the steps. My youngest son still hasn't forgiven me for that Christmas. On Christmas Eve, he and my husband went out and bought a regular tree and set it up in the dining room and moved their presents in there.

The next year I tried having a live tree. Four men struggled valiantly to carry a huge pot of dirt with a pear-shaped cedar into the house. They got it as far as the front hall and there it sat, looking like a giant cedar Buddha. After Christmas, the men returned and moved it to the side yard, where it promptly died. This cost quite a bit of money and cured me of my tree fixation.

It is not the tree, I decided. It is all the parties and everyone getting drunk. The following Christmas we took the children to the British Virgin Islands to spend the holiday on a sailboat. The downside of this adventure is that my two older sons now live in the islands and I have to travel nine hours to see them. Not to mention worry about them getting skin cancer. There are pitfalls everywhere in the Christmas game.

Another year my brothers and I took all our children to Wyoming to learn to ski. My parents came along, too. Everyone did learn to ski. But the children kept locking themselves in bathrooms to smoke marijuana, my one-eyed brother drove a Mercedes off the road in a snowstorm (causing me to have my first near-death—and only out-of-body—experience), and when I got home from the trip, I learned that I had pneumonia.

In recent years, three Christmases stand out in my mind. When my oldest grandson, Marshall, was five, I was at his house in New Orleans on Christmas morning. As soon as the presents were opened, I kissed my sons and their wives goodbye and, with my grandchild, began driving to my home in Arkansas. By sundown we were in the Delta in the middle of a flood. We checked into a hotel in Dumas and spent the evening at the local discount store. Marshall bought a detective set with a secret code concealed in the handle of the gun. He still remembers finding the hidden spring and pulling out the rolled-up piece of paper. He says it was at that moment that he began to want to learn to read.

The next morning we continued on our way. In Alma it began to snow, and we locked the keys in the car at a fast-food restaurant. Three members of the Alma football team came to our rescue and opened the door with a coat hanger.

That night, in my house on the mountain, I began to teach my grandchild to read and write the English language. I still have the scrap of paper on which he wrote, "Today we drove to Grandmother's house."

On another great Christmas, I stayed alone all day and wrote the last chapter of a novel. It snowed that year and I saw a white fox in the yard, although I have never been able to get anyone to believe it wasn't just a snow-covered dog.

Last year was an interesting Christmas. My youngest son, the one who can't forgive me for the ladder, was visiting with a friend just home from Russia. At 2:00 on Christmas Eve we learned that the person who had invited us to Christmas dinner was ill and had to cancel the party. We rushed to the grocery store; we bought a frozen turkey. We threw it into a bathtub and ran cold water on it. We made dressing. We mashed sweet potatoes. We ironed a tablecloth. We stayed up until three in the morning basting that turkey.

By noon the next day we had prepared a feast. Cooking a turkey is not so bad as long as there's some drama to it. Not that it tasted very good or that we ate much of it. Luckily, to make up for that, there were plenty of presents under the artificial, predecorated tree I had ordered from the florist. And best of all, the next day would be December 26 and it would all be over.

Finally, John Boy

Chris Gilmer

The Waltons live, and not just in syndication.

It is a long way from Harperville, Mississippi, to Harlem and further still from Lucky Cheng's drag queen restaurant in the East Village to the endless terrace rows of tomatoes which as a boy I tended with my grandfather. In September every year the bumper crop of tomatoes turned the candied-apple red color of my uncle's faded 1967 Ford Mustang which, much later and against my mother's better judgment, became my first car. The terraces were the longest rows in the field-sized garden, but I quickly learned that I could go fishing if by accident I hoed down a couple of Best Boy tomato plants, a small price for the family to pay by my scales of cosmic justice.

The bass pond was in sight of the garden, through one barbed wire fence and a pleasant walk if the charolais bull was in a good humor. If not, it was a brisk and dicey run to get settled onto the little pier made just for me and relax in relative safety, the bull smart enough to recognize the fragility of the pier, regally above swimming out to confront me, and content to wait for my return trek through his pasture. But the risk was better than a little boy's longing, standing in the garden almost able to touch my oasis of absolute joy. It was harder in fact than waiting on a cool December morning to open Christmas presents until after breakfast had been served, and Papaw enjoyed seeing how long I could hold out.

The garden is where Papaw and I talked about the Statue of Liberty and I recited the capitals of all 50 states—six years old, propped on the short-handled hoe he made especially for me—Sacramento, Little Rock, Boise, even Jackson which I had not seen all that many times. Grandpa Walton he was not in many ways, but he quit school in the third grade to plow the fields that fed eight sisters, and he had rattlesnake rattlers, real ones, in the belly of the fiddle on which he played "Listen to the Mockingbird" by ear. That was good enough for me. I would be the one to see Mt. Rushmore and the Golden Gate Bridge, he decreed. He had seen only Lookout Mountain once, but he bought me penny candy with dollars earned the hard way and years later sold a cow to pay my junior college tuition.

It is a long way from the pews of the Damascus Primitive Baptist Church where Mamaw and I sang "Mansion Over the Hilltop" from shaped-note songbooks with no accompaniment to an upscale gay piano bar in San Francisco where the chanteuse earned a twenty dollar tip for singing, no, channeling "Miss Celie's Blues" to me—finally John Boy—and the two chosen brothers whom my mother did not bear.

The Waltons have been with me my whole life, first winning Emmy Awards in prime time when I was a boy and still loving each other in syndication today as I strive for my waist size not to exceed my age. I am thirty-five years old this year. They populated the only television show new or old to which I could ever give ten hours for a rerun marathon and recite many of the well-loved speeches with John Boy and his family—Grandpa getting kicked out of the hospital when Grandma was so ill, Mary Ellen getting hurt in the car wreck and turning away from her husband, Olivia having to go to the sanatorium, Jim Bob learning about his twin brother who died at birth. The Waltons were real to me then, more real in many ways than my neighbors or schoolmates or friends. John and Olivia were my ideal parents, and the thought of all those brothers and sisters wishing me good night with the crickets and owls quietly serenading us to sleep was as mouth-watering to me as the aroma of country ham wafting before daybreak through my mamaw's hilltop house.

It was my solitary fantasy, so I always got to be John Boy, the eldest who thought deep thoughts and felt the hurts and joys of others as deeply as if they were his own. John Boy was a writer, and I wanted to be a writer. If he could get started in rural Virginia during the Great Depression, surely I could do it from rural Mississippi in the wake of Watergate. What I didn't count on was the loss of hope that happened to so many of us somewhere between his generation and mine. What I do count on is winning back that hope, but no longer with the help of John Boy and his family. I have learned that John and Olivia; John Boy, Mary Ellen, and Ben; Erin, Jason, Jim Bob, and Elizabeth; even Grandma, Grandpa, and the cousins and neighbors on Walton's Mountain, all have parallels in my own life and my own time. It is they who have resurrected my hope, and now it is my job to live fully into that hope today and tomorrow.

In my updated version of life on Walton's Mountain—a place of the heart rather than a place of real geography—Jim Bob and Jason are lovers, not brothers, and Elizabeth is a black woman. I am white. Erin and Ben are married, and my Erin is the one sister of my birth and my soul. My Ben is her husband, the first man with whom I ever felt fully comfortable, the brother-in-law with whom "brother" matters more than "in-law." Mary Ellen is a grandmother with two grown daughters of her own. The real Olivia neither loved her family more, nor was willing to define it more broadly, than my own mother. Versions of Corabeth Godsey and the old maid Baldwin ladies have been fixtures in my life for years, though it was my Corabeth who turned me on to martinis in real life rather than the Baldwins and their moonshine "recipe" which always brought some drama to their mountain. Granted when my family sits around the antique dining table, we would raise a few eyebrows if there weren't a wall between us and the street, but what interests me is that I define family—its essence, purpose, and beauty—exactly as Olivia and John Walton did when I watched wistfully them sitting around their own table on the 19-inch color television of my boyhood.

For a long while in my twenties I thought the Waltons were dead, or that they were never real. Those were my hardest years, when I wanted so much to be John Boy that it actually hurt to watch the reruns. I don't think much about those times anymore, because I have learned that I can travel from the magnolia tree in my Granny's yard all the way to Manhattan; I can snorkel Trunk Bay in the Virgin Islands with my Jim Bob and still honor the cane-pole fisher-woman who made a young boy chocolate cakes with hard icing which had gone to sugar. The distances of the heart are not so far anymore, nor so extreme. Unafraid of the future and unhaunted by the past, I am finally and joyfully my own John Boy, the real one's surrogate across time and space, him no longer envied for his simple goodness and elegant complexity, myself unable to juxtapose the two—until now.

Seldom one to be satisfied, however, I no longer want to be John Boy. Now I want to be Olivia, not a woman in body, but a mother in spirit. I aspire to be Olivia Walton in my soul, the center of gravity holding a beautiful solar system in place, planets and moons revolving in harmony around a sun, occasionally eclipsing each other or passing in different combinations from time to time into close orbits, always, however, essential components of our small unit of the universe. It seems I may get this wish, over time.

It is the natural course of life, is it not, for the mother to become the grandmother, for every family's John Boy to become its Olivia or John, as he or she chooses, and for the children of the brothers, sisters, and cousins to fill the home, to fill the world, with the promise and the hope of the next generation of Elizabeths and Jasons? Does it really matter if the same blood runs through all of the veins, if the same parents gave nurture to all of the children, if the chosen brothers and sisters hold primary allegiances to other families of their own births, if all of the women and men who were once girls and boys hoed in the same gardens with the same papaws? Does it not perhaps matter more that such a diverse group of people found each other, chose each other, and loved each other—in spite of, as well as because? This accomplishment is not a small one. In fact, I call it a miracle on Walton's Mountain as the terrain has redefined itself today.

Of course, I will only get to be Olivia for a short time, and then my new niece or perhaps one of her cousins will have taken over making the turkey and dressing for Christmas dinner without my even realizing that it has happened. All of a sudden the Olivia who bore me will be gone, and I will be Grandpa Walton trying to define my lifetime with photographs and memories as a season of love. That is indeed incentive not to waste time.

Christmas is the one season of the year when I never seem to waste time. From the distant past, my distant past, I remember standing in line with my father and mother at the Sears catalog store on Highway 35 in Forest, Mississippi, to sit in Santa's lap and tell him what I wanted for Christmas. I remember watching the mystery of Santa riding in the annual Christmas parade behind the junior high marching band, the La Petite Club's officers, and the moving crepe paper daises of homecoming queens, never knowing that Santa was a local insurance agent and that I was vexing myself for naught over how he would return to the North Pole in time. In the gentlest voice I have ever heard, I remember Mama reading "Miss Flora McFlimsey's Christmas" to my Erin and me every year, the story of an old doll which no one wanted and the hope which wrought her Christmas miracle, her transformation into the doll of a new little girl's heart. In the near past I remember my stepfather dressing as a pastoral Father Christmas to share his Polish heritage with our growing family of new brothers and sisters, and I remember drinking a bit too much champagne and mistaking one of my gifts, a wall hanging, for a serving tray, laughing harder at myself than the others were laughing at me. I have chosen to reconstitute that gift as a fine serving tray, a symbol to trigger a memory.

Is not Christmas about such miracles—small and large, new and old—and transformations, and promises fulfilled, and unpretentious charity, and hope? Must it be only about virgin births or saviors for the world, or can it sometimes just be about God making God's self known to others through us, however we each define that entity and process? And isn't it mostly about hope, because isn't hope the essential raw material for all of the rest?

I am not the one to self-righteously chastise our society for its commercialization of Christmas because I have been on more than a few of those frenetic jaunts to the mall to find the "perfect" last minute gift for someone who might already have three gifts under my tree. Like so many others, I have done it with a credit card already stuffed as full as the Christmas turkey. My gold and magenta lights traditionally adorn the biggest tree which I can both afford and fit into my living room, and holiday parties with a harpist and food piled high on silver trays are not uncommon on my Walton's Mountain.

Still, I would be fine if I never got to hire another harpist, serve another high-rise red velvet cake, or catch the "John" of my imagination under the mistletoe. Well, at least I would be fine with the first two. To the best of my knowledge, there was not one harpist in the entire county of my youth, and Papaw would have judged a silver tray to be a foolish and undependable indulgence.

All I really need are the people I love singing "Deck the Halls" or "Silent Night" as I play, often badly, the tunes on the piano I inherited from my big mama, the great-grandmother born on a cold January day in 1905. I need to know that when Granny is no longer with us, she will live on in her great-granddaughter and in the bright peacock watercolor that she painted for my parlor. I need to know if Jason and Jim Bob follow their own paths to Denver or Dover one day that Christmas will bring them home again—and I need to love them enough to help them pack their bags if the time comes for their move. I need to know that books will always be the best holiday remembrances for Mary Ellen and Corabeth, and that Elizabeth will endure long beyond the days when her sparkle of Diana Ross and legs of Tina Turner have faded. I'll be fine as long as Erin and Ben keep letting their children be my children, and if I can look in the mirror one Christmas Eve far from now and know that I have been half as good of an Olivia for my family as my mama, who rose the hard way from a cotton field, has been for hers. I will hope that I have done it with a portion of her grace, which no doubt runs through me if I can harness it. And finally, I'll be fine as long as the hope of finding my own John Walton lives in the deepest place within me and I keep saving him a seat on the porch swing. For now, others from my Walton's Mountain—too many more friends to name, but not too many to cherish—can keep his seat warm.

The gifts, the glitter, the glib . . . they are transient, flowers which bloom for only one season. Love is the one and only miracle that transcends and endures, the eternal perennial. Christmas, for me, brings the annual fulfillment of a simple and eloquent little prayer: "God help me to want what I have rather than to have what I want." Although I almost always remember to want what I have, for the other eleven months of the year I want what I want just the same as any man. Often, I yearn for it unspeakably. But as I consider each precious, unrepeatable Christmas moment on my own Walton's Mountain, as I contemplate new lines not visible the year before in older faces including my own, as I listen to love manifest itself in ways both easy and brave, I am radiantly transformed into a man who truly wants nothing more than what he has. For what I have, no, whom I have, is indeed the sum of all that I am. I aspire to be no more, and I pray to be no less.

At Christmas each year, like at no other time, I become a better man.

Christmas 1976

Caroline Langston

The baby chicks had been a present for Easter. They had just come from church—Mama, Daddy, Lila and Davis—and the little creatures were running loose on the family room floor, their tiny claws practically skating across the squares of waxed linoleum. "Look what the Easter Bunny brought you," Mama said, standing there holding the bag that matched her shoes, but Lila knew that couldn't be right. Maybe the Easter Bunny had brought the basket that was covered in purple cellophane, but she had seen the baby chicks for sale downtown at Henderson's Feed and Seed. One chick was bright pink and the other pale blue, and she got down on the floor, belly-first in her smocked dress, to cup the beating bodies in her hand.

Maybe they came from Jody, who had dropped out of college and would not go to church, but when he finally dragged himself out of bed for dinner at two o'clock in the afternoon, he only shrugged his shoulders, frowned at his eight-year-old sister and complained, "Do you know how *cruel* it is to dye them like that?"

Mama said, "Why do you have to be so awful all the time, Jody?" and Lila, confused, burst into tears. Then from his silent end of the dinner table, the place where he always sat dreaming, came Daddy's taut voice, in a tone that could have cut glass, "You all remember that this is Easter."

This was all before Daddy got sick. This was when it still looked like the

Bicentennial might turn out to be something after all, rather than the extended summer of disappointment that ensued. Streamers of red, white and blue crepe paper hung from the ceilings of every store downtown, months before the Fourth of July.

It was a summer of Independence Day sales. Everything in stores had the theme of Ben Franklin and Philadelphia, or Boston and Paul Revere: towels, decorative plates, the curtains that Jody balked at when Mama hung them in his room.

There was Mama, Daddy, Lila, Jody, and Davis. Davis had a summer job at the Cyclone fence yard, while Jody got promoted to assistant manager at the Acacia Theater downtown. At the Acacia Theater, a red velvet curtain closed in front of the screen after the feature was over. They couldn't go to movies on Saturday nights, Mama said, because that was the night that only black people went.

Their oldest sister Serena was with her husband in Kansas, where the army had sent him. Kansas, Lila imagined. Someplace stretched out like the word, flat and syrup golden. Not like Mississippi. The highway to Jackson was a row of hills covered in flowering green vines. The hills were steep, and here and there their sides were washed out into deep ravines that trucks sometimes fell into. "It's not ivy, Lila," Mama said from the passenger side of the front seat. "It's called kudzu." One day when Mama, Daddy and Lila were down at the beach in Biloxi, Daddy got so sick he could not come out of the motel room. All afternoon Lila sat very quiet at the shallow end of the pool, the blue cement steps snagging her bathing suit bottom.

In the beginning, the chicks lived in the warm place next to the kitchen stove, in a cardboard box lined with clean sheets of *Jackson Daily News*. But by the time that the smell grew overpowering and Mama insisted that they be exiled to the yard, the chickens had doubled in size, and small traces of white, like cirrus clouds, had begun to appear among the candy-pink and sky-blue feathers. Small traces of white that Lila outlined with her hand when she picked up each one in turn, singing to it, after she drove home with Davis from school. The pink one she named Ruby and the blue Sapphire.

It was true; they were growing. White feathers began to fill in so fast that the chickens looked splotched all over with some bizarre affliction. "Ugly old thing," Davis said one afternoon, kicking Ruby out of the way as he went to the backyard shed to leave his muddy boots. "How come I'm the only one that feeds them?" Mama said, lugging another manila bag of chicken feed out of the trunk and into the yard.

And then one day it was July.

Anyone by now would have expected the chicks to be dead. "You're supposed to drown them accidentally," Jody said from the sofa in the den, where he was stretched out reading a book called *Crime and Punishment*. This time, Mama did not scold him and Lila did not cry. Instead she went out to the backyard to the chicken pen—the old doghouse—to say hello.

But Daddy loved them. After he came home from the hospital the first time, he began to come out into the yard in the evenings, when it was cool. Jody would be at work and Davis up at the country club, and Mama inside the house cooking dinner behind the yellow-lit window.

The screen door opened and it would be Daddy. He took his time coming across the yard because it tired him out to walk. Then he would sit down in an old aluminum lawn chair next to the dog pen and let Lila entertain him with the chickens. Completely white now and no longer delicate, they had tough little orange claws that scooted across the grass, which at dusk was blue-green, like one of the colors in the 64 crayon box.

If either one happened to flap close enough to him, he would lean over in his chair, groaning a little, pick up Ruby or Sapphire, then speak to it in some kind of little chicken language that Lila had never before heard. The chickens always struggled wildly whenever Lila, or Mama, or Davis tried to pick one up, but when Daddy did it, they rested easy in his hand, wings folded smoothly against their sides. One night he told her that she was in possession of two future roosters: It was his fingers that felt the stiff combs beginning to emerge, pushing up like buds of teeth.

Sometimes during these evenings, Daddy looked around to see that no one else but Lila was watching, then pulled a crumpled pack of cigarettes out of his trousers pocket. "You mind if I smoke?" he said, just like she were grown up. No, Lila always answered, even though she knew he was strictly forbidden. The sky would be violet by now and the match would bloom brightly for a second in the darkness as he lit up. Then he would begin to tell her stories.

When he was a little boy in south Mississippi, he said, they had had a chicken coop in the back yard, next to the little house where the cook lived. This was a long time ago. Early in the mornings, before he went to school, it had been his job to take a cane basket off the back porch and go out to collect the eggs. There had been steaming cold mornings, when the heaters were barely lit, that he had crept out into the chill air and lifted out eggs still warm from the hens' bodies, hot little globes that his hand would just enclose. He would take them inside and the cook would fry them in a cast iron pan, the grease rising off them in clouds.

After she heard that story, Lila knew that she would have to get a hen.

He told her other stories, as well: about Christmas when there wasn't any money, and about taking the train from Jackson to McComb, then walking the whole fifteen miles back to the hamlet where he grew up. The Mississippi he talked about was like a whole other country, the way that Jody had talked about it when he came back from Europe. Not like Mississippi during the Bicentennial.

When he told her these stories, all of a sudden he did not sound like a father anymore. They sat in the cavern of the yard, the pecans hanging in ripe clusters from the tree overhead—somehow it had ended up to be August—the chickens darted about under the branches and he did not sound like a father. She was not sure what he did sound like, but it was not the way a father was supposed to talk to his children. They had been a family all together, like a picture, then her father had grown huge and broken the frame.

After a while there was always an interruption. Mama calling them to dinner. Or Jody finally coming home, visible through the back windows into the den, the blue light from the television set washing over him. Sometimes Daddy would start coughing and not be able to stop, and he would have to lean on Lila's shoulder to walk back into the house. Whenever this happened, Jody and Mama came running, and Lila knew that Mama could smell the cigarette on him.

Then it was fall and the evening visits stopped. Lila was in school again: fourth grade. They were doing multiplication tables this year, and were given slim leaflets from the Metropolitan Life Insurance Company that listed the table up to 12 times 12. Jody said that some churches taught that only 144,000 would get to heaven. "When are you planning on going back to college?" Mama asked him, but she did not sound as mad as before, because everything worried her instead. Serena called from Kansas to say that she was going to have a baby, and for a little while they were all happy.

It was an election year and everybody they knew was going to vote for Ford. Sometimes it seemed to Lila that the people quoted in newspapers and on television news always had the opposite opinion to what everybody she knew thought, except for maybe Jody. All television shows took place in Los Angeles, California, where people did absurd things like walk down the street in daylight wearing a bikini bathing suit.

Everything was white and bright in Los Angeles, but in Mississippi it rained. The sky hung dusky gray over the water tower in the mornings when Davis drove them to school. The pecans started to fall in the backyard, but nobody bothered to pick them up. When Daddy was little, he had told her that summer, he and his brothers gathered up all the pecans from the ground and shelled them into great boxes that would be emptied into Mason jars and put on pantry shelves. They would salt them and toast them and at Christmas the cook would make a pie. "That's how come I planted this one," he had said to Lila, pointing at the tree in the middle of the grass.

But this year the pecans stayed on the ground, and were soon followed by the leaves. One day Lila saw Jody—*Jody*—trying to rake them up and when she walked past he did not say a word. She walked close and saw that he was crying. The pecans swelled with water in the rain and blackened; sometimes Lila might step on one when she went out to feed the chickens and it would collapse, rotten and gummy, under her heel. But the chickens delighted at them, roving through the yard making groaning noises and pecking at the sodden ground.

Oh the chickens! They were practically full-size now and crowed all the time it seemed: from early in the bluish mornings when Lila was getting ready for school, to the middle of the football game on Sunday afternoon (Daddy's bed was set up in the den now), to sometimes late at night, two thin crows in the dark when Jody got back from wherever he had been. One day a neighbor knocked and asked if there was anything they could do to keep them quiet. Mama stood in the front doorway and said, "I think we have enough to worry about around here right now," and shut the door.

A few days later a man from the county showed up and Mama asked him in. He started to explain that it was illegal to have poultry inside the city limits, but when he saw Daddy asleep on the iron bed in the den, he finished his coffee and left, leaving a pamphlet titled "The Small Poultry Farm" from the County Extension Service. The chickens stayed, and nobody bothered them about it any more.

Now the red combs jutted stiffly out of their heads. Sometimes when Lila went to feed them (it was her job now), one would peck at her leg, leaving behind a stinging, V-shaped welt. Her legs grew mottled with purple and one day when he was awake Daddy espied them and said to her, "Why Lila, you're as bad off as Job."

Even as the weather began to turn cold, the chickens were indefatigable (that was what Mama said, standing by the window), scrambling around the backyard hunting for rotten pecans. But more and more it seemed to Lila that there was something empty and useless about all their energy: their day-long crowing as they moved in endless circles around the yard, while on the other side of the windows the family sat more and more still.

It was time to get that hen.

For Christmas was coming. The days were running short. One morning she got out of bed (bare feet stinging on the wood bedroom floor) to find out that Jimmy Carter was the thirty-ninth president of the United States. "Goddamn," Daddy said, when Mama woke him up to give him the news, and her mind stumbled on the strangeness of hearing him say that word.

Gradually, all traces of the Bicentennial were disappearing. The last bits of red, white and blue plastic bunting that had hung over Main Street all summer grew twisted around the power lines, and was not taken down until the day after Thanksgiving when it was finally removed to make way for the red and green tinsel garlands that lit up the downtown streets. George Washington's and Benjamin Franklin's bright cardboard faces disappeared from shop windows and bulletin boards at school and from the labels of products at the Piggly-Wiggly—they had never really belonged in this town anyway, so it was not strange to see them go. Everywhere there were bells, the tinny bells of recorded Christmas music, songs that were never about the Baby Jesus but were always about snow, skis, and sleighs, things that Lila had never seen before.

Still it was cold. Trails of frost laced the plate glass windows of the store-fronts downtown. She went into Henderson's Feed and Seed for the first time in all those months, but all the baby chickens had vanished and the store had a staleness like it might be closing forever, stacked with silent bags of fertilizer and rakes hanging askew on the wall, as if they had been frozen in motion. At the back of the store there were a bunch of men sitting around a potbellied stove, the kind of men that Mama would have described as being "from out in the county," who came into town and just sat and talked for hours. When she asked whether they had any hens for sale, the men just looked at her and chuckled, until one of them said something in a low voice about Daddy, and they all went quiet.

She hitched her coat around her and walked out of the store. Jody was waiting in Mama's Chrysler New Yorker with the heat on high, listening to the Jackson rock station. Somehow he had become her accomplice. "Drive," she said. Away, she thought. Anywhere. He went to the end of Main Street, then over the old river bridge that led to the city power plant, and made a turn on a grayed asphalt road.

They were in the country now, where everything was overgrown and filled with mysteries. They passed a black nightclub that had a blue and white Christmas tree in the front window.

Soon little houses and farms began to appear, dotting the sides of the road, and in the gullies between houses the kudzu vines were dead now, tangled like coils of rusted barbed wire. And then the most amazing thing happened: they began to see chickens. They passed a mint-green-painted shack with a chicken coop in back, and Lila said "Jody wait," but he was driving too fast. The next time they saw chickens they managed to stop, but when they went to the door of the faded shotgun house, the tiny, spry black woman who answered said that she could not help them. She needed every last egg she could get her hands on, she said. A draft blew through the folds of her checked summer dress. "You shouldn't blame her," Jody said as they walked back to the car.

They kept on driving. At the house a few miles down the road, the hens were not even in a pen, but rambled freely across a fenced-in yard, if a yard was what you could call it: it was more a grassless plot of dust with a farmhouse in the middle. The rooster was on the front porch, puffing up his feathers in the chill air, the small amber beads of his eyes darting angrily as they walked up the stairs. This time a white woman answered and held the screen door half open. She was small and round and blond, like a hen herself, Lila thought. Somewhere in the room behind her a television blared.

"What do you all want?" the woman said, eyeing them in a way that said she didn't get too many visitors. Even in the middle of the country she was dressed up in a bright turquoise top and pants and had on red lipstick just like she was going to town.

Lila and Jody said at the exact same time, "We want to buy one of your hens."

We want to buy one of your hens, and it was almost Christmas, the trees were bare black smudges, and Lila wanted to hold a hot new egg in the palm of her hand.

All of a sudden hope rose up in her insistently, like a yawn at the end of a very long day.

The woman just looked at them like she couldn't believe what they'd just said.

Out of his pocket Jody pulled a ten dollar bill.

It began to rain. Ever so slightly, the woman began to smile.

"Well," the woman sighed, "if y'all want to have one that bad, I'd be happy to sell you one." She came out of the house and the screen door flapped behind her. She wiped her hands on her pants, then walked down the slippery porch steps into the yard. The rain started to pick up, and dark spots began to appear on her stretch shirt. In one long motion, strange for someone so large, the woman sprang forward and caught up a black-and-white speckled hen, then rushed back onto the porch as the hen struggled and flapped her wings. Lila held out her arms and the woman set the hen into them, as Jody handed her the folded bill. "You got her?" she said. "I assume you all have a place outside you want to keep her, and you know all about the feed and all, right?" They nodded. "Do you people know anything at *all* about taking care of chickens?" she said as they walked back to the car, before finally giving up and calling behind her, "Well, Merry Christmas!"

All the way home the hen was unusually quiet and still, resting on the floor of the backseat in case she made a mess. The car filled with the smell of wet feathers. Lila lay flat on the backseat, her cheek against the cushion, stroking the hen's wings and the tiny crown of her head. What are you thinking, little chicken? she wondered. What am I going to name you?

She had done it, she had actually done it, and how Daddy would be surprised! She would go out in the cold morning and pick up eggs, and bring them back inside for the family to eat.

But when they started to walk through the garage door into the den, Mama stopped them there. "You can't bring that chicken in here. You don't know where it's been." There were tiny organisms living in the hen's feathers, she explained, and if any of them got into Daddy's lungs, they could make him sicker than he already was.

"This is not the time, this is not the time," Mama said to Jody, but Jody just shrugged his shoulders.

Then from behind her came Daddy's voice, so faint that Lila and Jody could not understand what he was saying. Mama went away, then came back a minute later. Daddy had said that if Lila would carry the hen around to the back, he would get out of bed and move over by the window. That way, Lila could just hold her up to the glass, and he would be able to see her.

Jody went inside and Lila walked around to the backyard gate. The hen had started to tremble in her arms, and Lila could tell that she was growing uneasy. "You can't OVER-handle them," she remembered Daddy saying. She tried to stroke her gently as she walked in front of the bank of windows that looked out from the den, especially when the roosters saw her and came running across the yard, flapping their wings and making a commotion, which only made it worse. Her shoes were soaking wet with rainwater now, and her teeth chattered. The surface of the windows was stippled with raindrops, reflecting the light so that it was hard to see through them.

On the other side were Mama, Daddy, Davis, and Jody. They were only a few feet away, Lila knew, but all the same, it suddenly felt like there was a vast space between them and her, as long as the road from here to Jackson, or the distance from the top to the bottom of a ravine.

Her father was standing next to the window.

He was not actually standing, she saw, but leaning against the frame. His limbs were so thin and bony they looked as though they could be carved out of elephant tusks. Her father smiled at her and put the palm of his hand against the window, and a little cloud of condensation formed around it. Lila lifted up the hen next to the window, right up next to his hand, which he moved back and forth slowly as if he could actually feel her through the glass. The hen started to tap her beak lightly at the window, like there was something to eat there. The faint tapping sound started to grow, until it seemed to be entirely surrounding them, and Lila realized that it had started sleeting.

"Come on back inside now," she heard Mama's voice call muffled through the glass.

Then something happened—Daddy must have lost his balance, because he stumbled and almost fell over, just managing to steady himself in time. But the motion startled the hen, who fluttered out of Lila's hands and jumped to the ground where she could escape.

Only Ruby and Sapphire were waiting. Rascally, balking at the top of their lungs, digging their tight claws into the clammy grass, they began to chase after the little hen as Lila stood frozen, not sure what to do next, not sure what they would do when they actually caught her. Just as the chickens were gaining on her, though, the hen managed to flap her checked wings just enough to jump into an aluminum lawn chair abandoned from the summer.

Ruby and Sapphire stopped. The seat of the lawn chair was slick with sleet and the hen's claws scratched against it as she tried to get a footing. But she couldn't. Finally she simply flopped down and gathered her feathers around her—waiting, in that still and eternal moment, for whatever would come to rescue her.

Quilts
Kiver for My Children

Clifton L. Taulbert

The winter of 1963 would not be unusually cold for those native to St. Louis, but it was to be my first "northern" winter, one of those winters that Ma Ponk and Ma Mae had often talked about. In order to get through that first winter, I would learn to dress warm with scarfs, ear muffs and lined gloves. And as the days got colder and the snow deeper, I would also learn to time the buses to the minute.

But more that anything, I would be saved from the cold weather by a box that arrived in mid-October from Glen Allan.

I had looked forward to getting a package from home since my arrival in St. Louis five months earlier. Every day I could not wait to get home from work to see if the mailman had brought me a package. And my waiting and hoping were not in vain.

I recall vividly the day I came home from work and Mama Beulah said, "Boy, you got a package upstairs from down south." Without stopping to do my normal chatting with the customers and the kinfolk in the confectionery, I rushed immediately upstairs to my shared bedroom. There on the foot of the bed was a medium-sized box wrapped in brown paper and tied with white cord string. It was addressed to Mr. Clifton Taulbert and it was from Ma Ponk. As I untied the tightly-wrapped box with the brown paper glued to the sides, I laughed. I remembered Ma Ponk's insistence on wrapping her boxes tightly so that those nosey post office people up north would have no idea of the contents.

Excitement mounted as I untied the package and wondered if Ma Ponk had mailed the box herself or had gotten one of my sisters or my brother to walk uptown and mail it for her. I could hardly wait. I sure wanted some genuine southern pecans. Ma Ponk always included a four pound bag of big soft-shelled pecans when she sent her sons Melvin and Sidney their winter boxes. She had been sending winter boxes north for almost thirty years now. Quilts and pecans, and on those very rare occasions, a plain cake from her sister, Aunt Willie Mae, would be included. I had helped her fix and wrap and mail those packages every autumn. Now she included me in her list of those getting a package.

I sniffed as I hurriedly opened the box, but I couldn't smell a cake or hear a rattle. As always Ma Ponk had wrapped her packages well. She would save up piles and piles of *Sunday Delta Democrat Times* newspapers and stuff the boxes so tightly that only air would move. Nothing would rattle. At last I got the last knot untied, then I struggled to open the box which had been glued shut. Finally the flaps opened. I pulled out the piles of newspaper and reached into the box. Indeed there was a four pound sack of soft-shelled pecans, picked, I knew from experience, by Ma Ponk's own hands from the big tree in her back yard.

Then, as I pulled out the sack of pecans, I felt the softness of material and I saw the start of a star, a brightly colored star. It was my quilt. Gently I pulled it from the box and laid it out across the bed. It was beautiful, Ma Ponk's version of the Star of David. The northern winters were said to be harsh, but now I would be prepared.

I hollered down the tall stairs, "Hey, y'all, I just opened my box! You got to see my quilt."

As I inspected the quilt I thought to myself of the skilled labor which had gone into its making. It had no big squares, but lots of small pieces, neatly stitched together in the shape of stars.

The ladies of Glen Allan pieced quilts with a passion and my grandmothers and aunts were among the more passionate ones. I was Ma Ponk's collector of scrap materials that she gleaned from Mrs. Knight, the town seamstress, and from other members of the community.

A quilt from Glen Allan was truly from the community, for representative scraps of brightly colored cloth came from all over the little town. Dresses and pants no longer worn and Sunday shirts unable to be patched all became part of the scrap heap. Running through Glen Allan, I'd occasionally be stopped by Miss Sissy or Miss Stell who had saved bags of old clothes for the quilters. This collection of materials and scraps no longer needed would become the blocks and squares of flowers, birds, and patterned stars that would eventually be stitched together to form the top of a quilt.

As I sat holding my quilt from home, I recalled vividly the start of the quilting season. When the fall winds entered the Delta, the ladies' minds turned to quilting. It seemed as if those of Ma Ponk's household always started the rounds to gather scraps of cloth needed for quilting. Securely tucked away in the loft at Ma Ponk's were the quilting frames, wooden poles that had grown smooth from the scores of tired hands and the years of use. Always one to give me my orders, Ma Ponk would see that the frames were taken down and the hooks securely placed in the ceiling. She never trusted me to tie the poles, she always did that herself. Once the frames were set up there was hardly enough room to move around in the little parlor room, but soon the frames were covered with the start of the quilt, and encamped all around it would be older women who for years had followed this time-honored tradition. By the light from the exposed sixty-watt bulb and the flickering flames from the wood stove, I could see the ladies, bespeckled, tired, some of them dipping snuff. They had worked all week at other jobs, but they somehow found the creative energy needed to do the quilting. They hummed, gossiped, and talked to themselves as the patterns from their minds began to take shape. I was not allowed to sit in the room, but I would pass by the open door a thousand times, hearing the gossip not meant for my ears while seeing them working hard at a gift of love. And as the patterns grew and the gossip stopped, the quilts were pieced to the sounds of Dr. Watts' hymns, and the news from up north.

When fall ushered in the quilting season, the men of Glen Allan also had their traditions. Now facing a lull in the field work, they would go off with their .22 rifles to hunt rabbits, squirrels, and possums. They would leave early in the morning, heading for the woods, leaving the women to do the quilting.

Though hunting and quilting were both traditional autumn events, it was the quilting that carried the hearts of the people and the warmth of the South up north. According to those ladies of the South, our southern bones would never adjust to the cold of the North. Quilts were needed and nothing less would do. Prized possessions by both Southerners and Northerners, these designs from the heart and mind were always secured in trunks or large chests-of-drawers. Piles of handmade quilts were a status symbol, a show of industry, skill, and love.

Quilts were treasures to be envied and coveted. Even today, some thirty years later, I sometimes hear my mother and others discussing with dismay the disappearance of Mama Pearl's quilts soon after she died. Quilts were rarely ever sold, but always passed on from one generation to the next. Most often when the older black Southerners died, there was little or no money left. Much of the land had been lost, stolen, or sold. The greatest treasures they had to pass down to their children were the quilts. Soon after a funeral was over, friends and kinfolk of the deceased would gather for food and memories, and the traditional sharing of the quilts. Each quilt had its own particular story and the material used represented the times of that person's life, the joy and the sadness he or she experienced.

As a child in mid-Delta Mississippi I had been part of that time-honored tradition of quilting. Not only did I collect the scraps, but I helped to box and pack the quilts that would be sent north to our relatives. Without fail, quilts maintained the connecting link between the Southerners that went north and those that stayed behind. Now I had gone north and the connection was unbroken. Ma Ponk had sent me her heart and the warmth of my community. As memories flooded my mind I could hear the old people in Glen Allan saying, "Kiver up chile, it'll keep the chill out."

I remembered the old folks and clung to my quilt, until at last my new St. Louis family came upstairs from the confectionery to admire my aunt's handiwork, and perhaps silently compare the skills of their own southern relatives. And as they came up to see the quilt, we also shared some of my home grown papershell pecans. We cracked the pecans with our teeth, savored their meats, and admired the beauty of the quilt. For those few moments, we were all back home.

Left alone again, I looked out the window, across Spring Street at Miss Missy's house. I knew that snow would soon cover all the debris of the summer. I held my "kiver" close to me and I smiled inside. At last, I had my quilt, and I could give Mama Beulah's back for storage in her trunk. "I'll use it tonight," I said as I folded it again and laid it across the foot of the bed.

My first winter turned out to be all that Ma Ponk and Ma Mae had told me. It seemed as if all the snow of my life had come down to greet me. There were drifts of snow higher than cars, blown up by a chill wind that cut straight through to your bones.

The winters of the South had seemed like a gentle intrusion into an otherwise intensive labor environment. Here in the North, however, the winters were brutal. Ma Ponk had warned me that the people up north did not keep their houses warm. Instead, they dressed heavily throughout the winter. The control of the thermostat in the living quarters above the confectionery showed the truth of Ma Ponk's fears. At night the heat all but disappeared. There were no green logs to throw into iron heaters and no buckets of coal to keep the fires going all night.

I was prepared to face those northern nights warmly covered with the stars of David pieced together by loving hands and made soft with matted cotton from the scraps left over by the field hands. This would be one of two that I would receive from down south, where quilts were the kiver that kept us warm.

The Morning Stove

Nancy Isonhood

I smell coal and kerosene, hear the match strike, and behind the darkness of my eyelids see a quick flash of light. Daddy does all this in the dark. He has done it so often he doesn't need a light. I know that Mama is still in their bed waiting for the room to warm, and soon I will smell bacon frying in the kitchen next to where we all sleep. And I know that Mama will cook extra bacon and biscuits that she will pack in Daddy's black lunch box, and I know that when I open my eyes Daddy will have on overalls with only one strap fastened and that he will have his back to me holding his hands close to the morning stove. I know all this because it has been this way all my life and I know it will never change.

Daddy will leave to drive a bulldozer for the county. My sister will ride the yellow school bus away from the house, the same bus I will ride next year, and then I will watch Mama go to the barn to milk and I will mark time by counting the only numbers I know. And I know, before I even open my eyes, that the morning stove will cause the windowpanes to sweat and that I will draw pictures on them while I wait for Mama. And I know that when Mama comes back from the barn she will give me warm milk for our cat, though she says she hates him, and then she will do what she does every day. She will clean what she cleaned yesterday.

I move closer to my sister in the bed we share and before we even touch I feel the warmth of her body. It is a magical time of the morning. In that twilight sleep, in that quiet morning silence, when everything is still and calm, we can be close.

But I also know that this morning, like every morning, my sister and I will argue over who will get Mama the eggs. And I know that though she is seven years older than I am, I am faster and will beat her to the loosened boards in the floor of the cold hall, and that we will stand and stare—her, with Mama's black eyes, and me, with Daddy's green ones, spitting words only we can hear—green and black mingling, until Mama calls for the eggs again, and that as we lift the board where the hen has built her nest under the house, she will turn her glassy eyes up at us and beneath her we will find warm, brown eggs.

Then I remember that today is different. It is the beginning of my sister's Christmas vacation from school. Today, Mama, my sister, and I will cut a tree and decorate it before Daddy comes home and we will bake the black walnut cookies that he loves so much. I snuggle closer to my sister and feel sleep crawling back inside of me, and I dream I see Daddy wearing his heavy boots. He is mashing the green hulls off the walnuts on the ground. I pick up the cleaned ones and drop them in a box. "Put them in front of the morning stove to dry," he says. Daddy is standing under the walnut tree looking up. Clusters of walnuts hang from the branches of the huge tree and the ground appears to be covered with green balls. My sister moves away from me. I wake up.

I open my eyes and see Daddy. He has one overall strap over his shoulder, like I knew he would, and he is watching us. He points to the window behind the bed. I arch my neck to look. I have heard about it, dreamed about it, but have never seen it. Daddy is smiling like he has delivered it himself.

Snow. The boards inside the house ooze with white dripping snow like the icing between the layers of Mama's coconut cakes. Snow curls and drips down the insides of the gray boards like winter's soft white handwriting. It has snowed. It has snowed inside and outside our house.

Snow. Snow. Beautiful white snow. All day snow. Snow that Mama turns into snow ice cream. Snow that changes the path to my grandmother's house, where we cut our Christmas tree, into something I have only seen on Christmas cards. Snowmen, snow women, snow children, snowballs, and all day Mama keeps the morning stove full so we stay warm.

When Daddy comes home, he opens his lunch box that smells of bacon and biscuits and long-gone sandwiches, and in it he has three Coca-Colas—one for my sister, one for me, and one for him and Mama to share. The snow crunches as Mama mashes it into glasses. The foaming Coke rises over the snow. We sit around the morning stove. All the lights are off except the ones on the Christmas tree. The room is a hazy rainbow of color. I take a black walnut cookie from the plate and then, in the glow of the Christmas lights, I see Mama smile at Daddy.

It is only three weeks until Christmas. No presents have been bought, the tree is not up, and the garland that needs to be draped over the gate lies in a pile on my grandchild's stroller in the garage.

I look at the black walnuts soaking in the big tub of water. I hate them. My jeans are wet up to my knees, a cold wind is blowing directly out of the north, and I have to get them picked out before Christmas, before we go to Mama's. Had I known that Daddy was going to die, I would have mashed the hulls off the walnuts when they were green, but he didn't give us any warning and I didn't know the walnut tree was going to blow over. I didn't know its roots were dead, that its feeder roots were decayed. How was I to know? It was still producing fruit. It was in full leaf when it fell.

I tried to peel the dry black hulls off, but they wouldn't budge. Now, I resort to soaking them to remove the hulls. A cold mist begins to fall as I dump the water and walnuts for the third time. I stomp on them. "Come off!" I yell. I stomp harder. Dark brown water stains my socks as the walnuts disappear into the muddy ground.

The wind is cold, but inside there is a chill even colder than the wind. I dig the walnuts from the mud and put them back into the tub of water.

I don't know how old the tree was. It had always been there. I had climbed its gnarled trunk and rested in its branches. I had been Jane waiting for Tarzan. I had swung on a tire roped to one of its branches. It had watched me grow. It had stood solidly and quietly watching as I turned from a child to a woman, a wife, and then a grandmother, and I never thought that some day it would be gone. But, when it fell, it fell perfectly. Had it fallen any other way, it would have ripped the house apart.

Four generations stared into the large, gaping hole. I should have gathered the walnuts then, but I didn't. I didn't know Daddy would die in less than three months. I didn't realize it was the last harvest.

Children play in Mama's yard as we drive up. I see wool caps and hot breaths crystallizing in cold air. A silver bow hangs from the mailbox. I see Daddy's last cat. His name is Pete. Mama has not given him away, though she says she hates him. Daddy's truck is still parked in his parking place. I want to see the huge black walnut tree, but the only indication that it was ever there is a large bare spot in the yard that has been filled with sand. There is no monument to what it meant to us. Only a pile of dirt marks its life.

When we walk in the back door, his recliner is empty. No green eyes dance and say, "Y'all come on in." The emptiness is huge. The Christmas tree is in the same place it has always been, but its colored lights have been replaced with white ones. Silver and white balls hang on its branches. The white lights give off an icy stare. Everything is void of color.

My sister and I hug as we usually do. *He loved me more*, I think, but do not say.

"Black walnut cookies," I say, as I offer forth the mound of aluminum foil. I think about that Christmas so long ago. Three Cokes, the cookies, Mama, Daddy, and us, and the morning stove there to keep us warm. I remember the snow and the snow ice cream that Mama made—the black walnut cookies. I thought things would never change, but *then* Daddy had been there. *Then*, there had been magic.

A great-grandchild says the blessing before we eat. I had wondered who would. The chair at the head of the table is empty. Others, who have no place to sit, take their plates to a table in the den. Daddy's chair remains empty. Mama takes the chair. Mama, who never sits down at the table, takes the chair. Mama, who always hovers from plate to plate, making sure everyone has everything. Mama takes the chair.

Mama and I are alone. It is late. The house is silent. A silence that falls hard and loud after children's screams and adult laughter have faded and gone. It is a silence where the clock ticks too loudly and the wind's howl around the north corner of the house is more mournful than usual.

"Might as well take down the tree," she says.

I wonder where the old decorations are. The decorations we made as children, the colored lights. I want to snatch the colorless blinking orbs from the tree.

"We could," I say. I get the boxes for the decorations. We stand side by side, woman and mother. I take down a silver ball. She places it in the box.

"The cookies were good," she says.

"No one really ate them," I say.

"I did," she says.

Another silence falls between us. In that silence I finally hear it. It is the cold, hard realization that Mama has heard every day and night since Daddy died. *He is gone.* He is really gone and it is her first Christmas without him since she was sixteen. Her children have long ago left home, and now her mate of sixty-one years is gone, and now the silence says she is alone.

"Why did you quit making them?" I ask.

"Too much trouble," she says.

"Yeah."

"He would have liked them," she says.

Tears slide down my face. I try to stop them. I can't. It is as if my eyes are melting. "I can't believe he's not here," I say. "I can't believe I'll never see him . . . hear him. . . ."

Mama puts her hands on my shoulders and turns me toward her. "I do," she says.

"Mama. I don't mean heaven—that I won't *ever* see him. I'm talking about *now*. I want to see him *now!*"

"I do see him now," she says.

"You don't understand," I start, but then I look into her eyes. A tiny silver thread spins between her black eyes and my green ones. We stare. We stare, feeling the thread turn and twist tighter and tighter. The air between us is thin. We are so close we share the same breath. *Flesh of my flesh,* I think. Mama touches my chin. "I do see him now," she says again. "Every time I look at your eyes, I see him."

Mama takes me in her arms. I put mine around her. I feel it. The warmth. The warmth of the morning stove. I close my eyes and smell bacon frying and kerosene and *I know* before morning, there will be snow. There will be snow inside and outside our house. And, like always, Mama will make snow ice cream.

Sermon with Meath

Barry Hannah

You could see into the basement quarters through big glass sliding doors the playroom, as they called it, of Webb Meath. Meath was seventeen and I was only thirteen. I could see him putting 45 rpm records on a machine and practicing dance steps by himself around the playroom. I was going to enter Meath's world fairly soon. He was on the verge of being a sissy, even though he was on the football team, not playing much until all was hopeless or well in hand in the last quarter. Then he would trot in with great earnestness and get some grass stain on his uniform for when he met his girlfriend, who had almost made the cheerleader squad and hung around these girls like an extra pal, no hard feelings. She was almost cute, too. But Meath was built like a soft bowling pin. Although tall, he didn't seem to have any strength in him, and he slouched, with a high burr haircut on him and the red, bowed lips of a woman, full and wet like that. Webb Meath was from Indiana, or perhaps Minnesota. They were Methodists in a heavily Baptist town, further alien.

Meath wanted to be a Methodist preacher. He would bring a Bible out where I and a couple of other buddies my age played at a wide board rope swing hung from an oak at the bottom of our property, right where the Meath meadow began, out there where we on Sundays had fierce touch-football games with fellows of all ages.

Meath would stand there with his Bible in hand, more than a foot taller, and watch our play sternly as if whatever we were doing was not quite right. For instance, plastic soldiers spread all out in attack with tanks, artillery, command bunkers, and fortresses of packed soil. We would air-bomb them too, with spark plugs, and fire into them with whitehead matches from shooters made of clothespins. Smoke and mouth gunfire and screams going on very seriously. Meath would observe us with pity on his face, but kind pity. We all liked Meath. He was gentle like a brother, and he was very strange. Meath would not interrupt, he would let us play ourselves out, then he would hunker down, peer at each of us sincerely, wet his lips, and begin preaching from the Book of Revelations, the Bible spread out in his big left hand. We would sit on our negligible butts with arms around our knees and listen for upwards of an hour.

The Eagle and the Bear and the Horsemen and the White Horse of Death and the minions and the princes and Joseph Stalin and the Hydrogen Bomb and the Daughters of Wrath. I don't think Meath had a very good grasp of all this, but he listed them well, and in that Northern voice somewhere between a whine and a song. His eyes would half shut as if it hurt to read these things. Many years later it would strike me that those who especially loved Revelations were nerds and dweebs and dorks who despised people and life on this planet, somewhat like the *Star Trek* crowd I saw at Iowa City who liked to get in elevators and discuss how this or that civilization was "utterly consumed." But I don't believe Meath hated this world. He wanted in it badly but something was very wrong. He was not winning and he had no joy being regular and mature. He did not dance well, his girl was not so special, he was awkward and had made only second team, and in the school halls he was galoot-like, slouching and puzzled as if lost among bad smells. Even we little guys noticed it.

That he had a good car and his people were well-off cut no ice. With another person it might have, but not with Meath. He stayed at the edge of the popular crowd, giving bad imitations of it. For instance, it was difficult for Meath to look casual. He seemed near tears often. I once saw him and his girl-friend having a quiet moment at the hall locker like you were supposed to, but both of them were red-faced and pouted-up as if nearly crying over some deep matter. It was my sense she wanted him to do things.

After Meath finished, he would begin playing with us and our soldiers, or whatever we had going, with more zeal by far than he had shown in the sermon. Meath would really get off into it, making machine-gun sounds and totally successful bomb explosions. His mouth would be red from wetting the kitchen matches on the head before striking them. You sailed them and they left true smoke like rockets, bursting into flame as they fell among the soldiers.

Then one afternoon he got very concerned and stared at his hands and we asked him what was wrong.

They don't think this is right, he said.

Who? What? I asked him.

Me hanging out with guys your age.

Oh. Why not?

It's queer, Dad said.

No. But we need your sermons.

Yes, that's true, said Meath, more confident now. He fell to playing with us again. Meath wasn't just hanging out with us. He was deeper in play than we were.

One other afternoon he said he thought we were mature enough to follow along in Revelations with our own Bibles, so I went up the hill to my house and got several Bibles. We had plenty. My mother was huge in the Baptist church. She was the president of the state Women's Missionary Union. We had had Mexicans and Chinese people in our house.

Where are you going with those? my mother wanted to know. I told her Meath was preaching from Revelations and wanted us to follow. Mother peered down the hill where Meath stood with my other pals. She had that Nay look in her eyes. Baptists are the Church of the New Testament, they say, but in the South they tend to be severe as in the Old. My mother didn't believe in dancing or too much fun on the Sabbath. I never saw her affectionate with my Pa, not once. If the doors of the church were open, we were in it. With revivals, six days a week. She insisted on tithing to such a comprehensive extent that my father complained even to me. He was afraid she would give everything to the church in the event he died, so he lived a good long time. He was from the Depression where a nickel was serious.

Children shouldn't try to understand that book, she said.

But there's Meath.

Yes. He's a large boy, isn't he? She looked very doubtful as I left with the Bibles. I knew it didn't look right to her and was guilty, a common condition of young Baptists. My mother was from Delta planters. Somehow this made her consumed by appearances. The *appearance* of evil was as grave as, say, yelling *hell* at the dinner table.

Then another afternoon, a Sunday, Meath became entirely strange. We were playing touch football. Meath was far and away the largest out there. There must have been sixteen of us from junior high, and Meath, on his perfect sunlit property. My team did a sweep and I blocked Meath at the knees. I cut him down. I was shocked that this huge boy went over with only a soft rubbery give to him. We scored but we looked back and there was Meath rolling on the ground, holding his shins and howling. It was a thing I could barely connect with my block. I couldn't have weighed more than ninety or so. He was two hundred. But he wailed and then just began clinching up, all red and weepy, going on in an embarrassing, thin Yankee whine. It was a preposterous act. We all hung our heads. Soon we went home. All joy was gone, and it made us feel bad. My friends and I began to despise Meath. We watched his failures and cheered for them bitterly.

He and the girl broke up. Meath prowled around even sadder. We liked this. Some older boy pointed out that Meath had a low ass. This was true and we adored it. His voice, that we liked before, got on our nerves. We moved the soldiers back onto my property, abandoning the great forts in his, and watched the rains of the spring melt them down. We would jump bikes off a ramp and then leap from the bike at the peak of the rise and grab a rope that swung out forty feet high into a fir tree, and fall through the branches, usually hurt and even bleeding, which was the point. Meath came down and watched us from his swing. We knew he wanted to join us.

His mouth's connected to his butthole, whispered the older boy.

What?

No guts, the boy explained. This was a rich one and we barked the rest of the day about it, taking furtive glances at Meath, whose face with its big woman's lips just hung there sissy and wanting, a splendid annoyance to our play. We learned to cut Meath, just cut him, drop our eyes in the halls of the school when he came near. This was a sweet new social skill. High adolescence was going to be a snap.

Meath was ending his senior year this spring. I don't recall how we knew this in the small town, but it was understood Meath's father was failing in business. His Southern adventure had not worked out. They were moving back North. When I looked down into Meath's playroom, where he still practiced dancing, I saw the gray air of failure all around him. Somebody had caught him wearing a letter jacket he had not earned in the nearby capital city, Jackson, and this was his certain end. You could sink no lower.

In a frame asbestos-siding house on the street that Meath's faced, down just about five houses on the north side, lived a family that was not genteel poor. They were really poor. They were white, of course, and their father, in his forties, was studying at the little Baptist college in our town to be a grade-school teacher. He had many children and it was said they never ate much but cornflakes. He could not support them at whatever he used to do, so now he was educating himself to move up to the position of teacher, but the four years and odd jobs meant even direr straights for his people. Nevertheless he had them in church every Sunday, heads all watered-down with combing, in sorry clothes but clean. He and his entire family were baptized one Wednesday night at Prayer Meeting, there in the pool under the stained glass scene of the Jordan River. Everybody cheered him, and my mother became positively tearful about their goodness and conversion. Mother was stern, but she was loving, profoundly, about new church people. I understand the success of the Baptists in converting the South nearly wholesale, through my mother.

But Mr. Tweedy, the poor man, came out of the pool on the preacher's arm all choked up and fighting off the water. Here was an adult who feared water. I turned my head and grinned at another hellion down the pew. At Christmas I helped my father deliver boxes of hams and fruit and cheese to the needy. All of the families were black except the Tweedys, nearly on our own street. This was odd. I felt humiliated for them, even though they were most appreciative, and showed no false pride. I knew this was biblical but it didn't sit right. I recall, also, the absence of damned near everything in the living room of that house. I believe there was a card table and orange crates.

So Mr. Tweedy was graduating, too. This spring he was getting his degree and already he was a substitute teacher in Jackson. Things were looking up. Mother and the neighbors applauded them. Providence, it seemed, was about to attend the new Christian Tweedys. Nothing could be better. The Lord had promised this.

But in April while Mr. Tweedy was driving his awful Ford to his school, a tornado came through Jackson, picked up only his car into the air and hurled him against something and killed him. All his plans and work meant this, and his children were now orphans, his skinny, bent wife a widow by celestial violence. I could not understand at all. Although I played constantly at war with my pals, I could never, I thought, have devised anything this cruel. My mother was hurt, too. But she said it had a purpose. All had a design.

But I stopped going to church, scandalizing her and driving her into long prayer talks with our pastor. She went around teary and solemn. My father told me the same thing as when my terrier Spot died of jaundice: Son, everything dies. He could not know how viciously irrelevant he was then. I started growing up cynical. I believe, in the matter of Christians, I became a little Saul before the road to Damascus, Saul the persecutor of the faith, before he saw the light and became St. Paul of the Gospels.

My mother came in my room and told me Meath had called me and several of the boys to meet him down at the swing. He had a special testimony for us. I could not believe she was approving of Meath. She was truly desperate. But I went down, though sourly, already despising Meath as he stood tall among some boys who had already arrived. Nobody sat down. That was all over. We just sort of made a rank and stepped back from Meath. He had no Bible, but he clasped his hands together and was looking at the ground prayerfully.

What's giving, Reverend? said the older boy.

We're all confused by what happened to Mr. Tweedy, I know, said Meath.

He was meek and humble, a hard-working Christian man, a resurrected man, who loved his wife and children. The meek should inherit the earth, the Savior said. But . . . Tweedy.

When Meath raised his face, there was one of those warm, evangelical smiles on him. He had let his hair grow out and it was swept back, all oily, and looked like black under shellac. I hadn't seen him lately and this was almost too much.

God has His reasons for poor Mr. Tweedy. He was using him as a testament to us. Mr. Tweedy is happy now.

Meath seemed to be imitating Tweedy in heaven with this insane, warm smile.

Tweedy is looking down telling us guys to just love and support one another and get right with the Lord!

There was a big gap of quiet then, and many of us looked down at the soil, too. Where the forts had been was only a dry mud. That was what God did to Mr. Tweedy, I recall thinking. Right back into the mud for daring to get better.

You only like Tweedy because he's lower than you, the older boy suddenly said to Meath. You love it that he was murdered by a tornado because it makes a creep like you feel lucky and right. You're using Tweedy to make us be your friend. But we ain't going to be your friends because you're chicken and a liar and that's the way it's always going to be.

I was astounded by what my friend said. He had really been winding up inside in his hatred for Meath, and I was shocked that I hated Meath almost this much, too. I had depended on Meath to be smooth and Northern-hip and a friendly guide to life.

Meath's warm new smile fell off and he just collapsed. He turned around and walked back to his two-story house with its glassed playroom. We could see him shaking with sobs. His mother was on the balcony waiting and watching him. We saw the sudden expression on her face, horror, and we left, to all parts of the subdivision. I felt a part of a mob that had stoned somebody and it was not that bad, it had a nice edge to it. That big Meath.

In college my roommate, a brilliant boy already long into botany and

Freud, and I baited Christers at the college. Many of them were pre-ministerial students perfecting their future roles. They came on like idiot-savants, quoting scripture perfectly and at great length, but baffled by almost everything else. We especially went at a short boy with a wide, pale face and thick, ashy whiskers on him. He wore thick glasses and was a quoting fool, get him started. He was only eighteen but already like a loony old man. He roomed with a new Christian Chinese fellow, rail-thin and just out of starvation, who wrote this hesitant Christian poetry on the slant for the campus literary magazine. It was utter banal coonshit, and we loved to read it aloud. We played loud Ray Charles and much jazz on the machine, smoked and drank lab alcohol, and shouted out what we would do if challenged by one of the nude pin-up girls on our wall. The Christers gathered and put us on all the prayer lists. The dorm counselor, a giant, one-eyed Christer, broke down and told us nothing came from our room but crap and corruption. But we made A's, anointed thus. Once I hid in the closet while my buddy pretended to be in a spiritual crisis, weeping and gnashing his teeth for the loony thick-glassed guy who was overjoyed at his chance to save him. I finally howled out. The boy was so out of it, he thought I was in a fit of contrition, too. Then I went down and pretended to the Christian Chinese boy that his poetry had driven me insane.

I am not proud remembering this. Once I thrashed a skinny Christer, a senior, with boxing gloves in the hall. He had been wanting to prove that Christers were strong too, but I routed him. I was cheered by the agnostic few around the hall, but this seemed cheap, at last, and I gave up on baiting. My roommate pal went straight to the state asylum for depression and alcoholism, and I felt so miserable and lonely I got married too early.

A couple of decades passed and I was in Chicago, reading some pages from my new book at the University, I think, when I saw something in the paper. That night I got a taxi and went out to see him. Meath was indeed a minister, Methodist, but in a small sort of hippie chapel on the edge of a bad and garish neighborhood where transvestites sported around nearly in ownership of the block. Meath was overjoyed to see me. He met me an hour before the service began and although I came wanting vaguely to apologize for our awful treatment of him twenty years ago, I never got the chance. He hugged me and acted as if we had been perfect boyhood chums. He bragged on good traits about me I didn't even remember, said he knew my imagination would pull me through. He too had been through divorce and bad times, although always a minister. He was stout, not much hair, but trimmer, more solid, and glowing with health. Mostly he was so delighted to see me.

At the service were some forty folks—some bums, some straight and prosperous men and women, and some truly ancient hippies, those phenomenal people who are fifty and have changed nothing. Meath began as if just chatting, then I sensed the sermon was in progress. He stood, no lectern, no altar, no height, in front of his flock, and spoke with a sane joy. Simply a good-looking, middle-aged man with a comfortable interior to him. He wore glasses. A loose hair sprang up at the back of his head and waved about. Everything counts, he said.

Everything counts but you must isolate this thing and not let it become mixed with others. You must look at it as a child would. You must not bring the heaviness of long-thinking and the burden of your hours to it. The lightness, the calm wonder and intensity of a child is what I mean. Picasso says at fifty, At last, I can paint like a child! That must have been paradise for him. Perhaps it waits for you.

Come unto me, all you that labor and are heavy laden, and I will give you rest. Take my yoke upon you and learn of me; for I am meek and lowly in heart. And you shall find rest unto your souls. For my yoke is easy, and my burden is light, speaks Christ.

Heaviness comes as you get older. But sufficient unto the day is the evil thereof, says the Savior. Look at the day alone and do not mix it with others. A child has no need of the future or the past. He is all times at once. You've only need of the day. The precious day. This day even more precious because my friend of long ago is here.

Meath pointed to me.

I can't remember, in my life so far, a happier time than this.

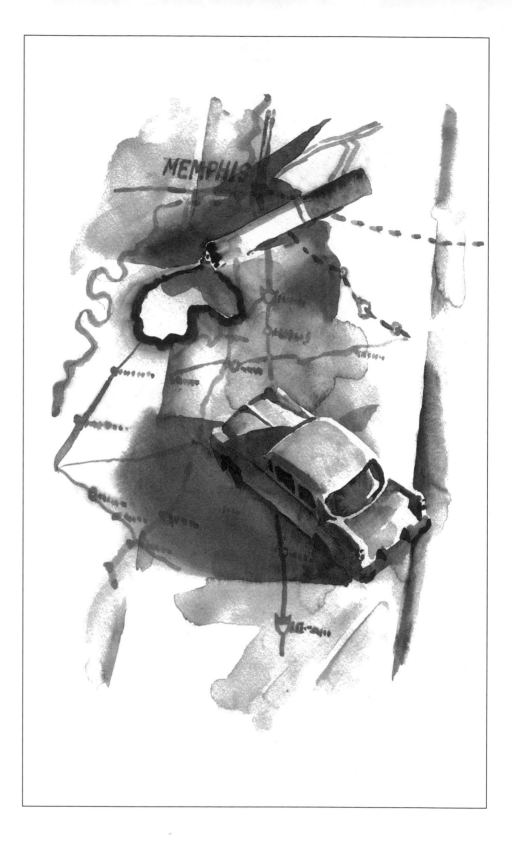

Home for Christmas

Charline R. McCord

We are right in the middle of watching *Friends* when Mama blurts out, "I want to go see my relations this Christmas!" I freeze like a deer in headlights and do not move my eyes from the television. Mama does not drive. Mama's family lives six hours away in Tennessee. I *knew* I should not have come to Mama's house tonight.

"Did you hear me, Janice?" Mama shouts. "MUTE that thing!" she yells, tossing a big fringy throw pillow at me and landing it right in the paper plate of dip I am using for my carrot sticks. Over the years Mama has made a zillion of these stuffed battering rams, and she has used them on me all my life.

I am ticked, so I snatch up the remote control and bump the volume down one number. "What?" I yell back, using my napkin to clean the dip off Mama's pillow.

"I want to spend Christmas with my relations!" she demands like a spoiled brat, completely forgetting how much she hates her family. Mama is totally unpredictable.

She *would* start on this right when I am waiting to see if Rachel is actually going to tell Ross the truth about her date. I jab my carrot stick around in my fuzzy dip and make a mental note to be super aggravating the next time Mama is watching *Who Wants To Be A Millionaire*. "What *are* you talking about?" I snap, breaking my carrot stick in half for effect.

"I'm talking about my *family*—F-A-M-I-L-Y," she spells out loud to her master's degreed daughter. "I want an old-fashioned family Christmas where everybody goes home for the holidays. I haven't seen Lola Ruth and Hortense and Carl and Murray in—well . . . since the funeral," she chokes out. Mama is referring to Daddy's funeral, which none of *us* are allowed to mention.

"Whatever made you think of that?" I ask innocently, trying to send this conversation in a whole new direction.

"Friends!" Mama wails, gesturing wildly toward the T.V. "Friends can't replace family—everybody knows that! Especially at Christmastime!" Mama has always been irritable with me.

"I never said they could," I tell Mama calmly and matter-of-factly. I am *trying* to appease her before this thing gets out of hand. But what I'm thinking is that Mama doesn't have many friends, so how would she know how they compare to family.

But I don't go there. Instead, I mumble, "Hortense is an oxymoron." I'm trying to make Mama *think* instead of *talk* so I can concentrate on the television.

"Why I ought to disinherit you!" Mama snaps back at me. "Your Aunt Hortense went two whole semesters to the Max Little Business College. She is *not* a moron!"

It is clear to me that my television viewing is over for tonight. I click the remote and watch the screen fade to a pinpoint of light. That is how bright my Mama is . . . my Mama and the whole Turner family. It makes me tired to think of it. "Mama," I sigh, "I didn't say Hortense was a moron. I said Hortense is an *oxymoron*—a contradiction in terms."

Mama's eyes are flashing and she's clutching another fringy throw pillow. "You've got half a second to explain that, Miss!" she threatens. Mama could've been a circus act she's so high-strung.

"Oh, for gosh sakes, Mama, *think about it!* There is no such thing as a *tense whore*—it's a ridiculous name!"

The pillow sails past the lampshade and slaps against the left side of my head just as the front door pops open. In waltzes Bam, just in time to snicker at me and take Mama's side. I wish you could see this. Bam's got on a leopard print spandex outfit that's so tight in the B & B it makes me blush. Bam is

Mama's favorite. Always has been. Mama thinks everything Bam does is plumb cute. "Let Bam take her to see her relations," I'm thinking. I snatch up a copy of *Southern Living* magazine so I won't be so bored.

"Mama," Bam coos, rolling her eyes at me and grabbing my paper plate of carrot sticks and Weight Watchers dip off the coffee table, "Steve and me are running a tad short for Christmas—can you spare us a *teeny* bit of cash, just a few measly hundred?"

That's our Bam, straight to the point and the pocketbook.

"Yuk," she chokes out in disgust as she tosses the plate of carrot sticks back onto the coffee table. "How do you eat this stuff?" Bam tries to be so subtle in front of Mama, but I catch the insult. I've got eyes—I can see that after three kids Bam still weighs 105 and every part of her body is leaping up and down, claiming total victory over mankind. I'm so ticked I'm flipping magazine pages as fast as I can. I blow right through the gardening section and don't even flinch at the pound cake recipes.

But Mama's in a *mood*, so she cranks up to preach Bam one of her famous sermons on character. "Betsy Ann McMillan," Mama says assertively, pur-posely omitting Bam's married name, "you and Steve can *NOT* maintain a higher standard of living than everybody you know—drive new automobiles with telephones in them and watch big screen T.V.'s, and then turn around and call on the rest of us, who are doing without, to bail you out of a bind." What Mama doesn't say is that Bam was the first person in town to have a scored concrete floor.

Bam is lighting a cigarette and raking her blonde hair behind one ear. Her leopard-print sunglasses are perched on top of her head, and she has kicked off her shoes and propped her bare, brown feet with fuchsia-painted toes in Mama's lap. "*Slut*," I think to myself. Bam needs behavior modification worse than anybody I know. She's only got one set of mannerisms, and they belong in the bedroom where she clearly spends most of her time.

She takes a long, slow drag on her cigarette, then tosses her head back and blows smoke at the ceiling fan. "Mama, that may be the dumbest thing you've ever said to me," Bam says, completely unscathed. "Think about it. If I lived like *you*, why I wouldn't even need *a mama*."

Mama sits right there and melts like she's been paid some kind of a compliment. Then she writes a check—*one* check to Bammie—and lord only knows how much she writes it for. No matter what she says or how she looks, please remember this: Mama has got money. Bam knows this better than anybody.

I get tired of watching Bam work a mother, a body, and a room—so I speak up and say, "Bam, Mama was just telling me that she wants to go to Tennessee for Christmas." Bam hates going to Tennessee, but Bam doesn't have the check in her hand yet, so she throws herself around Mama's neck and squeals: "Ohhh, Mama, that would be sooo much fun! Let's *all* go to Tennessee for Christmas!" This proves how things will totally backfire if your timing is the least bit off. Next thing I know, Mama and Bam have the Christmas trip to Tennessee all planned. We leave in three weeks, bright and early on Christmas Eve.

"You *hate* going to Tennessee," I snarl at Bam while Mama is out of the room popping popcorn.

Bam gives me a devilish grin as she slowly folds Mama's check. She makes a big production of slipping it between her boobs, which are heaving right over the edge of that leopard print top.

"Unlike *you*, Janice," Bam says with a haughty air, "I am *WAY* flexible . . . I don't care what state I pick up my gifts in." Then she does this real seductive maneuver off Mama's swooning sofa, easing that leopard skirt all the way up her tanned thigh. Bam used to be a dancer—may *still* be one for all I know. She twists her behind all the way to the kitchen phone, dials up Aunt Hortense, and locks in our visit. Mama is eating popcorn and grinning. Mama thinks Bam hung the moon.

Christmas Eve morning we are packing up to leave when the weatherman suddenly adds "chance of snow flurries" to his forecast. "Snow flurries!" I wail, racing to the window.

"Oh it's perfect!" Mama exclaims. "A white family Christmas!" I glance over my shoulder to see if she has a clue what she just said. Mama is standing in the middle of the floor with her hands clasped together under her chin like a praying angel. "We'll take the Buick," she says firmly, as if a Buick solves everything.

"If I've got to maneuver in snow, I want to be driving my own car," I huff, looking out at the overcast sky.

"The Buick is a heavier car with lots of room in the trunk," Mama persists. I turn to look at Mama again, and what I see this time is a difficulty with arms and legs.

"The Buick has been sitting up," I point out, choosing my words so as not to mention Daddy's death. "Besides, what we need is a U-Haul," I add, staring at all the food, gifts, and luggage Mama is busy stockpiling beside the front door.

"It's the season for giving," Mama chirps, dumping a heavy honey-baked ham in my arms. "Back seat," she orders.

"Mama, you're taking ham, turkey, dressing, chutney, cakes, pies, cookies, candy—what on earth have you left for Aunt Hortense and Aunt Lola Ruth to do?"

"Eat," Mama swipes. "They both *love* to eat." There is something in Mama's tone that I don't like. Clearly, she's mad about having to ride in my new red Chevrolet. I ignore her, grab a load of her stuff, and head out the door.

"Food in the backseat," Mama calls out bossily, "suitcases and gifts in the trunk."

I load everything into my own car the way I want to. The wind has picked up and it's freezing outside, but I hover under the trunk lid and arrange things properly. It'll be a long time before this vehicle is paid off, and I'm determined not to have Mama's ham juice riding with me for the next five years. I am very meticulous with my new car.

Mama comes out the door, lets out a sharp yell, and dashes back inside. I just grin; Mama *hates* cold weather. When she comes out again, she's bound herself up to look like Boris Yeltsin—long black overcoat, furry black hat, scarf, and gloves. My eyes slide down to her feet and I bust out laughing. She's got on her bright yellow gardening boots—the ones I call rubber ducky shoes.

"Humph," Mama says, tossing her head back to let me know her fashion conscience is uninjured by my laughter.

We finish packing the car and head over to Bam's house. The first icy mist begins to hit the windshield just as we pull into her driveway. Steve's outside loading the Jeep, and I can see the blonde heads of the kids, Scott and Lizzie, bobbing around in the backseat. Bam is nowhere in sight.

"Bam's drying her hair," Steve reports through my window like he's got everything at his place under tight control. Steve is a high school football coach, so he likes to pretend that all motion takes place according to a plan.

"Drying her hair!" I wail, pressing my whole body down on the horn. "I hope you know we're trying to outrun a snowstorm!"

"Calm down," Mama says as if *I* am the problem, "the weatherman only said 'flurries.' We're on an adventure here—a big Christmas adventure," she adds excitedly. We sit in the car and stare at Bam's carport door, watching for any sign of movement.

"Apparently you don't know the definition of an adventure," I reply. After all, somebody's got to make conversation. I refuse to sit here catatonic over Bam.

"Well, enlighten me," Mama snips.

"A situation only becomes an adventure," I explain, "when something goes wrong."

"There she is!" Steve bellows like Bob Barker. Our own Miss America appears at the carport door carrying three month old Justin.

"Finally!" I exclaim, gunning it out of the driveway and over to hit the interstate without once glancing in the rearview mirror to see if the Jeep is following.

"North toward home!" Mama crows in delight. Since moving to Mississippi, Mama has become a big Willie Morris fan. She digs around in a canvas bag by her feet and pulls out a Mississippi map.

"Mama," I say tiredly, "we don't need a map to go straight up Interstate 55."

"Well, you certainly will need one to negotiate your way around Memphis," she insists. She spreads the open map on her lap as if she is the designated navigator. Never mind that we are *hours* from Memphis.

It's a long drive, so I decide to act pleasant. "Well, this is exciting," I say, patting Mama's arm. "We're all going home for Christmas, just like you wanted. This'll be fun."

"Yes," Mama smiles. "Home for Christmas," she repeats, gazing out the window. "You know, Janice, it's a lot prettier in Tennessee. Tennessee has seasons—colorful falls. I miss seasons," she says wistfully. "I get sick of pine trees."

The car phone rings. I answer and it's little Lizzie, calling from the Jeep behind us. They're all hungry, she says. They haven't had breakfast. They want to get off at the Ridgeland exit and eat at the Shoney's breakfast bar.

"Fine," I say sarcastically. "Why, that's a fine idea, Lizzie. We've been on the road such a *long* time now and haven't stopped even once!"

"Right!" Lizzie says hurriedly, and slams down the phone.

We kill a full hour in Shoney's, and by the time we come out snow has completely whited out the windshields and is falling fast and solid. The kids go bonkers.

"WAHOO!" yells Scott. He takes off running, a flurry of arms and legs, then locks his feet and skids past eight or ten parked cars before disappearing under a gold Expedition.

Lizzie is skating circles on the sidewalk. "Loosen up!" she hollers at Mama and me as we support one another and creep across the enemy snow. "Why don't you two try to have a little fun sometime?"

Bam is laughing her head off, so proud of her sassy offspring. Steve lets out a shrill whistle and herds his whole team into the Jeep.

"Those kids are something else," I hear a man coming out behind me say.

We gingerly pick our way to the car. I am secretly glad that Mama's got on her rubber ducky boots. The kids are looking out the window and making fun of Mama and me. I can see Scott pointing at us and howling.

"Those kids need a keeper," Mama grumbles as she climbs into the car with a sigh. The kids have already gotten on Mama's nerves.

"Turn on some heat!" Mama demands before I can even get the key in the ignition. "It's COLD in here!"

"Mama," I say real slowly to reveal my exasperation, "I have to wait until the engine warms up." Mama not only doesn't drive, she knows *zip* about a car.

"I guess you'll freeze me all the way to Tennessee, and then turn me over to Hortense who'll freeze me some more," Mama grumbles. "She's so tight she won't heat that big old house. I'll have to sleep in pajamas, socks, and a robe."

I sigh and head up the entrance ramp to the interstate. "Mama, Aunt Hortense has plenty of bed linens. I'm sure you'll be just fine."

"Oh, yes, she certainly does!" Mama declares in that tone I heard earlier. "She's got every quilt your Grandmama Turner ever made—and wouldn't part with a one of them for the world!"

I've heard the quilt story half my life and I'm in *no* mood to hear it again. Especially when I'm all nerved up on Shoney's coffee and trying to drive through a snowstorm. I ignore Mama and concentrate on a slow, steady pace, keeping my wheels in the tracks of the car ahead of me.

"She's got the Star of David and the Double Wedding Ring quilts that mama made before she married," Mama drones on.

"Mama, try not to think about that right now," I urge politely.

We ride in silence for a few minutes. Suddenly Mama blurts out: "Did I ever tell you about the time Lola Ruth wrote me a letter and asked me if I'd GIVE my part of the land to her and Hortense since I probably wouldn't ever live up there again?"

"Yes, Mama," I groan, "you've told me about that letter a thousand times. You've even *shown* me the letter. I am intimately acquainted with all the sordid details of *the letter*, but that was a long time ago. Now please, settle down and think happy thoughts. We're going up here to have a big, congenial, family Christmas." My one nerve has stretched into an invisible thread.

The snow is coming down fast and hard, blowing straight into the windshield and making me jumpy as I hug the steering wheel and dodge the pounding of the enormous flakes. I can feel my tires sliding slightly sideways on the uncertain ice.

"*GIVE* my land," Mama erupts, ignoring my simple request.

"Damn it, Mama, *hush!*" I screech, accidentally hitting the brakes and spinning the car around in two perfect pirouettes before we slide off the shoulder and swirl to a stop headed South toward Jackson again. The Jeep passes us and everyone inside is laughing hysterically. Scott puts the window down and sticks his arm out giving me a thumbs up sign.

Mama folds her arms in front of her and looks out the side window smugly. "The Buick is a heavier car," she repeats like a parrot.

"Mama," I say in an exasperated and hateful tone that I have reserved for this moment, "this trip was YOUR idea. Nothing would do but you *had* to get to Tennessee for Christmas. You *had* to see your FAMILY! So we're going there. I'm trying to get you to your loved ones just as fast as I can—through wind, snow, sleet, hail, whatever! Now, you are either going to stop bitching about your family that you so desperately want to see, or you're going to *get out and walk.* Which is it going to be?" The tone of my voice is close to shattering glass.

Mama looks at me in utter astonishment. Two words escape her lips: *"Why, Janice!"* Then she folds her arms across her chest, sulls up, and stares straight ahead. I sit there, gripping the steering wheel, trying to calm the jitters from my icy spin and giving her ample time to exit. Finally, I crank the car and ease us back onto the road. The Jeep has been waiting up ahead, and it pulls back onto the road after we pass, then eases around us into the lead.

For the next 8 miles I am riding with an inanimate object. I am ecstatic. I have fought for and won a peaceful driving existence. Mama has not only ceased to complain, she has practically ceased to exist. I am the master of my destiny; I am the captain of my ship. I have wrested control! I smile a victor's smile.

The road has a good three inches of snow on it now, and I am glad to be following in the path of the Jeep. Snow is collecting in the trees and gradually transforming the landscape into an Ansel Adams–like photograph. I am trying to think when I last saw Mississippi in a winter coat, when Mama begins to rummage in her bag. I don't even look her way, but I chuckle to myself. I knew she couldn't remain a frozen statue too much longer. I am fiddling with the defroster when I hear a small click. Then I smell smoke. Mama has *lit a cigarette* in my new car! This is a deliberate, calculated attempt to spite me. Mama knows how I hate it when she smokes.

For a few minutes I drive in furious silence, letting Mama think she's getting away with this trick. I compose myself and wait until she has confidently smoked nearly half the cigarette. Then I announce in my deepest war voice: "I don't allow smoking in my new car."

Out of the corner of my eye, I see the end of Mama's cigarette light up bright red. She has taken another puff, refusing to acknowledge that I am addressing *her*. I clear my throat with authority, look up into the rearview mirror, and ease my foot off the accelerator, making her think there's about to be a *huge* showdown. She hits the power button, lowers her window just a crack, and pushes the cigarette out. She closes the window and resumes her sulled up, frozen posture. "Touché!" I think, picking up a little speed. I've got Mama under full control. We ride on down the road in blissful silence.

Suddenly I have a funny thought. I pop in a tape and begin my own little Christmas cantata. First, I sing a peppy rendition of *"Silent Night, Holy Night, All is calm, all is quiet."* Then I segue right into a verse of *"Do You Hear What I Hear?"* Mama gets furious when I make up my own words to a song, so next I belt out *"Jingle bells, jingle bells, jingle all the way, Oh what fun it is to ride in a brand new Chevrolet! Hey!"* Mama never flinches, but I know she's over there clenching her teeth.

A festive ten minutes have passed since the cigarette incident, but the smoke has not yet dissipated. I am thinking maybe I waited a bit too long to make Mama put the cigarette out. Suddenly, from the stone statue beside me, come the monotone words: "I think that cigarette blew in your backseat." I gasp, shriek, and lunge sideways between the seats. To my horror I glimpse a wisp of smoke feathering up behind Mama's seat.

"DAMN IT, MAMA!" I explode. I quickly angle the car off the road and slide onto the shoulder. Mama remains rock solid, while I leap out and use both hands to steady myself against the icy car. I stomp my way around the vehicle, snatch open the back door, and knock the devilish burning cigarette out onto the innocent snow. There, glaring me in the face, is an inch-long, blackened hole burned completely through my leather seat. I am clinging to the car door, hyperventilating, when the telephone rings. Of course, Mama won't budge. I retrace my steps and yank the phone out the open car door. "WHAT?" I shout.

"What on earth is going on back there?" Bam shrills into the receiver.

"I am putting out a FIRE!" I yell, glaring at Mama. "A fire *YOUR MOTHER* started in my backseat!" Bam convulses into laughter, so I slam the phone down. We drive all the way to a roadblock making only the sounds of tires crunching ice and windshield wipers slapping.

Just outside Oxford, we creep to a complete stop. Cars are backed up for as far as we can see. I am behind Steve's Jeep, with the motor running. We wait. A couple of people get out of cars, and Steve gets out too. There are at least six inches of snow on the ground now, and several men with heavy boots on walk up the road to see what's going on. Mama and I sit there in an awkward silence, but I am still glad for a break from gripping the steering wheel so tightly. I watch the men return and talk in a huddle. Steve gets back in the Jeep, and soon the phone rings. Just over the hill up ahead, he explains, two 18-wheelers have jack-knifed across the road, blocking both lanes of traffic. "We may be here all night," he says. "You probably ought to cut your motor off for a while and try to stay warm."

After an hour and a half, it is as cold inside the car as it is outside. Car doors open and people begin to get out and mingle. I decide to stretch my legs so I get out and leave Mama to sulk alone for a while. Scott and Lizzie are already outside playing in the snow, and three other kids have joined them.

A man from Louisiana is hauling a load of wood in the back of his pickup. He gets a couple of other guys to help him, and they unload some of the wood and start a large fire just off the shoulder of the road. People press up to the fire, warming their hands, introducing themselves, laughing, and talking. There are people from Alabama, Georgia, Mississippi, Louisiana, Arkansas, and Tennessee. There's even a couple from North Dakota, and one fellow trying to get back into snowy Illinois. A local man is explaining how long it could take to get a wrecker this far out to move the 18-wheelers and clear the road. He looks up and pauses to holler out, "Hold up a minute and I'll help you with that, ma'am!"

I look around and see Mama headed toward the fire carrying the honey-baked ham. The man with the pickup truck drops down his tailgate and soon food begins to appear from all directions. Everybody has something to contribute. I go to the car and help Mama bring back the red velvet cake and the fruitcake cookies. A crowd has gathered and someone has produced paper plates, napkins, and several thermoses of coffee. More wood is thrown on the fire. As I munch on one of Mama's fruitcake cookies and take all this in, I have two thoughts: one, that this is the most heart-warming demonstration of Christmas spirit I have ever witnessed; and two, that my anger at Mama has given way to pride. I watch her stomping around in her yellow rubber ducky boots, looking after people. I learn that the retired couple with the Winnebago are the ones who are somehow able to keep us supplied with hot coffee. Several of the men are going from car to car, offering to bring coffee or something to snack on to people who've elected to stay in their cars.

The crackling and popping of the fire is abruptly drowned out by the distant revving up of a motor. We look up in time to see a pickup truck pulling out of the lineup and onto the shoulder. The driver begins to make his way up the shoulder of the road, fishtailing left and right. He veers around our group gathered by the fire and spins past us, almost hitting a tree. As he guns it on up the shoulder, someone notices his New York license plate. "No time for the hospitality state," someone laughs.

"Yeah, he's gonna show us how to drive on ice," drawls another voice.

The New York truck careens past twelve or fifteen vehicles before it hits a dip in the shoulder and the left wheel drops into a hole and spins. The driver gooses it, causing the backend of the truck to whip around and then scoot backwards down the embankment. A loud cheer goes up for the New York driver, who may be a little rattled, but isn't hurt. Then someone chuckles: "So much for our driving lesson."

Two men leave the fire and slide down the embankment to check on the driver. Soon, three men clamor back up the bank and press in toward the fire. I'm eyeing the New Yorker and thinking how sheepish I'd feel if I had to join a group I'd just tried to blow past. Behind me a seductive voice says: "Hey, big guy, nice try. I *do* love a man with spirit!" I don't even have to turn around. It's Bam. She's left Steve in the car with the baby so she can flaunt and flirt with a Yankee Evel Knievel.

"Hey!" someone else yells. "I think they're moving a little up there!"

All heads turn northward and, sure enough, the cars up ahead are beginning to inch forward. The successive blasts of two mournful truck horns let us know the 18-wheelers have been cleared from the road. We are about to be on our way.

"MERRY CHRISTMAS!" people call out hurriedly. "Have a safe trip!"

People are suddenly shaking hands, hugging, wrapping up their food, and racing off toward their cars. I help Mama lug our food items back to the Chevrolet, and we jump in and crank the motor.

"Brrrrrr! I'm freezing!" I shudder, trying to thaw up Mama. Then, for insurance, I add: "That was a fantastic idea, Mama, bringing out the ham."

"Aren't you glad I didn't get out and walk way back there?" she says with a hoity-toity I'm-all-over-it attitude.

"Yeah," I laugh. "A get-together isn't really together without you."

"If we had stayed the night," Mama says with slight disappointment, "I was going to give out gifts in the morning."

We begin a slow crawl forward on the snow-crusted road. Mama and I are actually smiling as we look over and wave one more time to the couples from Arkansas and Georgia.

We make it just to the other side of Memphis before Steve waves us over at a fireworks tent. The kids are pleading to shoot fireworks tonight, something they can't do in the city. We're parked for a full half hour watching them race around the tables inside the tent grabbing some of everything. When they run squealing back to the Jeep, they've collected two huge grocery bags of everything from bottle rockets to cherry bombs.

"I don't want anything to do with those fireworks," Mama says glaring at me. "I don't trust anything with a short fuse."

I am too exhausted even to comment. Two more stops and three more hours later, we finally limp into Aunt Hortense's long driveway and the open arms of the two huge oak trees that Mama's great-great-granddaddy planted on either side of the drive. The house is lit up top to bottom, and a fresh covering of snow blankets everything. In one long window, the flashing, colored lights of the Christmas tree signal a jackpot—a safe haven from all offending elements of the outside world. It's been a long time since we pulled out of Jackson, Mississippi; we have fought, frozen, feasted, started fires, and made new friends, but we've reached the promised land at last.

Aunt Hortense and Uncle Carl live sixty-five miles west of Jackson, Tennessee, in the big two-story house in the country that Mama and her two sisters grew up in. HOME, they all call it. Aunt Lola Ruth and Uncle Murray live down the road, not even a mile away. They're all here waiting on us, including my five cousins and three of their children. I do the math and realize there will be nineteen people under one roof; surely that ought to be enough for Mama's family Christmas.

Everybody spills out and hugs everybody. "Girl, you look like a runway model!" Aunt Hortense gushes over Bam while Mama beams.

"And *you* take after your Grandmama Turner more every day," Aunt Lola Ruth sighs sadly, fixing a critical eye on *me*. She squeezes my left hand, studies it, then pats it sympathetically saying, "Honey, isn't there *one* eligible bachelor in your church?"

"Oh, nonsense!" cries an indignant Aunt Hortense. She yanks me out of the clutches of Aunt Lola Ruth and admonishes, "Janice can wait till she's forty years old to get married and still live in hell long enough!"

Bam smiles her beauty queen smile and glides inside to find the throne of her newest kingdom, while Mama stands there holding the baby and making zero effort to come to my defense. The kids race in all directions and beg Steve to stay outside and shoot fireworks until time to eat.

Cars are unloaded, gifts are placed under the tree, chattering women press into a warm, scented kitchen, and the bustle to serve up the Christmas Eve dinner officially begins. Aunt Lola Ruth informs impatient kids that gifts won't be opened until after dinner, because this is the way Mama and her sisters always did things at Home. I am watching the snow out the window, listening to the popping of firecrackers and the excited squeals of children, when Aunt Hortense breaks my reverie.

"Janice," Aunt Hortense snaps like a drill sergeant, "you're in charge of the dining room." She guides me to a stack of plates, napkins, and silverware, and suddenly I am appointed Martha Stewart and saddled with the huge task of magically transforming a rather ordinary dining room into a candlelit banquet hall for nineteen.

"Where is Bam?" I ask innocently, but everyone is too busy scurrying around to acknowledge a perfectly legitimate question. You'd think these folks would show some interest in a missing person report.

When the food is all spread out in grand fashion down the full length of the dining room table, Mama barks at me: "Janice, get everybody in from out-side—we're ready to eat." They can say what they want to about me, but the one thing I am in this family is indispensable.

I hike to the door like I am the only one who can do this job and yell for the guys to round up the kids and come on in. Soon we are overrun with gig-gling, snow-stamping confusion. The kids toss their grocery sacks of fireworks into a corner of the kitchen, and chase each other to various bathrooms to wash their hands. Finally, everyone assembles and finds a seat around the din-ing table, which consists of four satellite card tables that I have attached on the sides of either end to create a giant "I." The din of noise gradually dies down.

"Who would like to say the blessing for us?" Aunt Lola Ruth inquires with eyebrows raised.

"I will!" screams little 7-year-old Jeremy, flailing his arm in the air.

"Go ahead," Aunt Lola Ruth says, nodding and smiling her approval at Jeremy.

"Everybody hold hands," Jeremy orders, and a wave of protest ensues.

"I believe Jeremy is in charge of the blessing," Aunt Hortense says sternly, darting her eyes around the table to dare further objections. Hands begin to connect reluctantly, and Jeremy smiles to see his own idea taking shape. Mama is beside me, so I am forced to hold her hand. I try to focus on the fact that I *don't* have to hold Bam's hand. Bam would probably draw blood with those long, gilded, floosy nails of hers.

"Now, bow you heads," Jeremy grins, looking from one person to another and making no effort to bow his own head.

When all heads are bowed, the voice of Jeremy next instructs: "Beginning with Janice, we'll go around the table and everybody say a sentence of the Christmas prayer."

I am totally amused at how Jeremy has cleverly turned this prayer on us. Apparently he has no clear sense of what it means to "volunteer" to say the blessing. The funniest part is that I know Bam is sitting there steaming over being forced to talk publicly to God.

"Dear Lord," I say without missing a beat, "thank you for the wisdom of little Jeremy."

The prayer continues from person to person around the table until it reaches Bam. "Thank you that Mama had such a wonderful idea for a family Christmas," Bam says, still sucking up to Mama instead of God.

The prayer moves on until it comes back to Jeremy, who concludes with a hasty: "Thanks God for the great fireworks. . . ."

A soft whistle begins before Jeremy can say "Amen." We all hear it, open our eyes and look up. The whistle turns into a whine, and the whine into an explosion. Steve and Uncle Murray rise from their chairs and freeze in place. A *shwoosh* is followed by another whine and a new and bigger explosion. A full string of firecrackers relays off one another in rapid succession, and everyone understands it is coming from the kitchen. A new whine causes one of the boys to look at another and snicker, "cherry bomb," then a bottle rocket races through the air and pounds the ceiling. The noise and activity are picking up quickly; a number of things are exploding against walls and ceiling.

Steve cracks the door into the kitchen and peeks inside. The sounds of heavy attack, followed by thick gray smoke pour into the dining room. "Everybody out!" he yells, jerking his head back around the door facing. "Both bags are on fire!"

Naturally, I am squeezed into a corner spot on the back side of the table. I jump onto the seat of my chair and walk the row of abandoned chair seats beside me like stepping stones to make my getaway. I see Mama go out a window with the baby wrapped up in her arms. The kids are grabbing food off the table when Steve and Uncle Murray snatch them up, toss them over their shoulders, and haul them outside.

"*Oh! Oh! Oh! My house!*" Aunt Hortense stands in the center of the floor hollering with her skirt yanked up around her hips as if the flames are literally licking at her feet. "*It's burning to the ground!*" she wails frantically. The explosions in the kitchen have escalated to imitate a full scale air attack.

"*The gifts! The gifts! Someone help me get these gifts!*" Aunt Lola Ruth pleads. She drops to her knees under the Christmas tree and scoots around reading gift tags and snatching various packages out on the rug. When Uncle Carl tries to pull her toward the door, she bites his hand and fights him like a tiger.

"Just take the gifts," I demand breathlessly, stacking four large ones in

Uncle Carl's arms. "She's not going anywhere without them." I grab a few more and coax Aunt Lola Ruth out the door into the cold, clear, glistening, snow-covered night.

Outside, everyone huddles around a picnic table beneath the bare arms of another oak tree set out by Mama's great-great-granddaddy. Mama is bawling, and Bam goes over and takes the baby from her. Steve pulls a whistle from his pocket and showers down on it, scaring everyone into thinking that the fireworks have followed us outside.

"Head count everybody! Head count! Line up now!" Steve clenches the whistle between his teeth and barks orders around it. "We gotta make sure everybody's out of the house! Quiet now!"

The kids are all so cold and excited they're jigging up and down like they just might wet their pants. "Man! This is the BEST Christmas ever!" exclaims a wide-eyed Scott, earning himself a heavy thump on the head from Steve. Inside, a chaos of explosions continues as rocket after rocket slams against the kitchen windows and tries to force its way outside.

We go down the line, counting off, and stop on eighteen.

"Look around, who's missing?" Steve demands, making a quick inspection of the line.

Suddenly we're interested in a missing person. Everyone frantically looks around.

"It's the baby," Bam says, indicating the bundle in her arms. "The baby makes nineteen."

"Praise the Lord!" Aunt Hortense exclaims through tears. "Then we're all here, and that's what matters most."

"It's all my fault," Mama sobs loudly. "I've ruined the family Christmas and burned down the homeplace!"

Bam and I exchange a serious look and move toward Mama.

"Oh, nonsense," sniffs Aunt Hortense. "How could this be your fault? It's those damned sacks of firecrackers brought into my kitchen," she says sharply, looking straight at Steve. In twenty-six years this is only the second time I have heard Aunt Hortense curse.

"No, it's my fault!" Mama wails. "I dropped the sparklers down in the bags of fireworks. This is the second fire I've started today!" she shrieks, finally confessing her earlier crime.

"What sparklers?" Steve demands. "We didn't have any sparklers."

"Oh my gosh!" Lizzie squeals, throwing her hands on her cheeks. "Grandma's talking about our *lighting sticks*. When you called us in to eat, we laid our *lighting sticks* on the stove to cool off! That's what we use to *light* the fireworks," she explains to Mama.

"They looked like sparklers that belonged in the bags with the fireworks," Mama chokes out innocently.

"Well, now, they *do* look exactly like sparklers," Bam says defensively. She is perched on top of the picnic table, clutching the baby with one arm and wrapping the other one around Mama's waist.

"The fire truck's on the way," Steve reports nervously, glancing at his watch. "Listen," he says motioning for quiet. "I think the noise inside is dying down."

Everyone stands perfectly still and listens. I look up through the oak branches to be sure the Lord is watching Mama's latest mischief. The heavens are sprinkled with bright, clear starlight, and the moon is full. I think of the banquet feast still spread inside and the nineteen abandoned chairs looking for all the world like the Turner family got in on the Rapture after all. I hear Mama sniffle, and from across the fence behind us, comes the soft, gentle moo of a single cow.

Bam is gently rocking baby Justin in her arms, and little Jeremy begins singing to him: *"A-way in a man-ger, no crib for a bed."* The other kids press forward and join in, and by the second verse the adults begin to follow suit: *"The cat-tle are low-ing, the Ba-by a-wakes."* Bam, still perched atop the picnic table, is completely encircled by her family as everyone serenades her silent, watchful baby. I think how very different Bam looks in this glistening, otherworldly setting. She looks almost regal when the song ends, and I am caught off-guard when she suddenly looks up and smiles directly at me.

Mama is still wiping tears and shivering, when Aunt Lola Ruth thrusts a large gift at her. "Here," she orders. "Open a present. It'll cheer you up."

Mama sheepishly takes the package and slowly tears back the red and green gift wrap, letting the ribbon float down to rest on the festive snow. A new, much deeper sob escapes her. From inside the package Mama gently pulls her mother's Star of David quilt. New tears spring up and plunge down her cheeks as she silently envelopes herself in the long-awaited warmth of her mother's handiwork.

"Mama wanted you to have it," Aunt Hortense explains, "but she said you had to come home for Christmas to get it."

The men have gone inside the house, and Steve trots out to the oak tree to say the coast is clear—the fireworks display has played out in a mound of exhausted confetti, leaving only a few chinks in the walls and ceiling. The men are setting up fans to blow the smoke out.

"This is the BEST Christmas ever!" little Jeremy crows with renewed excitement as a flashing fire truck pulls into the driveway.

I am exhausted. I lean against the trunk of the magnificent oak and review the day's events. "Mama is finally right about one thing," I think to myself as I watch the firemen sprint into action. "Friends can't replace family. I don't have a single friend who could compete with *this*."

Big Red

Jerry L. Bustin

Saturday before Christmas Daddy says what we're going to do, and I shiver.

When I step off the back porch to get the metal barrel ready, the December winds slap my face numb.

Down at the pond slivers of ice run round the water's edge, and it's so cold when I reach for a bucket of water, my hands turn pale blue.

The cold north winds whip up and chap my face so much my nose runs.

I look back toward the house and see Daddy and Mama standing near the back door talking quiet and low, both looking serious as schoolteachers. Now and then they look out toward the hog pen, then down at me.

Mama goes back in the house, and Daddy takes long strides out toward the smokehouse.

I keep on dipping the cold water and pouring it into the scalding barrel.

Pretty soon Daddy comes from the smokehouse with a butcher knife half-near long as my arm, its blade curved like a rocking chair and pointed on end sharp as a pitch-fork.

I set chunks of wood afire round the scalding barrel, and keep on dipping and pouring more pond water in. I see Daddy go over to the emery wheel near the smokehouse and begin sharpening his long pointed knife.

In a few minutes Mama comes from the house wearing a checked apron round her waist, and slides the big wooden table over near the sizzling wash pot. She stands there and pokes the fire round the wash pot with her shoe toe and it catches up a right smart. She stands there over the hot wash pot warming her hands off the oozing flame and staring down my way.

The penned hogs squeal and take to running from end to end. I figure they must know or sense death, and I quiver inside.

I sure hope Daddy don't take Big Red, my big red shoat I got for Christmas last year.

Grandpa comes round the corner of the house wearing his long-sleeve wool shirt, his longjohns fastened up near his goosle, and he goes to whacking up firewood lickety split.

Grandpa won't smile, and Daddy won't look up, and Mama keeps on jabbering fast as she can, never stopping, even when Aunt Susie walks up holding her hands folded across her stomach.

"Need me a good mess o' brains, a lot a salt pork, some chitlins too, a good helpin' fer ever'body for Christmas morning," Mama says.

"I declare, that sho sounds good," Aunt Susie says, warming her hands at the wash pot.

"Can't get Rob-Dearl to slow down none—he jest works all the bloomin' time," Mama says.

"Sure 'nuff does, gonna kill hisself," Aunt Susie agrees. "But what if ya wuz alone—like me—Mim's been gone nigh a year now."

Their words ride like paper atop the winds and float on down to my ears. Mama turns to Grandpa and says, "Oughta check on your sister more, Susie is yore sister—lest you forget."

Grandpa grunts not looking up from chopping on wood.

I stoop down low and pull my last bucket of pond water out. I pour it into the scalding barrel and now the barrel is three-fourths full, like Daddy said fill it. And the red fire around the scalding barrel licks out and drinks up some spilled water making a popping noise. The barrel water begins to spit and sizzle and steam, sounding like a spewing fuse.

I hear the penned hogs squealing louder, and I look up toward the hog pen and see Daddy sloshing and bogging round in the sucking, pig mud after my pet shoat, Big Red. And Daddy's face is glowing redder than a coal, just like before he whips me, and his eyes are hard and gray as hickory.

The squealing pitches higher, and the other hogs huddle in the pen's corner watching Big Red kick and shake his hams as Daddy holds to his hind legs. Grandpa rushes up and locks his arms round Big Red's head, and Grandpa sconces his legs in the sucking mud while Daddy throws Big Red and they both drag Big Red from the pen.

I run off and hide behind a crooked sweet-gum tree, and hold my ears to shut out Big Red's squealing, but I can't muffle it back good. I hear a thud, a grunt, then another thud. My stomach flips over, and tears wedge from the curbs of my eyes, but I pinch them away.

I peep round the tree and see Daddy dropping the sledge hammer, and watch while Daddy and Grandpa tie a rope to Big Red's hind legs and look down toward the scalding barrel.

"Son, get up here and help us," Daddy yells.

I step out pigeon-toed, hands deep inside my pockets, hearing the scalding barrel sizzle, spit, and spew, getting scalding hot.

Daddy and Grandpa pull the rope ends over their shoulders. They lean forward grinding the rope into their thin muscles, and they move Big Red down toward me, neither looking at the other.

And Big Red's fat sides flounce and bounce like water in a sack, and they drag Big Red down might near up to the scalding barrel. Then Daddy takes his sharp-pointed butcher knife from his back pocket and sticks the sharp point of the blade up into Big Red's throat, ramming the blade all the way in, ripping the throat clean across, like cutting warm butter. Dark crimson blood pumps and sprays out, some of it spewing on Daddy's hands and arms, and Big Red makes a low, short grunt, and his big hams shiver one last time and I turn toward the pond to fetch another bucket of water.

"Here, stop that Son, grab hold of this here rope," Daddy says.

I reach down and try to pull like a man, my knees wobbling. I'm close enough to smell Big Red's sour mouth, and smell Daddy and Grandpa too. Daddy smells like greasy cars, Grandpa like old moth balls.

My heart leaps into my throat as we slosh Big Red up and down in the scalding barrel, the metal and pig hair smelling like burning feathers.

Daddy says it's plum cold today, and Grandpa agrees, as they ram Big Red's front hooves up and down, working him in the scalding water until he's might near steaming.

Then they roll Big Red over in the barrel and drag him back out. Daddy hooks a single-tree up to Big Red's back leg tendons, pitches a rope over the lowest sweet-gum limb, and hoists Big Red up pulley-fashion until the limb tilts, swaying Big Red's head barely off the ground. And Big Red swings there, his half cut-off head dripping blood, his throat and gristle and arteries sliced in two, his white tongue lagging out and clenched between his tiny yellow teeth, and I wonder if I should have done more to save him.

I turn to Mama standing beside the wash pot, but Mama says, "Son, get back over yonder and help yore Daddy scrape."

I go back to where Big Red swings from the limb, take a sharp knife, crawl up on a box, and begin to scrape Big Red's red hair off. Mama, Grandpa, and Aunt Susie come over and help too.

Then Daddy takes his long butcher knife and rips the stomach wide open, beginning carefully between the hind legs and going on down to the chest wall. Guts fall out and hang forward, puffing up like a balloon filled with air. When Daddy gets to the ribs he takes his hacksaw and saws down through the ribs, sawing them in two, and I help roll the guts forward toward a bucket, and the guts steam and spew as they drop from Big Red's stomach cavity. A sick smell comes out from near the entrails, and a slick, salt-like, briny wetness runs over my hands so I can't hold on to the guts good.

"Don't cut them guts, it'll ruin the meat, we'll need them for sausage and chitlins," Daddy says.

Daddy looks at Grandpa. "Take that head and go over there and get them brains out," Daddy commands Grandpa.

The warm guts groan and pop as they fall in the foot tub. In seconds, the wind blows them dry as stable dirt, and I reach down and touch them and they feel like an old man's fingers. Holding my head sideways, I help put the liver and heart and stomach into the foot tub.

I look at Big Red and hope his spirit has gone on up by now because there's not much left of him now except loins and hams and backbone, and a head that Grandpa has the ax over.

I look over at Big Red's eyes, and see they are white as smoked marble, see his tongue cut off and lagging in the grit.

I go and stand beside Grandpa and stare down into Big Red's colorless, marble eyes, and I see that Big Red is not there.

I run over beside Mama and stand looking at Daddy by the sweet-gum tree, see him quartering-up Big Red. A scream hides deep down inside me as Daddy brings each quarter to the wooden table where Aunt Susie and Mama wait with sharp knives to cut the meat into small squares and pitch it into the boiling wash pot.

The wash pot fire licks way out around the black, wrought iron pot, and chunks of fat meat thrown inside begin to sizzle and grease pops and spits and bubbles begin to belch-up from the bottom of the wash pot.

And suddenly, there beside the wooden table, there arises the sweet savor of frying hog meat, and it wafts across my nostrils making me hungry, and I feel ashamed.

"Go in the house and get some more rags," Mama says.

I hurry inside and hide in the closet, then catch my senses and pray to God to make all this a dream. Knowing it's not, and that Mama is waiting and will come looking, I slip from hiding and waddle along back outside.

Daddy glances at Mama, "Min'lee, you want more loins or cracklins?"

"Cracklins," she says. "We need the grease for lye soap—'sides, I'm gonna give a few cracklins to neighbors on Christmas morning."

Daddy cuts chunks of side meat off and hands it to Grandpa to cut up and put into the pot.

Daddy looks at me. "Son, help Grandpa take his cut-ups to the pot, and watch out for the spitting grease, it'll pop out and burn you."

Mama looks at Daddy. "Rob-Dearl, a mess of brains sho would taste good," she says.

Aunt Susie nods and wipes a driblet of dried snuff off the corner of her chin.

Grandpa points to the brains he's put in a dish pan sitting on the table, and Daddy tells Grandpa to take them on in the house.

The cracklins sizzle becoming brownish yellow; I watch them spew in the grease, and think of Big Red. The cold Christmas winds slip up and stick clean through my tattered, wool shirt. I look over at Daddy, and see how he's a little man, not even tall as the stall gate, with skin tougher than leather, and deep-set wrinkles underneath his sparkling brown eyes, and with a chin cut sharp and set in iron.

Mama won't stop talking. "Ain't enough for us if we have a bad winter, not with two boys to feed. Gonna starve this winter, Rob-Dear!"

Daddy keeps cutting meat and looking at Grandpa. "Get yourself and Miss Jessie a bundle of 'em tenderloins and big ham too—that'll be yore Christmas from us."

Mama turns red and looks away. She hushes talking for a minute, then she picks up a load of cracklins and totes them to the wash pot and stands there quietly looking into the wash pot and rubbing her chin. She looks up toward the back door, goes to the door, and motions Daddy to follow her inside.

In ten minutes or so they both return with solemn faces. Mama's face has softened some.

Mama says to Aunt Susie, "Get y'all a good mess of sausage. And a ham too. Some brains if ya want 'em. We'll all eat till we run out."

Aunt Susie smiles and says, "Reckon I will."

I stir the wash-pot with the wooden ladle, and take out a brown cracklin, trapping it against the pot with the spoon. I blow the cracklin cool, then take it into my mouth and chew, sloshing the rich pig juice around on my tongue. It tastes good, until I remember Big Red and my insides begin to crawl.

Mama wheels from the worktable and goes inside to make breakfast, saying back to me, "You did a right smart of work today, son—I'm gonna make you a special breakfast."

I sit and watch the last cracklins cook down to a golden brown, and hear Vintern's rattletrap, cut-off pickup clattering along the dirt road in front of the house headed to Bud's store, probably carrying Christmas moonshine. I see all the other hogs out there sulking round the hogpen with their heads down low, sniffing at the mud, being mosey-quiet, and missing Big Red, I reckon.

Mama pops her head out the screen door holding a skillet in her hand. "Come on in fer breakfast—ya bound to be starvin'."

Daddy, Grandpa, and Aunt Susie go wash up at the outside faucet, but I go on inside and take my place at the table.

"Here, Son, have you some of these scrambled eggs before they come in," Mama says raking me a plate full.

"You was hepful today—working 'side yore Daddy like you done," she whispers.

Bigness swells all over me. I fork the spongy eggs, packing a whole spoonful in my mouth.

I go over and sit under the pin oaks. The last, tiny leaves rattle like icicles on the tree limbs. Two Dominique hens and a rooster scratch over closer to the worktable, cocking their wild, red eyes on the cracklin piles. I gaze out toward the hog pen, hoping that Santa Claus remembers me.

Presents

Elizabeth Spencer

The beagle trotted down the quiet white path. When a squirrel jumped high up in a bare oak tree, he did not notice; when a blue jay floated past he did not turn his head. His tail was high, his gait steady, and he looked responsible for something. Sandy, the minute he came out of the wood to where she was sitting with her first cousin down by the lily pond, knew exactly the way in which he had been coming toward them. The beagle was serious and had no time for animals and birds. It was Christmas and he had come to see about the children. What if they had taken their shoes off? It was warm, but not that warm. They might be sitting on the damp ground, which could lead to a bad cold and missing school. They had had too much excitement and could be struck by crazy ideas at the best of times. If no one now remembered that school was going to resume, the beagle remembered. Somebody had to think of these things.

The two little girls were sitting on an ornamental stone bench, and though it was cold, they did not have their coats on. The beagle jumped up on the bench and sat down between them. He made a show of indifference, yawning a bit when Sandy's cousin Linda reached out and patted him. It was clear that he belonged to Sandy, for they did not notice one another at all.

At least, the adults, back at the house, would have said that he was Sandy's dog. The truth was, of course, that Sandy belonged to him. He never lay at her door or rambled along glued to her heels as a boy's dog will do. At night before the fire when she tried to romp with him, he always at once scrambled away. He growled, yelped if his ears were so much as touched, all but fiercely closed his teeth upon her, and pulling entirely free, shook his rumpled coat together. He was not amused. She was beneath his dignity; who did she think she was? He went off to the kitchen to see about his supper. But at times he lay near her with his head fixed between his white forepaws. He sat at her feet when she was studying. He chose his own length of time to start waiting for school to be out.

The two little girls sighed. Everything was over now. It had been building up all through the year, or at least ever since summer, when, having nothing else to do, somebody might say on a hot afternoon (holding their skirts up before the electric fan), "What you going to want for Christmas?" Since November, it had been definitely in the air, and since Thanksgiving it had been almost unbearable. At school there had been all the paper cutouts to do and paste in the windows, songs and programs and readings in the textbooks. At church they had the pageant to practice for, Christmas carols to sing, and Sunday School lessons about little baby Jesus. At home it was on the radio and the TV all the time, and it hid in the far backs of closets and was spread out on beds in chilly guest rooms, so that every door you might open somebody would say "Can't come in here, you'll see your present!" And if you drove way back in the country to pick up a quilt from an ancient colored woman, she would stand on the porch and the last thing she would say was: "Christmas comin', gonna snow." Everybody promised you snow, but it wouldn't snow. You could go out at night in the yard and shiver, squint your eyes out staring up at the crystal sky, imagine you felt one flake graze your cheek, but still it wouldn't snow. It would, however, be Christmas. Inch at a time, creeping closer day by day, the time would come. Now it had ended in a burst of tinsel, angel hair, lights, ribbon. Too much, far too much. Too long awaited, far too long, and gone in a flash. This accounted for the stillness. This accounted for the three of them sitting together down by the lily pond on a stone bench with nothing much to say.

"Did you get everything you wanted?" Linda asked. There had been about a million presents. The question was, in all the furore, if you could even remember what you wanted. Everyone went "Oh!" and "Look, just look!" "What'd you do it for?"

"Well, no, I didn't," said Sandy, just remembering. "There was one thing."

"What was it?" Linda pursued. Sated with gifts, tired from fitful dreams of the night before, from getting up early, shouting "Christmas gift!" being hugged by everybody, gorging on turkey, cranberries, candied sweet potatoes, ambrosia, fruitcake, and a hundred hot biscuits, the children found it simpler, not as far beyond the range of the appetite, to think of what they didn't get than what they did.

"I don't know," said Sandy, and hooked her fingers through the beagle's collar. "I can't remember."

Yet it had been most important at the time she was making out lists and wishing. This had all happened before; there was always something you didn't get. Either it cost too much, or the stores were all sold out, or the line discontinued, or they said she was too old, or too young, or they decided it was in bad taste. If you kept on begging maybe you got it anyway, like the brightly striped dress in the store window, which never looked right no matter how many people worked on it, or the rabbit's fur muff which not only kept her hands warm during church and held her Sunday School book, but also looked, as her mother had warned her, ridiculous. Whatever it had been this year, however, she hadn't campaigned for it hard enough; maybe she hadn't cared. Or maybe—this was the hard part—she knew in advance that something was liable to be the matter with it, turning it to no value in others' eyes, and so, eventually, in her own. So by now it—whatever it was—might as well be a shooting star over the cedar tree at night for whoever might be up and wishing. And in the way of stars it might just as well come swooping back her way sometime ages from now, maybe sooner. "I can't remember," she repeated, and like that, even the desire to left her.

"Mama got her silver dresser set," said Linda.

"I know it," Sandy said.

"It was gorgeous," Linda mused.

"Sure was," said Sandy, but she wasn't thinking of it, or of anything.

Quiet took a deeper hold; the ground looked swept on purpose. The sunshine had no color, it felt like Sunday without church. Could you be wide awake and asleep, both at once? Sandy was.

The dry brown winter leaves—silver-shaped leaves from some kind of oak—lay carpeted over the paving about the lily pond which had no lilies in it. Everybody had done their best all day and now turned into such good people: even the Negroes, sitting out back, had something nice to say to you if you went by. The beagle jumped down from the bench and trotted off into the woods. He came back with an old shoe sole in his mouth. He gave it to Sandy, laid it down in front of her. It was time to go.

The little girls began to walk home. Sandy did not see Linda very often. Linda lived twenty miles away, in a bigger town. She imitated her mother, which seemed to Sandy an odd thing to do. Sandy felt there must be a part of the world where all little girls imitated their mothers, but it was not a part that made her very curious. She was happier with the dog than that could ever make her. With no right to any idea of what Christmas was or wasn't (though he seemed caught up on it, the whole time), he trotted ahead of them, complete in some kind of knowledge.

When they got to the house, they found their mothers sitting in the front swing, just as they themselves had been sitting by the lily pond. The young women were in a good humor, for they liked each other, in spite of being in-laws, and they said, "Look, he's bringing them back. Did you ever?"

The whole day was the quiet color of the field gate which no one had ever painted, and many hands had worn smooth. Far out in the field, a flight of crows, thick as a black cloud, tilted to rest in a bare pecan tree, so that it seemed suddenly to have grown a treeful of coal-black leaves.

The two young mothers were talking of their husbands. "But then you know Jerry was always unselfish like that," said Linda's mother. "He'd give you his last cent."

"Just like Bob," said Sandy's mother.

"I think they could be brothers, even though they aren't any kin."

"I know it," said Sandy's mother. "They're just alike in so many ways. What have you got in your hand?" she said to Sandy.

"It's an old shoe sole," said Sandy. "The beagle brought it to me."

"The silly old dog," said Linda, suddenly wicked. "The ugly old hound dog."

"He's not silly," said Sandy. "He's not ugly." She had felt a start of anger which did not recede when Linda squirmed into the swing between her mother and Sandy's mother. The beagle accompanied Sandy into the house. Now they were out in the sun parlor where everybody sat.

"I never thought I'd see the day," said Aunt Jennie, "when a dog would be allowed inside this house." She leaned down to look the beagle in the eye. "You sassy little thing," she said.

"They worship one another," said Sandy's grandmother. "You know *he* was a Christmas present."

"I know he was. Cutest thing I ever saw. Don't you remember trying to keep him quiet on that Christmas Eve night, so she wouldn't guess? We smothered him in blankets. We put five alarm clocks in with him."

Sandy's brother Hernan came in. He was cramming a fistful of fruitcake in his mouth. "Sandy, there's a girl off at school that brought her horse with her. You ought to see him. She rides him every afternoon. Real pretty bay."

Hernan went to a military school. There was a girls' finishing school across the road from the boys' school.

"Reckon you want to take the beagle off to college with you?" said Sandy's granddaddy, coming up out of the newspaper. It seemed Granddaddy could arrange everything.

"Law, the beagle will be dead and gone by then," Aunt Jennie said. She thought everyone would be dead and gone sooner than they ever were, except those who had accidents and were removed before you could think about it.

"Some dogs live to be twelve or thirteen years old," said Sandy's grandmother.

"I knew a horse once that lived to be thirty-five years old," said her grandfather. "I certainly did," he said, and put the paper entirely aside to think it over. That particular horse's face came back to him now; you could tell.

"Turtles live to be five hundred!" cried Hernan, as though in triumph.

What were they saying? What did they mean?

Sandy eventually got all the way to the back porch, all the way out with the Negroes. "Thank you, ma'am, for the handkerchuffs, Sandy," said Elvira. "I meants to get you a present, but I didn't have no money."

"What was you gonna git her, Mama?" said Tommie, Elvira's boy, after a long time. He was sitting out on the steps, and when he said this he was making fun, just like Elvira. You gave presents to Negroes; they never gave presents to you.

Sandy went down the steps and sat down on the very bottom step with her back to Tommie, who was sitting up near the door, and to Elvira, who was sitting in a straight chair on the screen porch, taking her ease now all the dinner was finally over with and the dishwasher going. Elvira's husband Charlie had long ago eaten his big turkey dinner and gone home.

"A pair of pink socks, for Easter," said Elvira, comfortably, still making it up. "Easter the next thing."

"You ain't going to get me nothing," said Sandy, right out, talking without grammar, the way you did to Negroes.

"That's right," said Elvira, amiably. "I sho ain't."

Cold truth was what they had spoken.

The beagle, having stopped to lick up some onion dressing from the kitchen floor, pushed through the back door and came to sit down beside Sandy. He curled his tail around him neatly and looked out at the dun-colored winter yard and the mild bare sky. She held the shoe sole in her lap.

All Sandy's presents—the ones from the tree—were stacked in her room inside the house. She would go look at them some time later and be glad, she guessed, but just now all she wanted was to rest her hand on the smooth brown and white head. Far beyond horses and turtles he would endure, no matter what they said.

Land of the Giants

Carolyn Haines

My family is a tribe. Although there is no proof, I feel certain the descent from Hannibal is there, waiting for some genealogically-driven spinster aunt to find. Attila, too. Most members of my family, though, avoid the concept of researching the past. It's too hard to step over the bodies of the alcoholics and horse thieves that are only a generation in the grave. No telling what dark secrets are hidden back in ancient history.

We are from the land of the square-heads, that misunderstood legion of conquering Vikings, Swedes, Scots, and Irish controlled by land lust, family tradition, and a hot desire for a good fight and a stiff drink, no matter which order it arrives in.

I think that in me and my generation, the gene pool has grown weary, with the possible exceptions of my brothers. I desire no fight, no tradition, no land other than the small house and yard I currently own. I've noticed the same thing in my cousins and nieces and nephews. Compared to my parents and grandparents, we are a sedate and boring generation.

We don't raise hell the way we were brought up to do, and our lack of enthusiasm for mayhem has made the Christmas season a disappointment to some of the clan. That's why I'm on this volunteer mission to find something I don't even approve of. Duck hunters. Three of them lost in the Mississippi Delta's jewel, Sardis Lake, on the coldest Christmas morning in the memory of even my oldest aunt, Lila Belle, who is ninety-three. She still celebrates Christmas by drinking four shots of Highland Scotch before she will even consider starting the cornbread dressing. This morning, in celebration of the temperature gauge, which read eight degrees Fahrenheit, she had her first shot at four A.M., when she poured me a cup of coffee and disapprovingly packed some food for my lunch.

"You're gonna freeze your ass off for no good reason. Anybody stupid enough to go duck huntin' on Christmas Eve mornin' when it's nearly zero degrees is better off dead. I just hope it got 'em before they could breed. Enough stupid people behind the steerin' wheels of cars as it is."

"Aunt Lila, is that whiskey you're pourin' in the thermos?" I knew it was, but I was hoping that by calling attention to it she would come to her senses and realize that I would be out on a lake in my boat in sub-freezing temperatures.

"Of course, it's whiskey. Keeps the blood movin' through the veins." She added another healthy dose.

"Thanks." I took it from her and put it with the sandwiches she'd already prepared.

"Lulu, why are you doin' this?" she asked, and the pale blue of her eyes reminded me of all the stories she'd told about our relatives from the old country. They were a people who looked past the shores of their own land, beyond the limits of their own geography. They were conquerors.

"Somebody's got to hunt them," I said. It was true. The local sheriff's department had been searching all night. It was up to volunteers now, and I had a boat, a nice one that I used mostly for water skiing in the summer.

"You'd be a lot more help here puttin' together this Christmas dinner." Aunt Lila believed in a lot of rights for women, but holiday dinners were to be handmade from scratch with all tits and asses in the kitchen and working hard. The other gender was relegated to the den with televised sports, or out to the barn with some liquor and story-telling. These were the stories that wouldn't be allowed around the table in mixed company.

"Aunt Lila, what if it was Uncle Gus out there lost, maybe frozen?" Gus was her husband, and though he'd been dead for forty years, we always spoke of him as if he'd just walked out of the room for a moment.

She took her second shot of Scotch that morning before answering. "If it was Gus out there, I'd say let the bastard freeze. Gus had more sense than to be out duck huntin' on Christmas, no matter if it was a balmy day of thirty degrees."

I finished the eggs and bacon she'd insisted that I eat, put my plate in the sink, and kissed her on the cheek. She'd once been taller than me, but age had begun to stoop her a bit. It was hardly noticeable because it seemed that as she shrank she also got feistier.

"I'll be back as soon as I can," I promised.

"We're not waitin' dinner on you."

I smiled at her. "Please don't. I just hope those three men are alive and that we can find them soon. Imagine the kind of Christmas their family is having." I could tell by her look that she didn't figure that family had enough brains to suffer.

"When you leave, drive by your brother Alfred's house and make sure Toby's bicycle is out in the front yard. If it isn't, call me, and I'll call Wilbert and get him to go over and put it together."

"Sure." Alfred was known to get too drunk to put his children's Christmas presents together. At that house, Santa only brought presents in pieces and left instruction sheets scattered about the living room. Betty just told the kids that Santa had been running late and didn't have time to finish what he started, just like all other men. It seemed to satisfy the children, but I knew Toby was counting on the bicycle. He'd been waiting since October.

The boat was already hooked to the Passport, so I swung out Ellwood Street to Tallahatchie Avenue and drove slowly by my brother's house. The first thing I saw was not the bicycle parked at the front steps but Alfred himself. He was on his hands and knees in the front yard under the booger light and crawling in a circle like a rabid dog. I considered stopping and helping him into the house, seeing as how I was certain he'd lost all sense of direction. I kept driving. After all, we were descendants of Hannibal, who crossed the Alps on an elephant. Surely Alfred could find his way up the six steps to the front door. If not, Toby would be outside soon enough to find his bicycle, which, surprisingly, was all put together and parked on the front walk right by the steps. I did notice that it was a handsome red Schwinn. Good for Toby.

I drove on, hitting the outskirts of town in less than five minutes. Ebenezer is a tiny town, one of the old Delta crossroads that once served a purpose in breaking the long journey from Memphis to New Orleans. Now with interstates and fast cars, Ebenezer is nothing more than a blink.

At the U-Pick-Em I stopped, poured my thermos of "coffee" onto a frozen puddle that briefly steamed, gurgled, and then re-froze, before I went inside and filled up the thermos with unleaded coffee. It was too cold to drink and drive a boat. Way too cold. I didn't want to join the lost duck hunters in the land of the missing.

Once back in the car, I drove out to Sardis Lake, a huge body of fresh water that attracted all types of sportspeople. I wondered about the men, and it was mostly men, who would abandon their families on Christmas to freeze themselves to the bone for the pleasure of killing something. These people were almost as alien to me as my own family.

My cell phone began to ring as I was turning around at the landing to back the boat trailer into the water. On a summer day, this is an easy and pleasant job. On a day with eight-degree temperatures, it is something more of a chore.

I stopped the Passport. A mist hung over the lake in the pre-dawn light, giving it the look of a landscape on another, hotter planet. In the stillness there was the sound of a duck calling and the ringing of my phone.

"Hello," I said.

"Lulu, it's Marvel again. Your brother is killin' me." Anita's voice was clotted with tears. "He's snatched up the Christmas tree and gone outside with it. I'm standin' in the kitchen window watchin' him. I think he's lost his mind for sure this time."

Marvel and Anita fought every Christmas morning. They fought other times, too, but never as intensely as they did on baby Jesus' birthday. I didn't know if it was the religion, the holiday, or the financial pressures of being Santa that brought out the worst in Marvel. He'd once studied to become a priest, though our family was mostly Protestant. I think it was when he found out that priests were supposed to be celibate that he decided to marry Anita and start his own congregation. They had eight kids.

Since the battery plant had closed down and he'd lost his job as head of public relations, times weren't that great for my older brother. Especially Christmas. Especially this Christmas, when Marvel had just taken a new job as a long distance hauler for a trucking company. He'd been gone the two weeks before Christmas, which had Anita in a real snit.

"Anita, you know Christmas is hard on Marvel." It wouldn't do any good to tell her to leave him.

"He's a bastard."

"Just give him a little time alone. He'll calm down."

"The kids are all upstairs, too afraid to come down to get their presents from Santa."

"Anita, it's not even five o'clock. The kids should still be asleep."

"They were until that bastard started hollerin' and then jerked the Christmas tree up and took it out the front door. Just a minute, I want to see what he thinks he's going to do with our Christmas tree. Tommy found that tree in the woods and cut it down and brought it home all by himself, seein' as how his daddy couldn't be around to help."

"Marvel *had* to work." By lunchtime, when Anita and Marvel had made up, she would be repeating all of my words to the rest of the family.

"Hoo! Hoo!"

Anita's sudden screaming almost made me drop the phone.

"Anita, what's wrong?"

"Hoo! Lulu, you got to get over here right now. You got to come!"

"I can't, Anita, I'm huntin' for those lost duck hunters."

"Why, they been gone all day yesterday and all Christmas Eve. They're frozen already. Forget about them and get over here now. Marvel's thrown the Christmas tree down in the road and he's backin' up that eighteen wheeler."

There was a brief silence where only the sound of Anita's panting could be heard.

"Sweet Jesus!" she cried. "He ran over the Christmas tree with all the family ornaments and all the little twinkle lights." Her voice broke and she began to sob. "Lulu, girl, he ran over the Christmas tree."

Marvel had done some rash things in his life, but this time I wondered if he'd stepped over the line.

In counterpoint to Anita's crying was the sound of a lone duck circling the lake and calling. The cry seemed to hang in the fog, muted and drawn out, before it broke free and disappeared. In the east was the first hint of dawn.

I turned the heater up in the Passport, the blower whirring as Anita sobbed into the phone, too broken to even talk.

"Call Mama, Anita. Maybe she can talk some sense into Marvel."

"You think?"

By the note of hope in her voice, I knew she wasn't done with Marvel yet. It was Christmas, the season of miracles. Anita needed one.

"Call her and see. I've got to get out on the lake if I'm goin' to be any help at all."

"You be careful."

"Sure thing." I punched off the phone and debated leaving it in the car. But if I found the hunters and they were still alive, I'd need to call for help. I tucked it in the pocket of my down jacket, pulled on my insulated and water-proof gloves, and began the process of floating the boat.

I managed without getting wet, and once the Passport was out of the way of the ramp, I climbed into the boat and started out across the lake. If I thought it had been cold earlier, I learned the true definition of cold. The wind whipped tears out of my eyes, and they froze on my cheeks.

The morning search party was supposed to meet at Mabry's Landing about three miles east, and I was glad to be riding into the prospect of the sunrise. I doubted the sun would make it any warmer, but the light would *seem* warmer. I wondered if the duck hunters were somewhere along the lake, shivering and praying for dawn.

They were three brothers, only one of them still from around Ebenezer. Abbie Wilks was his name. The brothers who'd long moved away from Missis-sippi seeking fame and fortune in distant lands were Oscar and Fillingham. One was a computer consultant in the Silicon Valley and the other was a Con-Ed employee in New York City. They had come home for a Christmas hunting trip with their older brother, who'd remained in the family home and who'd been appointed guardian of the family traditions, which obviously included an idiotic duck-hunting trip. They hadn't been home in over twenty years. Now it was looking likely that they'd never leave again.

As I rounded a peninsula I saw the gathering of boats at Mabry's Landing and was glad I'd come. There were only four other boats there; I would make the fifth. The men turned at the sound of my motor, and if there was any animosity toward me, a single female, participating in what was once considered to be a man's role, they hid it well.

"Hey, Lulu," John Carroll called out. "Glad you could make it." The others nodded. Sheriff Bellcase was in one boat and he quickly outlined the search procedure. Other searchers had hunted throughout the night, but we would have the advantage of being able to see. A nighttime search on Sardis Lake is mostly futile, but it is also unavoidable. The attempt has to be made. We, the daytime searchers, had the best shot at actually doing something useful.

I aimed the boat for the section of shoreline that Sheriff Bellcase had appointed me. I was to move slowly around the edge of the lake, looking for any signs that the duck hunters might have dragged their boat up into the woods. Unless the men were alive and able to hail me, the chances that I, or any of the other volunteers, would actually find them were mighty slim. A deputy had gone for the tracking dogs up at Parchman prison farm, the state penitentiary. The best tracking hounds in the world are bred and raised there. By noon they would be running in the woods, hunting for a scent.

Once I was away from the other searchers and I'd cut back the throttle on the boat, I settled into the seat. I used my binoculars to scan the coastline and as far up into the trees as I could see. The marshy places on the lake, the small inlets where the water settled and the wind was cut by a fringe of trees, made the best hunting places. I found a likely spot and eased the boat into it, killing the motor and drifting toward shore. Gray light streamed from the trees, turning the last of the fog into wisps that danced into oblivion before my eyes.

I had a paddle that I used to keep the boat from getting too deep in the thick marsh grass. Mine was not a duck hunting boat but a summer craft, and I knew the dangers of shallow water filled with the sunken logs and detritus that hunters loved.

I was close enough to the shore that I could clearly see. No human had passed this way in several days. Pushing out into more open water, I started the motor and cruised along the shore to the next inlet.

The sun had risen above the trees, but the temperature was still well below freezing. It was Christmas morning, and all of the women in my family would be in my mother's kitchen, cooking the specialty dishes that had become their annual assignment. Cousin Jean made biscuits, and her daughter Addie the cranberry salad. My sister-in-law Wilda made the brussel sprouts and chestnuts, a recent addition to the menu that came with her more proper British background. Fried corn and the greenbean salad were always made by Cousin Gail. Aunt Rachel brought the mashed potatoes and the pumpkin pies. And on and on it went, the list of food so long that no single table could hold it. Several buffet lines had to be set up in the long dark hall that was never used except at Christmas.

Up through last year, I'd been assigned the coconut pie. I had a light hand with pastry and meringue. This year I'd refused any attempt to corral me into the food tradition. I said I would bake a pie when some of the men cooked, too. Such scandalous talk had earned me banishment from the kitchen, though Cousin Barry, who actually wanted to cook, sent me a rose cut from his garden and a handwritten thank you note. He had excellent penmanship.

A flock of ducks ruffled the water as they dragged their webbed feet and flapped their wings in the tremendous effort it took to hurl themselves into the air. It was a wonder they hadn't frozen on the edge of the lake, where ice continued to cling to the shore.

I loved the solitude of the lake. I opened my thermos and drank the black coffee, ignoring the almost painful bite of the steam against my frozen cheeks. I wondered where the lost duck-hunters might be. What had happened? Had the boat tipped and thrown them into the lake? Had they had engine trouble and pulled to the shore? Had some magical Christmas Eve miracle occurred, and they would reappear in three days time to proclaim a new message of hope for mankind?

I knew such blasphemy would get me into trouble if I spoke it aloud, but my thoughts were my own, and I could freely indulge them in the silence of the lake.

The ringing of my cell phone was like a guilty conscience, and I snatched it up and said hello before I thought. For some mysterious reason, I assumed it would be another of the volunteers calling to say the hunters had been found.

"Lulu, it's Billy."

Billy was my oldest brother. We'd once been close. "Merry Christmas, Billy." I wondered if there was anything merry in his life since his wife and kids had left him.

"Mama's torn up about the coconut pie. I just wanted to let you know I got Miss Velma to make one, and I'm takin' it and puttin' it on the table with your name beside it."

We always had a nice, hand-lettered nametag to put beside each dish to show who'd made it.

"Don't do that, Billy."

"I am, too."

"Billy, don't do it." I felt an amazing rage ignite. "I didn't bake a fucking pie, and I don't want the credit for one."

"This isn't about you, Lulu. It's about Mama. I'm puttin' your name on the pie, and I'm tellin' her you baked it and asked me to deliver it. And you'd better not tell her any different."

The line went dead. My fingers were too tired to dial him back. The entire year I'd fought about that pie until I'd made them believe I wouldn't bake it. Now it would be there, just as if I'd never opened my mouth.

I took deep breaths in the hopes of expelling the anger that there was no other way to get rid of. In my mind's eye, that pie was already on the tablecloth that Aunt Rae had hand-embroidered for us during the long years of her missionary work in the Amazon forest. I remembered the Christmas she came home for the first time since she'd accepted her mission ten years before. She'd brought the tablecloth, and we'd all held our breaths as she'd thrown it open and over the table, a waterfall of tiny stitches against the pure white cloth. It was a work of art, and she'd calmly said that once she returned to the Amazon on January fifth, she never intended to come back to Mississippi again. And she hadn't.

Mama said she'd gone native and probably had all of her teeth capped gold by now and had learned something a lot more interesting than the missionary position from some wild savage. I hoped so. It was the memory of Aunt Rae that finally made me release the anger and turn my attention back to the chore at hand—finding the lost hunters.

It wasn't just my family that was a mess. All of my friends suffered from the same thing. The Richfields down the road had decided not to have another family Christmas after John-John tried to kill his daughter-in-law by running her down in the family Cadillac. He'd gone straight through the plate glass window and into the family den, crushing the tree, all the presents, and the ten thousand dollar crystal collection that his wife had painstakingly purchased from all over Ireland.

It was rumored that John-John had caught the daughter-in-law stealing the family silver. She was suffering from a bad cocaine addiction that made a steady cash flow a necessity for survival. Her three-week stay in the local hospital was a Demerol paradise, which about made John-John insane, since he was paying for it.

And the Rupert Masons had had to call Sheriff Bellcase last Christmas to take their son to jail. He'd pulled a gun and threatened to kill himself. No one ever heard why, but there was talk that he'd found another lifestyle. Now the Masons go to Memphis to have Christmas lunch in the Peabody Hotel, where Buddy works as a waiter.

It crossed my mind that the duck hunters might have deliberately hidden themselves out in the woods in an effort to avoid Christmas. Perhaps they weren't lost at all, but happy to be out in the trees with no more responsibility than finding dry firewood to keep warm.

That possibility cheered me as I turned into another inlet. I saw the boat instantly. It was half-sunk and floating among the reedy grass. On the bank of the lake a black lab darted and jumped at me. Its mouth was moving open and shut, but no sound came out, and I suddenly realized that it had barked for so long in the cold that it no longer had any voice.

The sun was behind me, and I cut my engine and drifted up to the boat, my right hand reaching for the cell phone. In my waterproof gloves I reached my left hand into the water and caught the bowline of the boat, securing it to my boat and at the same time pulling it around so I could see below the seats on the off-chance that one of the hunters was still in there. It was empty, and I realized I'd forgotten Sheriff Bellcase's cell-phone number. I'd never expected to need it.

I called the sheriff's office and got them to radio him to call me. It took about twenty seconds for my phone to ring.

"I've got the boat," I told him. "No sign of the hunters, but their dog is on the bank." I gave him my location and eased my boat to shore.

The dog almost knocked me down as it rubbed against my legs, panting and peeing on my foot. Labs are normally not timid dogs. Ice crystals had frozen in the dog's coat and I did my best to brush them out. Whenever the animal stopped moving, it shivered uncontrollably. I'd packed some blankets and towels in my boat and I got some and wrapped the dog. He wore a collar that told me his name was Dammit. Abbie Wilks was a man with a sense of humor.

With the dog dragging a blanket beside me, I walked along the edge of the lake. There was no sign that a human had made it to shore. There were plenty of dog tracks, and the ice all along the shoreline had been broken where Dammit had jumped in and out of the lake. I used a stick to poke at the edges of the water. In this part of the lake the drop-off was steep. The men could not have waded ashore. They would have had to swim.

In the distance was the throb of a boat motor. My cell phone rang and I answered.

"Lulu, will you be home for dinner?" My mother sounded tired. I knew she'd been baking one turkey since five o'clock and supervising the frying of another. Fried turkey was a new tradition, only several years old. Loretta, a niece, took care of that, but it required my mother's constant attention.

"Maybe," I said. "I just found the boat."

There was a pause. "And the hunters?" she asked.

"I found their dog."

"I went to school with Fillingham," she said in a voice that was suddenly far away. "He made straight A's in geometry, and his socks never matched."

"I'm afraid they're all dead."

"His wife's a Yankee, you know. She's been up at the courthouse carryin' on because they don't have the National Guard out lookin'."

"I don't think it's gonna be necessary," I said. Dammit was leaning against my leg, shivering so much that I was afraid he might die. I held the phone against my shoulder and knelt down to pull the blanket tighter around the dog. I knotted it at his throat, creating a cape effect.

"I've invited Andrew to dinner," my mother said.

143

What was surprising was that the anger didn't boil up. Andrew and I had broken up over the summer after eight years of dating. Family expectations had been that we would marry. "I've got to go, Mama. Here comes the sheriff."

"Get home as soon as you can. I laid out that green sweater that looks so nice on you. You left it here when you moved out. Your old Levis are here, too. After a warm bath, you'll be hungry, I know. And we still have to open the rest of the presents."

Our family exchanged our gifts on Christmas Eve, had always done so. The Christmas Day presents were those from Santa, distant family, and friends.

"I'll be there as soon as I can. Merry Christmas, Mama."

"Try hard, honey. Toby is here and he's askin' for you. He had a little accident this morning."

"An accident?"

"Alfred didn't put his bicycle together right, and when Toby was goin' down Thrill Hill the handlebars and front wheel came off. He had eight stitches in his head and fifteen on his leg."

"Great." I could see the Frankenstein scar on a head already too large and too square for Ebenezer.

"He's okay, but he was askin' when you were gonna come."

"Tell him as soon as I can." I turned off the phone and watched as the boat bearing Sheriff Bellcase approached. He was standing, his gaze directed at the dark black water of the lake.

Finally he looked up and waved, signaling me out to meet him. I took the blanket off Dammit so the dog could jump into the boat without hanging himself. I boarded carefully, and in one mighty leap he was beside me.

The duck-hunter's boat was still tied to mine, and I dragged it slowly behind me as I pushed away from the bank with the paddle and finally started the motor.

Dammit started doing his soundless bark as he stared over the side of the boat. Out of curiosity, I leaned over. The man was floating about three feet beneath the surface, his face white, his eyes wide open and a milky brown. The red flannel of his shirt undulated softly on his chest, giving the illusion that perhaps he breathed there beneath the water.

"Sheriff!" I waved frantically and then leaned back down to watch as the body drifted beneath the boat. I rushed to the other side and saw him again, floating gently away on a dark current that was invisible to me. Below him was another form, a half-glimpsed shadow of a man drifting closer to the bottom.

Turning the boat in a circle, I tried to find the bodies again, but the churn from the propeller had chopped up bits of marsh grass and weeds, and they cluttered the water. They were gone.

The sheriff floated up beside me, and I told him what I'd seen.

"Which ones was it?" he asked.

I shook my head. "I didn't know any of them."

For a long moment he stared into the lake. "Go on home and get you some Christmas dinner, Lulu. It doesn't matter when we hunt for these men now."

"The other one may be alive." I didn't believe it even as I said it.

"Go on home. We'll get some hooks and a drag-line. As cold as it is, it could take the bodies a week to pop up. The families are already hysterical. It'll be best to finish it now, but watching a body dragged up by a hook isn't something you need to see."

"I wonder what happened?" My hand was on the dog's collar as I held him in my boat.

"Take their boat back with you, and tell the deputy at the landing not to let anyone near it, okay?"

I nodded. "What about the dog? You think the family will want him?"

Sheriff Bellcase looked at the trembling lab and then at me. "I doubt they'll want to take him to California or New York. Abbie didn't have anyone else around here." He looked at the shore of the lake as if there was a message in the trees. "Merry Christmas, Lulu," he said. "Think of all the boys and girls who asked for a dog for Christmas and didn't get one."

"Merry Christmas, Sheriff," I said. My hand held Dammit's collar as I eased the boat away from shore and out into the lake.

As I picked up speed, the air grew bitterly cold, until once again the wind whipped tears from my eyes and froze them solid on my face.

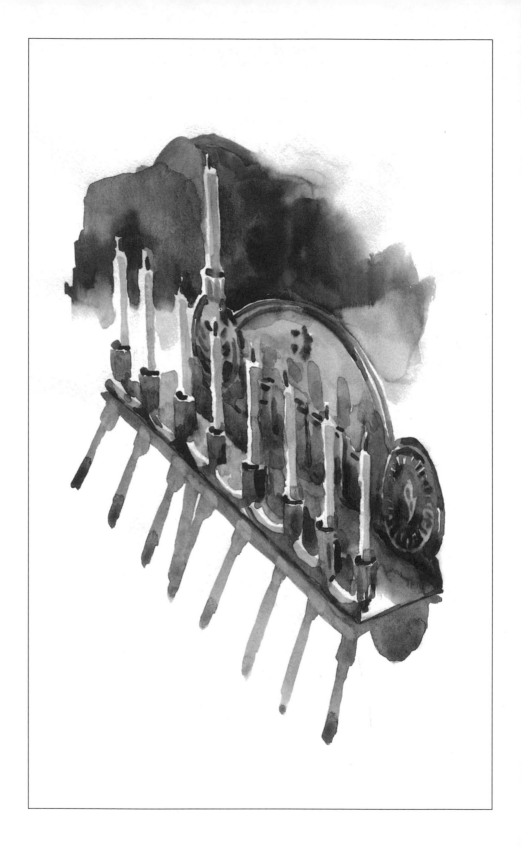

The Peddler's Grandson

Growing Up Jewish in Mississippi

Edward Cohen

My parents weren't concerned about my attending this Christian-affiliated kindergarten. Episcopalians were considered to be the most educated and tolerant of the Christians, and there were no prayers at St. Andrew's. Most important to my mother, however, was the fact that St. Andrew's was simply the best kindergarten, where drawing and French were taught; the paramount Jewish canon of education prevailed over any discomfort about sending her child to a school named after a saint.

In the photo of my class, seven of us are seated at tables, drawing, and behind us are two teachers, their hair neatly permed. Everyone is looking at the camera, as instructed—except me. I am determinedly, fixedly, looking down at my drawing. There is something willful about the stare of this small, blond, sensitive-looking boy. Like any child, I wanted to be the same, but simultaneously I raged against it.

My divided loyalties, my ethnic acrobatics to fit in while I remained apart, continued throughout my years at Boyd Elementary. In those days, every morning began with the teacher reciting a prayer, and every prayer ended with "In Jesus' name." The prayers, particularly the ending, made me feel sacrilegious, disloyal to my parents and Tottie and to myself. We Jews didn't believe in Jesus, didn't believe he was the son of God, though I knew by this time that everybody else did. I thought about not bowing my head so I wouldn't be

147

participating. I tried not closing my eyes but I still heard the prayer. It was just three words, "In Jesus' name," but they were inestimably important, to my classmates in their acceptance of them, to me in my rejection of what everyone else believed. I never even considered protesting. I was a child, one who knew better than most the First Commandment of childhood.

When I was ten, the teacher announced that there would be a Christmas pageant and asked who wanted to participate. I looked around at my classmates, their raised hands waving like the banners of Crusader regiments. They had no conflicting feelings. I felt again the weight of otherness. We didn't celebrate Christmas for the same reason we didn't say "In Jesus' name." Christmas seemed not only alien but dangerous, and staying apart from it was in some way integral to my very identity.

I stared down at my desk, studying its carvings and stains with ferocious attention. I was very aware of Christmas because of my father's clothing store, where the holiday season was the busiest time of the year. There, unlike at our home, Christmas decorations (safely secular images of Santa and his reindeer) went up. Christmas gifts of candy were given out to regular customers, though the customers' greetings of "Merry Christmas" were returned with the more neutral "Happy holidays."

I watched Miss Holderfield copy down the Christian children's names for the pageant. I recalled the year I had begged my mother for a Christmas tree. It had seemed like a fun and harmless thing, with all the presents under it and the lights and decorations. In those days, when every house and every neighborhood was lit up in festive solidarity, our home couldn't have been more conspicuously dark than if, like the Israelites in Egypt, we had daubed blood over our doors.

My mother refused, at first patiently, defusing my argument about the store's decoration by simply ignoring it. We had Hanukkah, a minor military holiday transformed by the combined pressure from thousands of Jewish children over the years into a substitute Christmas, with a present each night for the eight nights we lit candles. But I wanted a tree.

Exasperated finally, she said it would have to be in my room with the door shut because she wouldn't have any Christmas tree in her window. It was characteristic of her that she didn't take the easier approach of some Jewish parents, who, without rabbinical sanction, were buying small, squat Christmas trees and renaming them Hanukkah bushes. They'd put a Star of David at the top and hang little figures of the Maccabee warriors and a few incongruous Santas for variety. To my mother, this was nothing more than an agronomical ruse. Anyway, a Hanukkah bush wasn't what I wanted.

I got a small artificial tree and set it up by myself in my room, placing some decorations my father had given me from the store on its green metal bristles. For the eight nights of Hanukkah, after my parents and I lit the candles in the menorah to celebrate the biblical miracle of the oil lantern continuing to burn in the temple, I shut myself in my room and plugged in my tree—the modern miracle of the Jewish Christmas tree. This solitary celebration, watching my single lonely strand of lights blinking, with my eight saved-up unopened Hanukkah presents underneath, was profoundly dispiriting. (My participation in Easter egg hunts, which my mother inexplicably allowed, was equally unsatisfying; I worried that at any moment I would be exposed as an impostor and forced to give back all my eggs.)

As Miss Holderfield's volunteer sheet for the pageant filled, I held back. That night, when I brought up the Christmas pageant to my parents, I had very mixed feelings. I dreaded being branded by my classmates as different, as on the High Holydays, but I also felt that participating in the pageant would be some kind of betrayal. The pageant, after all, was going to enact the birth of Jesus, and there was no getting around that with ecumenical Santas or so-called Hanukkah bushes.

My mother decided the issue much as she had the Christmas tree affair, with accommodation but without acquiescence. The ruling of the family Sanhedrin Jewish court was that I could not play Jesus or any of the major figures. I could work backstage, or, if absolutely necessary, I could play a rock or other inanimate object. I didn't know how to explain these fine casting differences to my teacher, so I opted for pulling the curtains, hidden, while onstage all the Jewish roles were played by Christians.

With such a small role, I spent most of the rehearsal time sitting forgotten in the empty auditorium, while onstage everyone else, students and teachers, were caught up in the spirit of something that eluded me. They were all members of a giant club from which I alone was excluded. Every Sunday the club's members went almost as one to churches and then afterward to Morrison's Cafeteria. They talked year-round of the unbearable excitement and yearning for Christmas Eve and of rising early to fall upon their presents like hungry wolf puppies. They sent and received Christmas cards (that sad substitute, Hanukkah cards, had not been invented). The club was extremely easy to enter. All I had to do was give up everything.

My parents attended the pageant, of course. I was their son, and having themselves been raised in the South, they knew of the compromises necessary. My mother smiled the way she did at the ecumenical canasta games, while my father was as proud of me pulling the curtain as he would have been if I had played Moses in a Passover pageant. I could see them from backstage, surrounded by the other parents, for whom attendance was not a minor act of apostasy. I opened and closed the curtains, participating but invisible, part of it but apart.

At the end when I took my bow with the Three Wise Men, the rock, the tree, and the rest, I was comforted to see my parents out there, smiling and clapping, as if we were just like everybody else.

Christmas Lights

Jacqueline Wheelock

I t was a sultry Friday morning in 1950, three days before Christmas, and ten-year-old Julia Dothan was sitting in the forked trunk of a massive live oak. She was hoping for a visit from the Singing River Electric truck, when the skinny, blond-haired boy from just outside the edge of the Settlement walked right by her and up to the front door. Through the years he had come ever so often, and never had they exchanged a smidgen of communication—no, not so much as one gesture. "This time," thought Julia, "he want to stay and play. I can tell." But she let him pass his usual note off to her mama, without saying a word, and turn on his roughened bare heels to run back down the road. To tell the truth, part of Julia's intuitive power about what the boy wanted that day came from the fact that she was a little lonesome herself, what with Mama busy cooking Christmas sweets and Daddy asleep in the back room because he had worked all night firing the boiler at the sawmill. So in a whimsical moment, she called out to the boy's quickly disappearing form.

"Hey! Hey, white boy! You wanna play with me?"

"Can't," he said from the distance, slowing down but never turning.

"I got marbles," she called rather pleadingly, "and—and a rocking horse."

His shoulders tensed, and he stopped in the sandy road. But he would not turn around.

"Can't," he said again and picked up speed once more.

· · ·

Elizabeth Dothan, eight months along, was still standing in the doorway minutes after the boy turned the corner. Her unborn child brushed the screen door as the rest of her stood inches behind. She clutched the note the boy had left and called to her daughter.

"Julia, git down outta that tree and come here!"

"Yes ma'am."

Julia quickly slid down out of the oak, marking her skin with the grooved bark of the old tree and separating the skirt of her dress from its bodice.

"Goodness, Julia! You done tore another one of Miss Bess's dresses off the waist?" said her mother, removing a safety pin from the bib of her apron and trying to bend to where the skirt and bodice were severed. "Now you listen to me, young lady. No matter what I might think of that boy that jes left here, his name is *Bufkin*, Bufkin Rankins, and I think I heard your daddy call him Buffy once or twice. You can call him Bufkin, and you can call him Buffy. But you cannot call him 'white boy.' Do you hear me?"

"Yes ma'am."

Julia stood perfectly still while her mother carefully pinned the sections of the dress back together.

"We don't do that 'round here. As long as he's got a name, you use it."

"Yes ma'am."

But Julia thought to herself after her mama went back into the house, "All these times he done been here, I ain't never said *nothing* to him. First time I try to make friends, Mama gits to fussin' 'bout the way I do it."

It crossed Julia's mind, too, as she regained her lookout in the crevice of the ancient tree, that the note from the boy could very well interfere with the coming of the electric truck. But she quickly tucked that somewhere beneath her active thinking. Her daddy had promised and that was that.

Watching her father through the north window, bringing the holly tree down from the edge of the cemetery late that same evening, had been worrisome to Julia, though it had never bothered her before. Before, she would have been pleased because the holly tree always meant Christmas day was almost here, and furthermore, it meant the annual fireworks celebration, held in her own front yard each Saturday before Christmas, would be coming up the next day. This year, though, Julia longed for a different kind of tree, a tree that demanded electric lights, one that spoke to the neighbors from the front room window, telling them that the Dothans were finally in tune. For weeks now, every other house in the Settlement had glowed in the night with the wonder of electricity, while Julia sat watching soot gather inside the globes of the old coal oil lamps. And now, sitting in the front room of their four-room clapboard house, looking at the tree stuffed into a Luzianne Coffee can, she had proof enough that there would be no electric lights for Christmas this year, no parti-colored lighted bulbs draped about the rich green of a cedar tree like the ones she had recently seen on the streets of Pascagoula. No, just the same old pale green of the wild holly leaf and the flame of its winter berries, colors that had once delighted her this time of year but now made her want to shed hot, offended tears. She had loved being in town with her father last week, looking through the window of the old International Harvester truck at all the Christmas lights winking and waving from front room windows and storefronts alike. She recalled, for just a moment, that there had been a picture (stretching the length of a tall billboard) of a little boy with metal braces on his legs—right in the middle of the holiday decorations—saying "Help Fight Polio," but that was all right. It was Christmastime, and the enchantment of the lights had made everything mystical, even the sadness of the billboard.

They could have had lights this Christmas. She knew they could. The house was almost ready because Mr. Ollie's handprints (he was the community electrician) were all around the carved-out circles on the unpainted ceiling, circles that were dead center in the tops of all four rooms, letting air in around thick fingers of black wires left hanging abruptly—incompletely. All they needed was juice, as Mama called it. Just a little bit of juice from those new high-flying outside wires that had been saturating the Settlement skies for months. After all, it was 1950; half the century was gone (teacher said so), and electricity had been flowing through those kinds of wires, stretched upon tall sleek naked poles smelling of creosote, for years.

"If Daddy had jes sent for the Singing River Electric Truck," she sighed. "If he had jes. . . . But no, he had to spend his money on them fire poppers out in the shed, *and* whatever else it is that always brings that white boy here, over and over, with them notes."

There were few secrets in this African American Mississippi Gulf Coast community simply known as the Settlement, so everybody knew that there was a cloud hanging over Julia Dothan's family. Even her school friends knew that her father Zachary Dothan had left for the county just west of the Settlement one rainy night in December of 1940, chasing down a drunken white man named Hank Rankins, only to return three days later to a yearling son dead of pneumonia, a new baby girl named Julia, and a nearly destroyed wife, sad and bitter to this day. Everybody knew that Liz Dothan had lost an ailing child and delivered a breech one—all in the same night, and the grown folks shook their heads and clucked their tongues and said that Zach should have been there. Even the white folks said that Hank Rankins had been a "no 'count scoundrel," drinking all the time with the colored folks at Ethelee's Place when he should have been taking care of his own. But they also said—black and white and always in the same breath—that Zach was a good man. "Your daddy a good man," they would say to Julia—and no more. That frustrated her because she already knew that. Didn't he bring her pralines from town? And didn't he sing lonesome songs out into the sheets of rain as she sat on the front porch in his lap of a summer morning? Didn't he make her a "big girl's" rocking horse when she was eight? And doesn't he call her his "Julie Girl" and tuck her in every night before he goes to fire the boiler? But to Julia there were gaps in his goodness, times when suddenly he was not there—times that nobody explained, not even Mama.

So here he was in the front room that hot Friday night in December, holly tree duly seated in the coffee can, singing to her "Prettiest Little Girl in the County-O; 'Cause her Papa told her so" (just like she was still five) and preparing their house, inside and out, for tomorrow's fireworks celebration while everybody else in the Settlement, for the first time, had Christmas lights twinkling and seemingly taunting Julia from their own front room windows.

"Come on now, help me, Julie Girl," said Zach. "It's time to fix this here tree up."

She helped him pull out old silver and gold Christmas tinsel and cracked mirror ornaments and used tinfoil icicles. Carefully, she placed them on the couch.

"Look at that," said Zach, slapping his thigh with abandon, and laughing that throaty laugh that was his alone. "I got me a young'un big enough to help git ready for Christmas." He pulled a small package from the bulging pocket of his checkered flannel shirt and reached toward Julia. "And here's something I made 'specially for you." It was a wooden figurine, painstakingly carved into the shape of a tiny delicate angel, painted a soft yellow with "Julia" and "Dothan" etched on either wing. "Now put that on your tree for as long as you live and know Daddy go'n always fly with you wheresoever you go." Julia quietly hung the angel on the tree.

She watched her father spread open the intricate tissue folds of the red paper Christmas bell. Huge and faded, the bell looked ancient and meaningless to her as he attached it to the wire that Mr. Ollie had left hanging.

And then from the kitchen she heard Mama clear her throat in that familiar manner reserved for confrontation. The coal oil lamp threw her pregnant shadow against the wall behind the cookstove as she put in a fresh lichen-covered oak log.

"Mama don't really want to be in the family way," thought Julia. "She scared, I think." And to Julia, looking at the shadow from the front room, her mother appeared alien and bizarre.

"Looks like we ain't go'n git the juice before Christmas," Mama said from the kitchen.

Silence.

"I'm pretty sho I heard you say the truck was coming today, Zach—didn't I?"

Silence.

Julia could hear her mother replacing one of the iron eyes over the fire of the cookstove, and then she saw her move into the doorway between the kitchen and the front room and lean on the facing.

"Mr. Ollie ain't been here today to put up no light bulb sockets, so I guess it was Hank Rankins' house you stopped by before you went tree huntin' this evenin'."

"Um."

"I jes wanna know one thing from you. How long is them notes go'n rule our life?"

Silence.

"What else did you do? Did you stop at the grocery store and call the Singing River Electric Company to tell them we didn't want to be hooked up after all? I thought you had already paid the deposit?"

"I can git it back; I have to."

"Because of Buffy 'nem?"

"Um."

Julia, still unraveling all the old tinsel garlands, thought "Mama know she pickin' at Daddy now, jes pickin' and pickin' at him. But she can't stop."

"All them cedars growing out there, Zach, but I see you still brought the holly, even after Julia begged for a cedar this year—with electric lights."

"Holly always suited us before," said Zach. "Got it's own natural beautification to start with—them pretty red berries and all. A cedar tree ain't got no decorations, none a'tall. When we finish with this holly, won't be a cedar tree that can touch it. Ain't that so, Julia?"

In an unguarded moment, Julia looked up and met with a plea in her father's eyes—a desperate request for a way out that she had never seen before. She saw the line of haphazardly drawn anguish resting in the folds of Zach's forehead. But it was too late. Julia was primed to turn loose the tide of unshed tears which she had stemmed for hours now. She was about to bawl, partly from anger and disappointment; partly from love and confusion. She understood that her father wanted peace, but right then she wanted her lights more than she wanted his peace. And, after all, he had promised a cedar tree with lights. When the words came, the tears followed.

"But you promised, Daddy," she sobbed. "You said 'By the Saturday before Christmas, we'll have them lights.' That's what you said. Everybody—the Holloways, Cousin Mack 'nem—everybody got Christmas lights 'cept us. Is we that poor?"

"No," interrupted Mama, her voice high and tremulous. "No, we ain't that poor."

Julia knew very well that they were no poorer than anyone else in the Settlement. Her father had always provided warmth and clothing, and she had never seen him follow the others through the path to Ethelee's honky tonk. But more than once there had been special mysterious sacrifices for no apparent reason, like the year when she was seven and had to wear last year's Easter dress, and the time Mama, her eyes cold and moist, chopped the Christmas ham in half, while Daddy dropped his head and quickly disappeared with the better part of it. And there was the time he was supposed to take Julia, for the first time, fishing in the Pascagoula River but he never showed up. And from time to time when she would try to find answers about her daddy from people like the old midwife Miss Bess, they froze and said, "Your daddy a good man." But one thing never changed. As far back as Julia's memory served her, no matter how tight the money was, Zach always had the Saturday before Christmas fireworks celebration. So Julia knew they were not *that* poor. She simply did not understand yet that every toy and trinket Zach brought to her from town had to be accounted for in their meager income. He had constructed in his own mind what he called a budget, but in reality, it was a monthly shuffle that Zach did, dancing around Peter to bow to Paul, trying to keep some semblance of happiness in his household. And anything—anything at all that rocked that skilled performance could cause the music to come to a halt. Somehow, though, each year since 1941, he had managed to have his fireworks.

"Yes, we poor, but we ain't that poor," continued Julia's mother. "Your daddy works at the sawmill everyday like everybody else 'round here. You see all them fire poppers out in the smokehouse? That's money that could 'a been spent to put sockets in them ceilings and git that electric truck to this house."

"Uh oh," thought Julia drying her face with the back of her hands. "They fixin' to git started."

They didn't argue often, but when they did, and the fireworks celebration got all mixed into it, that meant the little dead boy was coming up too—the little baby that was somehow connected to the blond boy and the notes. That was the cloud that they were under.

"Now Liz," said Zach. "Don't git on the celebration. You know how much the Settlement enjoys it every year. You know . . ."

"Naw, I don't know nothin', nothin' 'cept this: It ain't the Settlement—it ain't *them* that's got to have it. It's *you*. You got to have that Christmas celebration to numb your mind—to keep you from remembering the night your baby boy died. You might as well had drunk white lightnin' that night in the Harrison County woods with Hank, 'cause one habit gone wild is jes as bad as another. You tryin' to make up for bein' out there frolickin' around lookin' for your white friend when you should 'a been here takin' care of your own, but ain't no celebration go'n do it—do you hear me? Nothin' in this world can ever make it up 'cept you put my li'l boy back in my arms."

As soon as the words escaped her lips, Julia's mother took on that self-defeated look that she always did after she crushed the spirit of her mate.

"She can't help it," thought Julia. "She jes can't help it; I reckon it hurts too bad."

Julia had learned that no matter how hard her mother tried to bury the past, over the months the hurt pushed its way back to the surface and erupted violently—always upon Daddy. He turned from the holly tree and looked at his daughter.

"Julie Girl," he said, his voice low and hoarse. "Christmas ain't 'bout no lights—no decorations of no kind, and it ain't 'bout no fireworks neither. Christmas is 'bout lovin' your neighbor—lovin' him so hard that you willin' to try to be what he needs when he needs it." And then he turned to his wife.

"Liz, I wasn't frolickin' and you know it." He laid the old gaudy tinsel down across a cane bottom chair. "It's gittin' time for me to go to the mill and fire the boiler." Zach walked out and slammed the door.

"Mama?" asked Julia. "Do you hate that li'l white boy?"

"No, Julia. I don't hate him. I don't hate him."

In truth, the Saturday before Christmas had always been a special time for her, because at the heart of it was a birthday celebration for Julia herself. Her true birthday—earlier in the month—was a death day too, always mourned by her mother and quietly and painfully ignored by her father. But on this day, this special Saturday evening each December—when children came to play in the sandy yard and grown folks watched the fireworks in the evening skies—on this one day, it was understood that nobody would ever mention the hurt of that haunting day; the one her mother always looked sad about, even through the holiday baking and cleaning and even now that she'd swallowed the baby seed and her stomach was the size of a spring melon (Julia knew better than that baby seed stuff; she was ten for goodness sakes). So now *Julia's* day was here, and she had managed to set aside disappointment for joy.

The front yard was charged. Fired up with scores of Settlement people hungry for excitement. Even the path to Ethelee's honky tonk was confused with the comings and goings of fence riders wanting to be in both places at once.

Old lady Bess Hollingsworth, the fading midwife whose back door Julia could see across the expanse of winter-brown grass, took baby steps up the sandy road toward Zach's celebration, the toes of her shoes hacked away to expose dark crimped roots which were themselves once strong healthy toes. Julia skipped to within feet of her old neighbor. Then she saw Bess stop and look past her through the short distance to Liz Dothan as she greeted people gathering in the yard. "Don't think she go'n make it another month," she muttered, until her musings were interrupted by the familiar voice of the young girl poised in the road to greet her.

"Better hurry up, Miss Bess," called Julia. "Daddy 'bout to light the first sparkle!"

"Humph!" said Bess, her fists resting in the curves of her sides. "I was lookin' at Zach when he clumb out the womb, the wrong way, jes like you did. He start that fire poppin' without me and I'll shove him right back into Paradise—right now, big as he think he is! And as for you, li'l woman, you come here to me."

Julia moved further toward Bess and stopped short. She wanted to ask what a womb was, but she thought better of it. She looked down at her dusty dress and then up into Bess's face.

"Miss Bess, you ain't fixin' to pinch my meat, is you?"

Bess stood in her tracks, lips quivering with laughter, trying to maintain a stern face.

"I sho in the Dickens is. If I see where you done ripped and tore that dress your mama asked me to make, I'm go'n git me a piece o' that meat wheresoever I can find a hole."

"Ain't no holes, Miss Bess. I jes looked."

"Better not be."

"Yes ma'am."

But just to be on the safe side, Julia held a decided distance from Miss Bess, and then she waved "Merry Christmas" to the old midwife as she turned and raced back through the crowd toward the western corner of the front yard, where Zach was systematically arranging his fireworks by the little sunlight that remained. Without looking up, he said "Go tell your mama we 'bout to git started."

The energy was palpable as the children darted through and around the crowd of grown-up merrymakers. Even the dark moisture-laden clouds that had rushed in within the hour added to the electricity in the air. And Julia, able to forget for a while that she had no Christmas lights, was ecstatic, lost in the sheer fun of having other children in her yard. Cousin Mack's daughter Neecy was there talking about the Betsy Wetsy doll she hoped to get for Christmas, and both of Neecy's big brothers were there too, telling about the big game you could get with a BB gun if you just knew how to aim right. Then Julia saw two more of her schoolmates riding up, children whom she saw only at the Settlement School for Coloreds because they lived on the south end of the Settlement—thirteen-year-old Bertha Holloway, absorbed in the thrill and confusion of adolescence, and her mischievous eleven-year-old brother Langston, with whom Julia had a contentious relationship at best and a hostile one at worst. She did not see the shy watchful eyes peering nor the wisps of long blond hair blowing around the eastern corner of the house at precisely the same time Langston Holloway was hopping down from the bed of his father's new Ford truck.

"I betcha I can beat you playin' marbles, Julia," said Langston, already daringly kicking up sand with the toe of his shoe.

"You jes sayin' that, Langston Holloway, 'cause it's almost dark and I wouldn't have time to beat you. Anyway, my daddy 'bout to light the first sparkle, and I got to find my mama. I ain't got no time to be beatin' you playin' no marbles right now."

"You ain't nothin' but a Li'l Miss Muffett, *Julie Girl*. You can't play no marbles."

"I done told you, Langston Holloway" shouted Julia, stomping her foot with mounting irritation. "Don't you be tryin' to call me no Julie Girl. Don't nobody call me that but my daddy! Anyway, I can play with whatever I please. One thing I can do anytime I want to is bust your marbles wide open. Put 'em on the ground, right now, and I'll tear you up," said Julia, forgetting all about her father's instructions. She started to rub her palms together. "Boy, 'member who it was took all your marbles on the last day of school? Jes throw 'em down there. I betcha I'll make you pee in your pants longer than you did in the first grade!"

"Ha, ha, ha," laughed Cousin Mack's thirteen and fifteen-year-old boys who were hanging back from the younger children but still within earshot. "Come on man," said one brother to the other. "These ain't nothin' but young'uns. Some prob'ly still need diapers, from what I'm hearin'."

Julia saw Langston's face drop. He was mortified by the cruel unearthing of that unmanly accident so long ago—in front of so many of his peers. She knew he would be compelled to retaliate.

"Well, at least I ain't got no dead brother that everybody always whispering 'bout," said Langston loudly—harshly, "and I don't have to go 'round still blowin' out coal oil lamps like you do while everybody else got juice comin' into their houses, 'cause my daddy got us hooked up to the power lines. We got the juice, and we got CHRISTMAS LIGHTS!"

With the clouds now covering the heavens, it was almost dark, but the whiteness of Buffy's feet and the lightness of his hair stood out as he appeared like a specter and sent Langston flying backwards into the sandbed road. Julia, stunned by the sudden appearance, stood there gaping for an undetermined stretch of seconds and then jumped onto Buffy's back, fists balled, eyes squinted, pounding his back like a drummer in a high school parade.

"What you doin' boy? I don't need nobody to fight for me!"

She tried to pull him off Langston, who screamed for his mother as his sister weaved through the crowd searching for her.

"Stop it, white boy," said Julia. "What you doin' hanging 'round here anyways. Nothin' but colored people here. Can't you see that?"

He scrambled to his feet. Langston had gotten in a punch or two, and blood streamed from Buffy's nose onto the collar of his thin shirt, washed so many times that the most delicate fingernail could sever it.

"Y-you asked me in; you said I c-could play."

"I ain't said no such a thing."

"Did too; yesterday, y-you said marbles and r-r-rocking horse. Did too."

Julia was flabbergasted. She had forgotten the lonely invitation offered on yesterday—eons ago. And now, in front of her guests, it had come back to haunt her in a boy she hadn't said more than ten words to in her whole life. What was more, she knew he had something to do with her father's strange behavior and the absence of Christmas lights. She decided right then—whether her mother did or not—she hated Bufkin Rankins.

"I didn't mean for you to come runnin' over here *now!* Who you think you is to be fightin' for me? Jes go on home, boy! Why don't you jes go on home!"

Buffy ran down the road under the canopy of an impending storm, while Langston flew into his mother's arms, screaming like a colicky baby.

Through the path, Ethelee's honky tonk spewed a continuous stream of blues, while Zach placed into the hands of every available man "a sparkle of hope," as he called it. Sparklers, Roman candles and one-inch and three-inch fire crackers were all featured attractions, but Zach always liked to start with the sparklers—to soften the mood, he said. Just after each man received his sparkle of hope, it was time for reverence. So the preacher offered devotion and the men stood in a circle next to their women and sang "Silent Night," lighted sparkler in hand. The Holloways from the south end of the Settlement, Zach's cousin Mack and his wife—people from every back road of the community, all crowded around with their children nudging each other in the warm December evening. And Zach and Liz, anger and hurt carefully placed back on the shelf, stood rigidly next to each other setting the mood with rich harmony—she softly providing the melody, he triumphantly offering bass with a touch of alto.

Silent night, Holy night.

"What happened over there with Buffy?" whispered Zach to Liz.

All is calm, all is bright.

"How I'm supposed to know?" snapped Liz.

Round yon virgin, mother and child;

"Well, I thought maybe you might 'a been in that part of the yard when it happened."

Holy infant so tender and mild;

"All I can tell you is that by the time I got over there, all the young'uns was doin' all right. Langston went cryin' to his mama, and Bufkin shot down the road like a bullet out the wild west. Julia go'n need a talkin' to, though, 'cause from the looks of her clothes, she must 'a been fightin' somebody over there like a alley cat. I made her put on clean clothes, and she's all right now."

Sleep in heavenly peace. Sleep in heavenly peace.

Devotion was over, the sparklers now dwindled down to wisps of slate. And everybody was stepping back, widening the fluid circle to let the celebration begin. Only Miss Bess noticed that Liz moved a little stiffer than she had an hour ago.

Zach made a miniature circus ring of the Roman candles by sticking them into the sand. Julia watched her father carefully light each Roman candle—carefully but swiftly enough so that none would explode too quickly in his wake. All the children were gathered in tightly from their yard play, spellbound by the beautiful soft balls of colored fire projected into the warm sky, creating a progressive circle and leaving behind puffs of holiday smoke.

"O-o-o-o-o-o!"

Some of the fire rainbows projected as high as fifty feet while others met their demise at twenty, but the drama was sure and steady.

"Ah-h-h-h-h!"

Now Zach, holding the last Roman candle in his hand, began to motion to the crowd to move in closer to observe his roundup. He loved this part because not only did it seemingly give the fireballs an opportunity to shoot farther, it gave the crowd, especially the children, a sense of daring. Julia knew that he would laugh vigorously, viscerally (he always did)—as though some delectable tiding of joy, which all the other Yuletide celebrants were ignorant of, had been whispered to his soul. He lit the match to the stem and began to circle it like a cowpoke preparing for the capture of a steer. With each fireball he made his motion. Round and round and round—Red! Round and round and round—Green! Round and round and round—Yellow! Round and round and round—Orange! Round and round and round—Purple!

"One more," shouted Zach, "and it's got to be blue."

The crowd stood in hushed anticipation.

Round and round. Round and round. Round and . . . nothing. No color. Only thin pale smoke floating on an evening breeze which had started up with the clouds at sunset.

"*Aw-w-w-w-w!*"

The disappointed sounds of the crowd trailed off into the wind, and for the first time that day, a shudder shook Julia's frame.

"No matter, Zach," said Mack. "It was real pretty, jes that last one messed up, that's all. Can't win 'em all."

"Yeah, you sho right," said Zach, but disappointment and a hint of the ominous had eclipsed his enthusiasm.

"Come on, Mack. Help me with the fire poppers now to end up the show."

"FIRE POPPIN' TIME!" yelled Mack.

Little ones began to place their hands close to their ears as Zach laid rows of firecrackers on top of lined-up tin cans. Other adults, men and women, made sure the children were a safe distance away—enough to enjoy the show and not be frightened—to keep excitement, but be shielded from danger. Zach carefully began to light the stems of whole packs of firecrackers and the immediacy of the noise was startling. Firecrackers popping unrhythmically, sporadically.

"*YEA! YEA! YEA!*"

POP! POP! POP! POP! POP! POP! POP!

Children dug their index fingers into their ears and huddled close to their mothers, but they did not close their eyes, because the light drew them. The last of the firecrackers yielded up a final POP! POP! and then

"Oh! Oh! Oh, Lord! Oh no!"

The wail of a woman mingled with the fireworks, as lightning ripped the skies and raindrops, large and hot, pelted the dense crowd.

"Zach!" shouted his Cousin Mack. "Zach, Zach! Your wife, she in trouble man. Stop the fire poppers!"

Zach dropped a string of red firecrackers, still exploding, and pressing through the throng, his arms pushing outward like an expert breaststroker, he made his way to his wife who stood locked in a cramp, her abdomen gently cradled in both her hands, her contorted face drenched with the sudden onslaught of rain.

"Aw Lord," thought Zach. "Aw my Lord; not again."

He gently lifted his wife, her hands still cradling the unborn child.

"Don't you worry none, honey," said Zach. "Don't worry 'bout a thing. We'll be in town to the hospital in no time. Lemme carry you to the porch and I'll git the truck started. Jes, please, don't you worry."

"It's too late, Zach. Rainin' too hard; hurtin' too bad. Git me to the bed and git Miss Bess." And then she whispered, "Don't put me through this again, Lord. Please don't take another one o' my chill'un."

"I'm here," said the old midwife who had picked her way against the crowd that was trying to get out of the rain. "Miss Bess is here jes like she always been, and this time everything go'n be all right."

Most of the guests were running to their cars for cover, while others were simply running. A few women, empathizing with Liz's distress, offered help, yelling through the din of the rain that Julia should go home with them.

"Naw, I thank you," said Zach carefully moving toward the porch, "but me and Miss Bess ought to be able to make it, and Julia ain't go'n be at peace nowhere else but at the house."

The women frowned on this arrangement, but it was raining so hard that they did not argue.

"It's too soon, Miss Bess," said Liz. "It's much too soon."

Julia, who had made it to her father, was clinging to his leg, sobbing and choking with fear of the new cloud threatening her family.

Julia felt her daddy settling her onto the couch, while old lady Bess, moving about with surprising speed behind the dividing curtains of the back bedroom, calmly and firmly issued orders strong enough to be heard throughout the four rooms. "Hot water, Zach. Clean cloths too; make 'em white if you can."

Zach, his loyalties torn between the pain of his wife and the fear of his daughter, knelt to lay the oak logs over the kindling in the heater of the front room. Then he heard a loud banging on the door.

"Who that comin' in all this rain?" said Julia, jumping up from the couch.

"Wait," said Zach. "Let Daddy see who it is."

Zach opened the door, and the driven rain rushed across the porch—past a thin, pale, shivering figure—into his face.

"Buffy?! What you doin' here in all this weather, child?"

The boy stood there dripping onto the linoleum, his shoulders hunched in a posture of uncertainty, his palms opening and shutting like the louvered blinds of a meddling neighbor. Most of the blood on his shirt collar, left over from the earlier fight, showed now as only barely perceptible streaks of pink. Julia pulled herself tight upon the studio couch and turned her head away.

"You jes as wet as you can be," said Zach, helping the boy out of his shirt. "Sit there by the heater so you can dry out a li'l bit. Go on, sit down. Now, why you here? Be quick now, son," said Zach, striking a match to the light-wood. "I got a needy wife in there. I can't stay with you long."

The boy hesitated before allowing Zach to steer him close to the heater, but the touch of the older man's hand seemed to strike a familiar chord of reassurance, a blend of trust, hope, and gentleness—familiar to Buffy, yet always wondrously new. He sat down on the floor—shaking, his back forming a toppled U. Turning, he looked up at Zach.

"He act like that's his daddy," thought Julia.

"S-somebody from Ethelee's stopped by and t-told us what happened at the fire poppin'," said Buffy.

"All right, son; it's all right. What you tryin' to tell us?"

"Mama said some of us oughta be here. Said we needed to r-r-rep'ersent."

"Oh, I see," said Zach, smiling and glancing toward Julia who had now covered her entire head with an old army blanket. "Well now that sounds fine, mighty fine. You stay in here with Julia and 'rep'ersent.' That's what you do. That be fine, mighty fine."

Zach hurried back through the kitchen and behind the dividing curtains where the pace of his wife's moans quickened, while Julia, the heat of the blanket forcing her to seek air, sat glowering at the boy. The celebration was ruined;

her mama was dying, and now the white boy was here—wet, and intrusive as usual.

"Well? Where your note this time?"

"Ain't got no n-note. My Mama said for me to come and sit with y'all. Said I might could bring in some wood or somethin'."

"We don't need no wood," said Julia, stoking the embers of her anger. Something about this boy—some struggle inside him which she was unable to articulate—something was disarming her, unraveling her rage like gale winds through loosely plaited grass, and she didn't like it.

There was quiet between the two children for a while as they watched the fresh oak logs burn down, reverting the fire-red belly of the tin heater to its original charcoal gray. The moans of Julia's mother pierced the silence; the thunder boomed and the holly tree trembled, Julia slapped her hands across her ears, and Buffy, his bare back lit by the jagged threads of lightning, crouched ever closer to the heater.

"Anyhow, my mama sick in there. Can't you hear her?"

Buffy nodded his head in assent.

"Well, why don't you go on back home then?"

"Can't."

"'Can't. Can't.' Is that all you know how to say, boy?"

He shook his head negatively—decisively, this time sending raindrops flying from the tips of his hair, landing and sizzling against the sides of the heater.

Buffy had much more to say—a whole unsaid story. At least, unsaid by *him*, for it seemed to this eldest overburdened child that his mother (whose very marrow was the telling and retelling of the Hank and Zach story) had, without interruption, spooned the tale to him throughout all the hungry mornings and every cold night of his entire life.

"Y-your mama—in there—sh-she ain't sick," he ventured.

"What you say?" Julia leaned forward to the edge of the couch and balled up her fists. "You tryin' to say my mama jes puttin' on in there, boy? Don't you hear her gruntin'?"

Buffy continued to hold his head down, and now he had begun to rock himself slightly, speaking toward the heater as though it might consume his chancy words before they reached Julia's hostile ears. "J-j-just go'n b-be a baby borned," he said.

The lightning glowed against the boy's bare back and Julia, fists more clenched than balled now, could see the stark outline of his skeleton.

"How you know so much about babies bein' borned, anyhow?"

"G-got f-f-four li'l brothers, 'sides my sister next t-to me. They d-daddy's gone too."

It seemed to Julia that the warmer the room became, the more the boy shook. She thought of offering him the blanket, but fear and anger would not permit her. Instead, seeing the lightning set the holly tree aglow, she opened her fists and covered her ears once more in preparation for the next round of thunder, and as it rolled eastward toward Mobile, she blurted out, loudly and somewhat off-key: "What's them notes about you always bringin' my daddy?"

"S-she writes 'em. My mama writes 'em—wh-when we git t-too hungry or somethin'."

"Hungry? Where your daddy be?"

"Dead."

"Dead? He up in Miss Martha's graveyard, like my brother?"

"N-no. He's in the white folks' graveyard."

Julia's hostility was waning with each roll of thunder. She knew it and she was powerless to stop it. She had heard that a lot of people lived in that Rankins house, but seven people living in a space hardly any bigger than a two-seated outhouse, now that was really something—even for poor Settlement black folks, not to mention white folks. Then her mother's groans became louder, and Julia's mind was jerked back into the crisis at hand.

"Can't you hear that?" she whispered. "My mama real sick. Is she go'n die, Buffy?"

He shot a guarded glance in her direction. A half-smile, fleeting and unsteady, passed over his face. *Nobody calls me "Buffy" 'cept Mr. Zach and sometimes . . .*

" . . . Grace," mumbled the boy, unaware.

"Say what? Grace? Who's Grace? My name ain't no Grace!"

Julia's voice startled him, setting his rocking rhythm off balance. "Huh? Oh—uh, Grace, sh-she's my li'l sister, the one wh-what's got the Polio."

"Polio!"

Looking at Buffy from the perch of her self-styled couch-throne, a new disturbance swept over Julia, as though the distant billboard from town now loomed close and large in the darkness of her own front yard. She stared down upon him, feeling what she did not know yet.

"Polio? You mean like the little boy with the braces on his legs on the big sign in town?" she asked.

"D-don't know. I—I reckon so. Ain't n-never been to town since my daddy died."

"What happened to your daddy? How did he die?"

Buffy turned and looked at her squarely—incredulously. "Y-you mean you don't know?"

Julia had always loved stories, but looking into the boy's face at that moment made her wonder if she wanted to hear this one. She started to jump up and run behind the dividing curtains as fast as she could, but when she saw his palms opening and closing again, she sensed that he was as scared to tell the story as she was to hear it. She slid off the couch onto the floor and sat with her legs crossed campfire-style, chin resting in the heels of her hands, signaling to him that she was ready to hear the story that he had heard so many times but had never told a soul. He turned his face back to the fire, and heaved a slow unsteady breath. Then, haltingly and with painful deliberation, he began to rehearse the story in his mother's voice—noun for noun and pronoun for pronoun, exactly as she had spoken it to him:

"Wh-when Zach's young'un was about to be borned, just t-two days 'fore your daddy left us, I . . . "

"Buffy, why come. . . ?"

Julia was about to question his mode of telling when she recognized that the house had now become still, mimicking the calm steady eye of a hurricane staring down at its subjects before it blinks one last time. Even the cadenced groans of Julia's mother were almost imperceptible. It silenced her, allowing the boy to continue.

"I . . . had to make myself obliged to Zach—me, a white girl—'cause your daddy left us—me and you and little Grace who was j-just one year old. Ever'-body always s-s-said the only person your daddy'd listen to when he got in his moonshine was Zach. Anybody else was in for a good c-cussin'."

The boy stopped abruptly for what seemed to Julia an endless season, but she could see that he was trembling even more and, perhaps, thinking—strug-gling with the next words he would say as though his first telling of his mother's story—its accuracy and order—were as important as the story itself. So she waited until he began again slowly, cautiously.

"Little Grace had took a fever. And nothin'—no qu-quinine, no pine-top tea—nothin' would bring it down. So I left you (you was two) with hot baby Grace (she was one) and I run over there and begged Zach to find your daddy. His wife d-didn't like it, bein' in a family way and havin' a li'l half-sick boy of her own, b-b-but Zach hugged his wife tight and said he'd be back before the night was over."

The rain came hard again, smothering the renewed wails of Liz Dothan behind the dividing curtain. Julia scooted closer to the boy's back—ostensibly so that she could hear him better—and wondered, as he punctuated his story with long silences, what it might be like to have a brother that would fight for you in the sand and tell you stories by the fire. Then he began again and she leaned in to hear him recount, more sure-footedly now and with inadvertent patches of his own voice, how sometimes his mama has to send notes when "Grace won't be 'bated by nobody but Mr. Zach," and how sometimes Grace gits agitated, tired of walkin' with them braces and she won't be calmed unless Julia's daddy comes and tells her a story or sings her a song. "Yesterday," he added, "Grace n-needed medicine."

Then, among the rain and thunder and groans of Julia's mother, a song from behind the dividing curtains threaded its way through the kitchen and into the listening of the children.

Jesus, Jesus; O what a wonderful child.
Jesus, O Jesus; so holy, meek, and mild.
New life and hope to all he brings,
Listen to the angels sing,
Glory, glory, glo-o-ry to the newborn King!

Julia scooted closer toward Buffy until she was shoulder to shoulder with him. She was still scared of his story. But she knew she had to know the end.

"Well, Buffy, is you go'n tell me what happened when my daddy found yours or not?"

He smiled shyly, pulled his legs up campfire-style like hers, and began again, telling the story into the night, slowly—and with his heart, until gradually it became his own.

"M-m-my daddy, he was s-sick in the woods o' Harrison County. S-sick from drinkin' bad liquor, when Mr. Zach found him, so he—m'daddy—got the promise from your daddy, c-c-cause your daddy knowed just where to find him."

Hearing that word, "promise," Julia started to get upset again, recalling the promise of the Christmas lights which her daddy had broken just yesterday. But she saw that Buffy was shivering less now, and she understood that somehow, somewhere during the coupling of this stormy night with the pain and wonder of childbirth, Buffy's feelings had become worthwhile.

"My d-daddy was laughin' just 'fore he died," said Buffy. "Mr. Zach said so—'laughin' like life had done pl-played s-some kind of b-bad j-joke on him' is what Mr. Zach said. Then m'daddy stopped, real quick like, and, and he reached for Mr. Zach's hand—like a h-handshake, you know—and he whispered 'My young'uns is in your hands now, 'specially Grace.' That was what he s-said."

Julia tried to settle herself for what she believed would be another stretch of Buffy's quiet, though now the sounds of the storm had become to her both terrible and wonderful—threatening and soothing, and without even turning around, she felt her father's presence behind her. Then she noticed a strange new expression gather across Buffy's brow, as he began trying to recite something, this time not of his own nor of his mother's making. Something sweet, deep-seated, sustaining—as though (Hank's and Zach's story notwithstanding) he were about to deliver the most important lines he had ever heard:

"J-Jonathan—Jonathan said t-to David. Jonathan said; J-J-Jon-Jonathan said to . . ." Julia watched the boy try the line over and over. "J-Jonathan s-said t-to David . . . ," until a voice, strong and precious to both children, blended with the boy's:

"Jonathan said to David. Go in peace for we have sworn friendship with each other in the name of the Lord, saying, 'The Lord is witness between you and me, and between your descendants and my descendants forever.' I Samuel 20:42"

"How ya'll young'uns doin' in here?" said Zach. "Is Buffy re'persentin'?"

"Do I have a li'l sister yet? Can I come in now?" said Julia.

"Not yet, but it won't be long now, Julie Girl. Now remember Buffy, you the man in here, so you keep takin' care o' my li'l girl."

"Y-yes sir."

"How come my daddy didn't come home that night, Buffy? Then maybe my mama wouldn't be so mad and hurtin' all the time. Maybe . . ."

"It was r-rainin', that's why. R-rainin' down horses and hushpuppies—that's what my mama always says. Rained so hard 'til the Escatawpa River Bridge washed out and Mr. Zach didn't git back to the Settlement to see 'bout his own family for th-three days. When he did git here, you had been borned, b-but your li'l br-br-brother, he had died."

Liz Dothan ushered a defining scream through the brushes of rain, coating and recoating the tin roof. It was Julia, now, who started to softly rock and cry, cry and rock.

"My mama dyin' in there Buffy. She dyin'. Jes like my brother, she go'n be dead."

"N-no, she ain't go'n die, Julia," said Buffy. And he awkwardly, gingerly patted her clenched fists.

"The Lord is witness between you and me," he said over and over, "and between your descendants and my descendants." And the two children rocked together as the screams lengthened in pitch and intensity and the storm pounded relentlessly, mercilessly. They could hear Miss Bess behind the dividing curtains singing "Away in a Manger," and finally they heard Julia's mother say "Lord ha'm mercy; Lord, ha'm mercy."

Then the world outside went dark.

For the first time in hours, Buffy moved to the window and looked out south toward the sandbed road. "The juice is gone," he said. "Ain't nobody in the Settlement got no more lights."

And then he turned from the window, hearing a little cry, soft and sweet like Sunday.

"What's that Buffy? You hear that?"

"I-I do."

"I got me a li'l sister! Must be done climbed outta the womb!"

Miss Bess called from behind the dividing curtain, and Julia sprang up, leaving Buffy near the holly tree by the south window.

When she passed through the dividing curtains, her daddy was sitting in the corner, his head in his hands. And her mama, as soaked as the rain-washed countryside, hair spread fan-like over the pillow, was holding a little bundle. She looked over at Julia and then up at Miss Bess.

"Miss Bess, he . . ."

"He!" interrupted Julia. "I got me a li'l brother? Can I see him?"

"Lots of young'uns borned after only eight months don't make it," said Bess sensing Liz's fear. "Jes don't seem to th'ive for some reason. But this one? I ain't so sho you didn't miscount. This one go'n make it. I seen a lot of new young'uns in my day, and this one go'n make it."

Julia's mother's smile was big and wide and peaceful, first at Miss Bess then at Julia. She pulled back the cover and Julia peered into the squirming blanket. The infant smiled.

"Jes gas," said Miss Bess. "Jes a li'l gas."

Then Liz Dothan called to her husband.

"Zach? You mighty quiet over there. Ain't you go'n git in on all this excitement?"

He raised his head, and Julia could see the tears in his eyes. All he said was "Um."

Julia moved back into the front room.

"Buffy! Buffy! Where you at? Come see my baby brother! Buffy?"

But the room was empty. Buffy was gone. Julia ran to the window, hoping to see the pale feet or maybe the yellow hair, but all was dark. The storm had passed now and a stillness lay over the land. In the whole of the Settlement, no Christmas lights shone. Not one cedar tree lit up the night. Julia turned to look at her own Christmas tree. The green leaves of the holly glistened. And the red berries glowed in the light of the coal oil lamp.

Poets, Plumbers, and the Baby Jesus

Marion Barnwell

"Get in here, Rex," Marie commands through the intercom after hearing the buzzer. Then she buzzes him through the outer gate and goes to the door of her slave quarter apartment of crumbling brick and opens it just as Rex starts to knock.

"Hey, Marie," he says, adjusting the collar of a navy blazer. "Like my new blazer? How'd you know it was me?"

Hands on ample hips, she gives him a look. "Now who else in the entire city of New Orleans would be comin' over here on Christmas night?" She pronounces it *Oil-yuns*, a sure sign she's a native. "'Scuse my appearance, darlin'," she says, refastening the buttons done up wrong on her Minnie Mouse robe, "but, oooh, I'm so mad I don't know whether to get drunk or—or eat a rat biscuit."

"Something wrong? What're you doing?" Rex asks, wide-eyed, as she takes off fuzzy pink slippers, pulls on rubber boots.

"You darn tootin', something's wrong. My pipes busted. That's what. Now who you think I'm gonna get to fix 'em on Christmas night? And as if that wasn't enough," she adds, grumbling and pulling at her boots, "my cat's run off again."

"Precious gone again? When?" he asks. Not waiting for an answer, he starts up the spiral staircase in the corner of the living room behind a drooping Christmas tree, setting ornaments in motion.

"Now where are you going?" Marie stops tugging at her boots, watches him ascend the stairs, then shakes her head. "Not again." After he is out of earshot, she mutters aloud, "She won't ever be worthy of his trust if he don't stop spying on her. I swear."

"What's that, Marie?" he calls down. "I just wanted to be sure you're safe. Just going out on the balcony to make sure. . . ." His voice trails off. Soon, he reappears, hiking his pants. "Hey, you got a flood up there. My shoes are wet. I tell you you're not safe, Marie, not on a night like this."

"Not safe? Because of some ole busted pipes?"

"I'm not talking about the pipes. You can't be too careful. On Christmas night there's no telling who's out on the streets of the Quarter. Burglars, muggers, rapists!" He raises his hands, waves them in warning.

"Out on my balcony? Now look, darlin', I haven't got time for burglars or rapists and so on and so forth. What I need is a plumber. Till I get one, you take this mop and get back up there!"

She puts the mop in his upraised hand. The steam goes out of him. "What? Well, okay. But I'm 'fraid I'm not much of a handyman."

"No handyman job either. Just mop."

He starts up the stairs, this time very slowly. "Guess you turned off the water, huh? You know you could try Plumber's Inc. I think they come out on holidays."

The phone rings. Marie sighs, and answers the phone. "Yes, this is Marie Clooney. You did? You will? Hot dog! Bye now." Still holding the phone to her ear, she does a little dance. "God bless him. Bless his little heart! He's coming! Rex, he's coming!" She goes to the staircase, hollers up. "Rex! I got Teebo Hebert. He's coming!" No answer. "Rex? Where you at, Rex?"

Breathing heavily, she labors up the stairs. Near the top, she can see Rex out on the balcony, staring across the alley into his own apartment. She watches. "Just look at that," she says to herself. "He oughtta be ashamed. Spying on Savannah like that."

Rex turns around, jumps when he sees her watching. "Oh, Marie, you scared me. I didn't know you—"

"See any burglars or rapists this time?"

"No ma'am. I just wanted to be sure—"

Gingerly she steps into the bedroom. "Here's something to be sure of. This floor is wet." She stamps her boots. "See? Now give me that mop. You get some towels. This water's gon' ruin my furniture." She mops furiously. "Go on."

Rex scratches his head. "I—I don't know where you keep your towels."

"Well, use your imagination! There are two rooms up here and we're standing in one of them." He goes off, tentatively opens the bathroom door, turns on the light.

He returns with a stack of towels. "Here you go."

"Thanks." She snatches them, opens them up, throws them at the legs of the furniture. "Now start wiping."

"Yes ma'am."

"And don't call me ma'am. Makes me feel old." The phone rings. Standing next to it, Rex jumps, startled. He looks at Marie. She nods. He picks it up. "Hello. No, he's not. He's . . ." Marie mouths something at him, gestures wildly. "Just a minute." He puts his hand over the receiver. "What?"

"Just tell them he's not here right now," she whispers urgently.

He looks at her curiously, shrugs. "Hello. I'm sorry. He's not here right now? What? Just a minute." Again, he puts his hand over the receiver. "The man wants to know when he'll be back."

"Tell him not for awhile," she whispers.

"Hello. Sir, he won't be back for, uh, quite a while. May I take a message? I see. Thank you." He hangs up. "It was a man from Citadel Life Insurance. Says he'll call back."

"Life insurance! Ha! Now that's a good one. But why on God's green earth would he be calling on Christmas night?"

"Why'd you do that? Why'd you pretend he was alive just then?"

"A woman's gotta protect herself. A woman living all alone. Can't expect anybody else to do it," she mutters to herself.

"When'd he die, anyway?"

"Who?"

"Who? MR. CLOONEY!"

"Oh. How long you been here?"

"Me? What does that have to do with it? I've been here four months. I started teaching at UNO back last August."

"Well, Canyon's been dead twenty years. Gall bladder busted. Just like these pipes. God bless his soul."

"Twenty years," he repeats, then whistles. "Canyon?"

"Yeah, you know, like the Grand Canyon." She extends her arms.

"How come you never remarried?"

"Just never did." She stops mopping, looks around the room. "Guess we're through here." She looks at herself in the dresser mirror. "Look at me. I'm a mess." She pushes at her fire engine red hair, checks her teeth. Rex looks too, straightens his button-down collar, brushes his beard. He takes off his horn-rimmed glasses, looks again uncertainly. "Come on. Long as you're here, you can help me take my tree down."

He raises an eyebrow, follows her down the stairs. She plucks the star off the top and a couple of ornaments as she descends. "Why're you taking it down? It's still Christmas."

"Can't you see it's dead? I bought it way back in October. Feel that. Dead as a run-over sun-dried toad frog. I think I'll start on a Valentine box right away. Like the ones Camellia Anne and Gloria and me made back in fourth grade. I'll make flowers out of crepe paper, cover a box, and cut a hole in the top to put all my valentines in. Oh, it'll be swell."

"And I'll send you a valentine."

"Will you, darlin'? Come on, help me with this string of lights."

Marie hums while they work on the tree. Rex looks nervously up the staircase from time to time. "Marie, I'm kinda worried about Savannah. I don't think she's got her heart in our marriage like she used to. You know what I mean?"

"Now Rex, let me tell you something. I'm a pretty good judge of character. Especially women 'cause I work with 'em all day down at Bayou Belle. And Savannah comes in a lot. Fact is, I like her. Some women treat salesladies like they're just another mannikin. But not Savannah. And she listens when I tell her what looks good on her. Some of the clothes Josephine picks out at market, well," she holds her nose, "phew—ee. Like that godawful looking lavender ultrasuede suit she bought. I tell you, that suit would look good on only one kind of person."

"What?" Rex asks, bewildered.

"A dead one. Yep, it'd go real well with the pallor of the dead."

"Marie, why are you talking about dead people? I mean, what does it have to do with me? All I want to know is what to do about Savannah."

"How in the world am I s'posed to know? All I can tell you is spying's not the answer."

"Did you and, uh, Canyon ever have trouble?"

"Not us. People said we looked alike and that meant our marriage was made in heaven." She sighs.

"Well, then, you were lucky."

"Yeah, right," she says, sarcastically.

"No, I mean it. At least you had it good for a while."

"I guess so. I get lonely though. I miss him. He was a kind man. You know what he said before he died?"

"What?"

She tucks her chin in chest, deepens her voice, "'Be sure to water the plants and take care of Precious when I'm gone.' Then he died. And then Precious died and I had to get a new cat, and now he's run off. And there's rats in this place. And I hate 'em. I just hate 'em. With Precious gone, they run wild. If I didn't put rat biscuits out every night, they'd be runnin' the joint, I swear."

"Now let me get this straight," says Rex, stroking his beard and looking around for rats, "you named him Precious after . . . the *other* Precious."

She nods. "Yeah. That way I'm keeping my promise to Canyon, see, to take care of Precious." She opens a box of rat biscuits, randomly throws them around. While her back is turned, Rex starts back up the stairs.

"You oughtta quit spying on her, Rex."

"I thought I heard something," he says weakly, still climbing.

Her features soften. "Well, maybe I know what it's like to . . . spy."

"You spied on Canyon?"

She looks at him coyly. "Who said anything about Canyon?"

The buzzer sounds. "Oh, I bet that's Teebo." She goes to the intercom, then opens the door. "Mr. Teebo Hebert! If you don't look good enough to kiss." He backs off. "And to come on Christmas night, too."

"Well, I was on my way to—to see somebody anyway," he says, sticking his hands in his pockets. Small, muscular, and compact, he wears only a teeshirt and jeans.

"Wait'll you see upstairs. It's Lake Pontchartrain up there. Hope you brought your—what are those little boats called?"

"Pirogues," says Rex from the stairs.

"Oh, ain't he a smart one. A hotshot professor of history out at UNO. Teebo, Rex McCloud. Rex, this is Teebo. The best plumber in New Orleans."

"Hey, mon. I think I've seen you around in the Quarter, no?" Teebo asks in a thick Cajun accent. He shakes Rex's hand.

"Maybe. I've been here four months now."

Marie leans towards Teebo, confidingly. "He's protecting me from burglars and all manner of marauders. Now go up there and look at the mess. The pipes just busted away. I tell you, anybody who'll come out on Christmas night has my gratitude."

"Yeah, well, I've got six kids, me. They at home screamin' 'n actin' like rootin' pigs. This a relief, this," he says. Then he notices the steep spiral stairs, eyes them warily. "I think," he adds. Marie and Rex watch him ascend the stairs, then disappear. They wait, silent, motionless. "'AY, MARIE. YOU GOT A LADDER?" Teebo yells.

"BEHIND THE DOOR," she yells back. She waits a minute, then hollers, "YOU FIND IT?"

"Yeah," Teebo answers. Another moment passes. "'AY, MARIE. YOU GOT A WRENCH?"

She goes to the kitchen, takes a wrench out of a drawer, motions to Rex to take it up. Again, she watches, waits.

"'AY MARIE. YOU GOT A MOP?"

"REX, SHOW HIM WHERE THE MOP IS," she yells, irritated now. "I swear, sometimes I wonder if I'm not better off without a man."

A few minutes later, Teebo and Rex come down.

"Well?" Marie asks.

"Nothing to it," answers Teebo.

"You fixed 'em, darlin'? Oh, Mr. Teebo Hebert, I swear." She throws her arms around his neck. He struggles to get out of her grasp. "Tell you what. How 'bout a nice stiff drink of Bourbon?"

"Me too," says Rex.

"Good. You fix 'em, Rex."

Leaving Rex to fix the drinks, they go outside to a tiny courtyard enclosed by a vine-covered brick wall. A statue of Buddha overlooks a goldfish pond bordered by jasmine, camellias, and a banana tree. Rex comes out, struggling to balance glasses, an ice bucket, a carafe of water. "Here's to plumbers and the baby Jesus," Marie announces lustily, clinking her glass with the others. "So how'd you fix 'em?"

Rex starts to answer, "I just—"

"Not the drinks, silly," Marie interrupts. "The pipes."

"Oh, they just needed a little coupling."

Rex and Marie look at each other, then Marie says wistfully, "Aw, a little coupling." They sigh.

Marie takes a long sip. They settle in green metal lawn chairs grouped near the fishpond. "Where else but the Crescent City can a person sit outside on Christmas night. Reminds me of my honeymoon. DAMMIT!"

Rex jumps. "What is it? What's the matter?"

"I swear it was a mosquito. Just look at my arm."

"You know, chère, if you just let 'em finish sucking, they don't leave a welt."

Marie gapes at him, speechless. Rex rises, starts inside. "I'll just be a minute."

"You gotta quit that spying, Rex."

"Spying?" asks Teebo. "I thought you said he was protecting you."

"That's what *he* says. But what he's really doing is spying on his own wife."

Incensed, Rex returns. "I was not," he retorts.

"Were too," says Marie.

"Spying on his wife! You can't do that, mon. Where's your self-respect?" Then in a lower decibel, "Where's your wife?"

"They live in the apartment across the street," Marie explains. "From my balcony, he can see straight into his own bedroom. Can't you, Rex?"

"What's she doing?" asks Teebo, alarmed.

"Said she was gonna wash out her stockings," Rex mutters disconsolately.

"Now lemme get this straight, me. You left your wife at home alone on Christmas night so you could spy on her?" asks Teebo, his voice rising. "And where does she think *you* are?"

"I told her I was going to visit my old aunt out on the lakefront."

"This is not making sense to me, mon. You got to help me here."

"She's got a lover," Rex blurts. He springs out of his chair, upending it. "I know it! And I won't stand for it! Do you hear?"

Marie goes over, pats his arm. "Shush now. It's all right darlin'."

"Hey, mon, take it easy. Be cool." He rights the chair, pours Rex another drink. "Now sit down and listen while I tell you a story." He strokes his mustache. "How to begin?" Dancing on the balls of his feet, he begins to pace. "Once there was a beautiful woman named Ginger . . . perfect in every way," he says, eyeing Marie, then Rex before going on, "except one." He stops, takes a drink, rubs the back of his neck, considering. "She was married. And this ole guy, whose name was . . . Teebo, just like me, ole Teebo, he falls in love with her, see?"

"How'd he meet her?" Marie asks.

"That don' matter, that. Okay, she worked at a newspaper stand. Well, it so happened that Ginger, beautiful Ginger, got off work the same time ole Teebo did. So they started having a drink together every afternoon and before long, one thing led to another. 'Cause everybody needs a little spice in their lives. Hee, hee. Get it, chère? Spice, Ginger? Hee, hee."

Rex crosses his legs. "I don't know what this has to do with me," he says impatiently.

Teebo points a silencing finger. "Patience! One day, ole Teebo decides to visit Ginger at her house on his lunch hour since she don't have to work that day, see? Well, he picks the wrong day, the one day the husband has decided to take the afternoon off and come home. But he must've smelled a rat 'cause when he comes into the bedroom he's got a shotgun, a shotgun fully loaded with buckshot, that. By that time I—I mean Teebo, ole Teebo has hidden in the closet, see."

"Oh, my soul! Another mosquito." She swats her arm. "Look at my arm," she says to Rex. "Do you see any blood?"

"Now, listen!" Teebo commands. "So there's pore ole Teebo hiding in the closet, naked as a jaybird, when the mad husband opens the closet door and starts firing away. Then he loads up my—his ass with buckshot. He can't sit down for a month, mon."

"But I still don't see," says Rex, protesting.

"Shhh," says Marie. "Do you hear something? Maybe it's my Precious. Here, Precious," she calls. "Here, kitty, kitty, kitty."

A pajamaed leg appears over the wall behind them. Marie's face lights up. "It's Myers," she says with a delighted sigh.

"*What is precious is never to forget,*" Myers says, hoisting his other leg over the wall. He almost falls, catches himself, careful not to spill the drink in his hand. "*The essential delight of the blood drawn from ageless springs. . . .*" He is clearly intoxicated, possibly with liquor, certainly with words. He gains his footing, still reciting. "*Breaking through rocks in worlds before our earth.*" He bows. "There's one more verse but I can't seem to remember." He looks at Marie as if waiting to be admitted through an invisible door. "May I?"

"You scared me, Myers. Of course. Come in," she says shyly, then moves back as if there is a door. "Hand me that glass. I'll fix you a refill." She pours whiskey, adds ice. "There. But you see you're interrupting. Teebo here," she points, "is telling us a story. And we're about to get to the point. Listen, now. Go on, Teebo."

"Well," says Teebo, scratching his head. "I, uh, say, who is this guy anyway, chère?"

"This is Myers Sinclair," she says with meaning. "Myers, this is Teebo. And I think you know Rex. Go on, Teebo," she urges.

"The point is, Rex, for all that buckshot he got in his ass, Teebo didn't—"

"Excuse me," interrupts Myers. "I thought *you* were Teebo."

"Yes, yes, I am," Teebo answers impatiently. "It's just a manner of speaking, mon. You had to be here for the first of it."

"Just sit down and listen, Myers," says Marie gently. "We'll catch you up on the rest of it later."

"Well, if you don't want me here, I'll just—" He gets up, starts towards the wall.

"No, stay, Myers. Just listen," says Rex.

"Okey dokey," he says, sitting on the edge of the fishpond. He turns, looks at Buddha, tries to copy his cross-legged position. He loses his balance, tries again.

"The point is, Rex," says Teebo, "with all that buckshot up my ass, I didn't stop seeing Ginger!"

"You mean," says Myers calmly, legs now crossed serenely, "*Teebo* didn't stop seeing Ginger."

"Right!" Marie shouts happily, clapping her hands.

"Okay, so . . . ," says Rex. "You're saying that—that there's nothing I can do if Savannah wants to cheat on me."

Dancing like a boxer, Teebo punches Rex in the shoulder. "Right, mon! Attaboy! Now you cooking, you."

"Okay. Tell you what I'll do. I'll just go up those stairs. . . ." Teebo and Marie moan. "NO, wait. Listen. I'm going up, take just one more look and then I'm through spying FOREVER! Okay?" Disbelieving, they wave him off.

Myers steps onto the ledge of the fishpond as if taking the stage. *"Born of the sun, they traveled a short while toward the sun,"* he says.

"Marie! Teebo! Come quick," Rex yells from upstairs.

They rush away, clamor up the stairs, leaving Myers still reciting. *"And left the vivid air signed with their honor,"* he finishes with a flourish before he realizes they've gone.

"That's mighty pretty. Did you write that? Are you a poet?" a young woman asks, entering the courtyard through the gate.

"'S that my Annie?"

"No, it's Kitty. I was resting in the doorway there when I thought I heard somebody calling my name. Then I heard some yelling. It was weird. Anything wrong?"

"My, you took my breath there for a minute," says Myers. "Are you sure you're not my Annie?" He steps off the fishpond, looks at her closely. She is dressed in a teeshirt, beads, a denim jacket.

"Who's your Annie?"

"My daughter who ran away."

"I ran away too. But I'm not your Annie. Where'd she go to?"

"You like to ask hard questions, don't you?"

"Not anymore than anybody else. Ask me something. Anything. Go ahead."

"Where'd you come from?"

"Over on Dumaine Street."

"I mean or-i-gin-ally," he says carefully so as not to slur his words. "Nobody's *from* Dumaine."

"Mississippi."

"Oh? Where?"

"A little town you never heard of."

"Try me."

"It's in the Delta. A little town called Shy. You know where the Delta is?"

"I ought to."

"Bet you don't. Most people assume it's near here, you know, near the mouth of the river. But it's not."

"I know."

"Okay, smarty, where is it then?"

He takes a deep breath, extends his arms as if about to perform an aria. *"The Delta begins in the lobby of the Peabody Hotel and ends on Catfish Row in Vicksburg."*

"Gee, that's pretty. Did you make it up?"

He smiles into his hand, thrilled to find a new, untapped audience.

They hear a loud crash, then a door slamming. "What was that?" asks Kitty.

"HANG ON, SAVANNAH, WE'RE COMING!" yells Rex, running through the courtyard and then out into the street, followed closely by Marie and Teebo. Dumbfounded, Kitty watches them disappear.

Afraid of losing her attention, Myers talks fast. "I'm from Possum Creek myself. Up north of Benoit. Shy, huh? Gotta be a story in that name. Lessee. When the train came in, they were one bale shy of a load." She stares at him. He scratches his head. "Or maybe, when the compress foreman totaled up the cotton, they were one bale shy." She stares harder. "Well, it's gotta have something to do with cotton. Okay, I got it! They had a big hail storm, see. It's so bad it's gon' be in all the papers. Some reporter comes up to the bigtime cotton planter who owns half the town, asks him how he feels about the hailstorm that's just destroyed his crop. So he thinks a minute, then says to the reporter, 'We're in shy cotton now!'" Myers slaps his knee, then holds his side, laughing.

"It's possible. So you're from Possum Creek. That explains how you knew where the Delta is. 'Course you mighta known anyway. You seem to know a lot."

Myers straightens, rocks back on his heels. "Well, now, Kitty, tell me. Are you shy?"

She laughs, getting it. "No, I'm not shy. Been better if I was."

"What do you mean? You're not sorry we struck up this conversation?"

"No, it's not that. I was thinking about my husband."

"Husband? You're married?"

"Not anymore. I came to New Orleans on a senior trip two, three years ago. That's when I met him. Said he was a photographer, wanted to take my picture for a magazine, wanted to make me famous. Next thing I knew, we were married. Then he left. Left me high and dry," she says wistfully. "Never heard from him again."

"Oh, my. And the pictures. The pictures that were gonna make you famous? Were they kind of, you know, ooh la la?"

"Some were. But it didn't matter."

"Didn't matter!"

"No."

"But, my dear, why not?"

"It was all a trick, see. He didn't put any film in the camera."

"So what did your folks think?"

"They didn't think anything. There's twelve of us kids."

He whistles. "Good God Almighty."

"So it's better if I don't complicate things up for them."

"You never go visit?"

"Sometimes. But they don't ask questions. Even if they did, by the time Mama's got the chicken fried and she might think to ask 'So how's Dewayne?' somebody always wants seconds. You can count on that."

"WE GOT HIM!" hollers Teebo. He crashes through the gate dragging a tall, gangly fellow by the collar.

"How do you do," says Myers politely to the stranger.

"He was trying to steal her purse," says Rex, following Teebo and the stranger. "Can you believe it?"

"Oh, my goodness," says Kitty.

"Get a good holt on him, boys," says Marie. "I'll call the police."

"He cut our phone wire," says Savannah, a willowy blonde. She puts her arms around Rex's neck, clinging to him.

"It's all right now, sweetheart," he says, holding her. "Just relax. I'm here. We'll call the phone company in the morning."

"Why'd you do it, mon?" asks Teebo, letting go of the stranger, but pushing him a little. "Who are you anyway?"

"My name's, uh, Pete. I was hungry, see. Tried to steal the lady's purse, that's all."

"Well, if he was hungry," says Kitty sympathetically.

"I got the police. They'll be here right away," says Marie.

Teebo starts laughing, holding his sides. "Hee, hee. So the NOPD will be here right away. That's funny, chère."

"So Pete, what do you do?" asks Myers. "When you're not burgling, that is."

"I'm an accountant. Or used to be before I—I fell on hard times."

Teebo goes into another convulsion of laughter. "Hee, hee. So you were settling accounts over there at Savannah's, eh mon?"

"Don't tease him. Anybody can see he's troubled. And hungry," says Kitty.

"Say, what are you? Some kind of social worker?" asks Teebo.

"Maybe I am. What if I am?"

"I think it's fine," says Myers.

"Anybody want a drink?" asks Marie, holding up a nearly empty bottle.

"Say, you got any red wine?" asks Pete.

"Hee, hee. We s'posed to believe this man Pete is an accountant who drinks red wine?"

Myers stands up, brings himself to his full height. He is incensed. "Well, I don't see why not. After all, we just heard a man named Teebo tell a story about a man named *Teebo*—but not the *same* Teebo—who falls in love with a woman named Ginger and hides in a closet and gets his bee-hind loaded up with buckshot."

"I was going to see her tonight, Marie, after I fixed your pipes," says Teebo. "That's why I was glad you called me to come. But I've changed my mind now, chère. I'm not going."

"What? You aren't?" asks Marie, smiling.

"Naah. When I told that story about—about Teebo, I felt kinda—kinda . . ." he scratches his head. "I keep thinking about my wife at home on Christmas night with those six kids rooting around, hollering like hogs, ya know, chère?"

"Come on, Pete," says Rex. "I'll take you next door and buy you a hamburger while we wait for the police."

"Hey, mon. Not serious, are you?" Teebo asks. He looks hard at Rex. "Okay, then. I better go with you, me."

"Now that's sweet," says Kitty, approvingly.

Myers has resumed his seat on the ledge of the fishpond. "Come over here, Kitty," he says, "and sit by me."

"Come to my apartment with me, Marie," says Savannah. "I've got you a Christmas present."

Marie watches Myers and Kitty. Reluctantly, she allows Savannah to drag her away.

"So what happened to her?" Kitty asks Myers. "What happened to your daughter, Annie? How'd she disappear?"

"Her mother and I were at her college graduation. Jackson, Mississippi. Late May. We were sitting in chairs outdoors in the broiling sun. You know how hot that is, Mississippi in late May. And we were waiting for her to cross the stage. 'S' is a long way down."

"I'm sorry. 'S'?"

"Sinclair. Annie Sinclair." Kitty nods.

"And my wife was wearing a white eyelet blouse. Finally, the 'S's came marching across the stage. 'Sandifer, Sargeant, Springsteen.' But no Sinclair. Where was my Annie? When we got home, I had to peel the eyelet off my wife's back. She was sunburned through every little bitty hole. She blamed me. Divorced me soon after."

"And you never heard from Annie again?"

"My wife did. She wrote her a letter, said adults were just too boring and she had decided she didn't want to be one. Said all we thought about was getting 'Yard of the Month.'"

"That is so sad," says Kitty, wiping her eyes.

"Yep. And then my wife left me for Charlie Baldwin. Old Charlie Baldwin. I, who peeled the eyelet off her back."

"So then what'd you do?"

"Left my job at the bank in Possum Creek. Came here to write poetry. *"The desires fall across their bodies like blossoms,"* he says, sinking into a reverie.

"That's so pretty. And you wrote it?"

"Ah, no, a greater one than I wrote that. But I could show you some poems I did write. Want to see them?" He stands, offers his arm.

"Sure I do. Annie would be so proud of you. You're not boring now." He gallantly helps her over the wall.

Marie and Savannah return to the patio through the gate. Marie is dressed in a silk blouse and patchwork skirt. "I feel so pretty, Savannah. You knew I had my eye on this outfit, didn't you?"

"Yeah, I remembered. You do look pretty."

"I should get rid of these boots, though," she says, raising a foot. "Um. Savannah? I don't mean to pry but Pete's not a burglar, is he?"

"Uh . . . no."

"Oooh, I was afraid of that. But who is he? You better go on and tell me about him."

"He's John."

"No, Pete. Who's John?"

"That's his real name. John. He's just . . . somebody I saw on the street."

"On the street! Oh, my stars."

"No, no. That made it sound worse than it is. I was on my way to the A&P the other day, see, when this humongus dog came up. His leash was dragging the ground behind him. And he bared his teeth and started to snap at my ankles."

"When was this?"

"When? Oh, Tuesday, I guess."

"That's it! That's the day Precious disappeared. Don't you see? That dog probably chased him off."

"Huh? Well, anyway, I was so scared. I've never been so scared in my life. I mean my hair was standing on end. And this big bubble of fear was just blowing up inside me. I could see the dog was getting ready to bite. I know he sensed how scared I was. You're not supposed to do that, you know. Let 'em know how scared you are."

"Stop! My knees have turned to jelly," says Marie. "I gotta sit down. Here. In the swing." They sit in a double swing suspended from a tree near the fishpond. "So what happened? Go on."

"Well, this man comes up and grabs the leash. And I look up. And it's John."

"So you knew him?"

"'Course I did, Marie."

"Dear God in Heaven if that isn't a relief!"

"We went to high school together. He was Mr. Yazoo City High and I was Miss."

"Well, bless my buttons. Why didn't you say you knew him? So then what?"

"Then we went to Tujaque's for lunch. And then this afternoon, just when the Christmas letdown set in, the phone rang and it was John. He just got divorced, so he's spending the holidays with his brother and his family. And he said he was lonesome, so he asked was there any way he could see me. Well, Rex had just asked me to go with him to the lakefront to see his old aunt and I had said no because I wanted to wash out my pantyhose. So I said to John, 'Okay, but just for a little while.'"

"Oh, Savannah."

"Marie, you think Rex is so nice because he comes over here and does every little thing you ask him to." Marie rolls her eyes. "But you oughta try to live with him. All the man ever does is read. Boring old books about the Civil War. *The Civil War, Volume I, The Civil War, Volume II, The Civil War, Volume III.* If that man comes out with another volume, I swear I'll spit. And me? I just wanted to have a little fun. But nooo. Ole stuff face hangs practically upside down on your balcony and sees us. I swear, nobody ever gets caught but me."

"Teebo did," Marie puts in. "Teebo got his bee-hind shot up with buck-shot."

"Me, I get caught for just thinking about it."

"So you and John weren't—"

"We *were* kissing. But that's all."

"So when Rex caught you kissing, you—"

"We pretended John was a burglar. Oh, Marie, you think I'm terrible, don't you? What should I do?"

"I think you should tell Rex the truth, but then I guess I don't know much about it," she admits.

"Guess you don't 'cause you've been faithful to Canyon for practically all your life and he's dead."

Marie gives her a look.

"Well, it's true."

"Not so faithful."

"Really? Tell me," she implores eagerly.

Marie shrugs, picks up the bottle. "Empty. Lemme get us something to drink." She goes in, comes back with a bottle of wine and some glasses on a tray. "It's no use. I—I have, I *had* the wildest crush on—on Myers. That is I did till tonight. Then he disappeared into the night with that young girl."

"You don't think Myers and that young girl are . . . Marie, that's perverted. He's old enough to be her father."

"Savannah, you must promise me you won't tell. And when Rex comes back, you've got to straighten things out."

"I've seen the way Myers looks at you, Marie. I think he likes you. Why, just wait'll he comes back and sees you all dressed up."

"You think so?" Marie asks, smoothing her skirt. She lifts a foot, sees her boot. "Oh, shoot, Savannah. I'm too old for this. You know that balloon of fear you talked about? Well, I've got it bad. He is cute, though, isn't he? The way he climbs over that wall? But, oh, he's so cultivated, Savannah. And I'm—I'm—"

"Earthy. Well, he's not all that cultivated. I mean the man does walk around in his pajamas."

Rex returns through the gate, followed by John, then Teebo. "So you and Savannah knew each other in high school, eh? Small world. You shoulda told me."

"Hey, chère, guess what?" Teebo says to Marie. "Turns out Savannah and Pete here, uh, make that John, are old friends, aren't you, Savannah? And get a loada this, mon. John here was in Rex's fraternity."

"Ha, ha! Can you beat that, Savannah? He's a KA! Put it there, bro," says Rex, giving John an elaborate handshake.

"Shine on, shine on harvest moon," sings Myers, throwing a leg over the wall. "Come on, Miss Kitty, our friends are back. Here's Teebo and Marie and Rex and Savannah and Pete."

"It's John," says John.

"Okay . . . John . . . then," Myers says uncertainly. Then he brightens, snaps his fingers. "Hey, I got it. You want to tell us something, a—a story. And you think you gotta change your name. But you see, in this group," he says, spreading his arms to indicate the others, "you don't have to change your name to tell a story. Right, Teebo?"

John looks at him, not getting it, while the others laugh. "Hey, guys," he says finally, punching Rex on the shoulder, "it's late. I don't think the police are coming. Y'all mind if I go on home? My brother's probably worried."

"Goodbye, John," Savannah calls as if he's already far away. The rest of them catch the spirit. "Goodbye, John," they all cry enthusiastically. "Goodbye, John. So long, John."

"His name's John, huh?" asks Myers. "Well, isn't that something." He notices Marie. "Well, isn't *this* something." He moves closer, takes in her new outfit. Then he walks all around her, looking at her in admiration. "Mar-ree," he sings, "the dawn is breaking. Ma-reee." He takes a seat in the swing. "Marie, come over here and sit by me." He pulls her to him, nuzzles her neck, growling.

"Let's all have some wine," says Savannah, pouring and handing out glasses. "One for you too, Sexy Rexy," she says to Rex. He looks up adoringly.

"How 'bout a toast, Mr. Sinclair," says Kitty.

"*Mister* Sinclair?" asks Marie hopefully.

Myers stretches out his arms, opens his mouth. Nothing comes out. He ponders this, scratching his head. "Now isn't that funny? I seem to be at a loss for words. Can you imagine? Me at a loss for words."

"Here's to plumbers," says Marie, then adds shyly, "and poets. And the baby Jesus."

"Hear, hear," says Myers.

"Hear, hear," say the others. They clink their glasses, then settle into chairs.

"Shhh," says Marie. "Did you hear something?" An orange cat sashays in, springs for her lap. "Precious," she coos, "where have you been?"

"I had a cat just like that once," says Kitty.

Teebo looks at Kitty as if for the first time. "Why don't you come sit here, chère," he says, patting the chair beside him. "I want to hear all about that cat, me."

Christmases Gone Revisited

Willie Morris

The town was so wonderfully contained for me in those Christmases of early childhood that I could hardly have asked for anything else: the lights aglitter in front of the established homes on the hills and down in the flat places, the main street with its decorations stretching away to the bend in the murky river—a different place altogether from the scorched vistas of its summers. The cruelty and madness of adolescence would come later, plenty of time for that. There was an electricity in the very atmosphere then, having to do, I know now, with being little and with pride in the sudden luster, and when we went caroling and gave our Christmas baskets to the poor white people in the neglected apartment houses and the Negroes in the shacks on stilts in the swamp bottoms, on those cool crisp nights after school had turned out for the holidays, I would look into the Delta at the evening star bright and high in the skies and think to myself: There is the Star itself, the one that guided them to the new child. To this day when I hear "O Little Town of Bethlehem," that town for me is really Yazoo. Once, many years later, I sat at a bar on eastern Long Island on Christmas Eve overhearing two Madison Avenue executives as they plotted in vivid and profane detail how to have their boss fired by the first of the year, and I thought: where did it all go?

Where does memory begin? I remember a Christmas pageant in the church when we were five years old. Our teacher had borrowed one of the infant Turner twins to be Jesus, promising the Turners that no one would drop her on the floor. The Baby Jesus himself was never treated so gingerly. They only let us use her in the dress rehearsal and the real evening. Kay King was Mary, I was Joseph, and Bubba Barrier was the innkeeper. When I knocked on the door, Bubba was supposed to open it, thrust his head out, and say, in a booming injunction: *"No room in the inn!"* We had practiced it to adult perfection. But when the night came, Bubba was flustered by the dozens of parents and relatives crowding the church sanctuary. When I knocked on the door of the inn, he opened it with diffidence and said: "Willie, we done run out of space."

For me those mornings of Christmas were warm with the familiar ritual. We would wake up shortly after dawn in our house in Yazoo—my mother, my father, my dog Old Skip, and I. Old Skip would have rousted me out of sleep with his cold wet nose, then pull the blankets off me with his teeth to make sure I did not stay in the bed any longer. No worry about that on *this* day. We would open the presents. My mother would play three or four carols on the Steinway baby grand—then we would have the sparsest of breakfasts to save room for the feast to come. Under the purple Mississippi clouds which, much as I prayed for it, never brought snow, we drove the forty miles south to be with my grandmother, Mamie, my grandfather, Percy, and my two old incorrigible great-aunts, Maggie and Susie, who were born during the Civil War. The drive itself is etched in my heart, the tiny hamlets of the plain where white and black children played outside with the acquisitions of the day, the sad unpainted country stores with the patent medicine posters trimmed in tinsel, and finally the splendid glimpse of the capitol dome and the ride down State Street to the little brick house on North Jefferson. When Old Skip saw the house he would bound out the door like a fox, and I was not far behind.

They would be there on the gallery under the magnolia tree waiting for us, the four of them, and we would all go inside to wild hosannas and exultant embracings to exchange our gifts—modest items for sure, because we were not rich—and examine what we had given each other, and then sit down and catch up on our tidings. And the smells from the kitchen! The fat turkey and giblet gravy and cornbread stuffing and sweet potatoes with melted marshmallows and the nectar and ambrosia and roasted pecans and mincemeat pies. Old Skip hovered around the oven and my two great-aunts bumped into each other every now and again and wished each other Merry Christmas, while the rest of us sank into the chairs by the fire in the parlor and awaited what my grandmother Mamie was making for us. Christmas songs wafted from the chimes of the church down the way and the crackle of firecrackers came from the neighboring lawns, and my grandmother would dart out of the kitchen with Old Skip at her heels and say: "Almost done now!"

Then, at eleven in the morning, never later, we would sit at the ancient table which had been my great-great-grandmother's: my grandfather Percy and my father at opposite ends, my mother and great-aunts on one side of it, my grandmother and I on the other, Old Skip poised next to my chair expecting his favors. We would sit there for two hours, it seemed, all of them talking about vanished Christmases, and people long since departed from the earth. The clock on the mantle would sound each quarter hour, and my great-aunts would ask for more servings and say: "My, ain't this *good?*"

I would look around me every year at each of them, and feel Old Skip's nose on my hand, as if all this were designed for me alone. Then, after the rattling of dishes, we would settle in the parlor again, drowsy and fulfilled, and talk away the afternoon. Finally my grandmother, standing before us by the fire, would gaze about the room and always say, in her tone at once poignant and bemused: "Oh, well, another Christmas come and gone."

They themselves are all gone now, each one of them: Mamie and Percy and Maggie and Susie, buried in a crumbling graveyard on a hill; my mother and father in the cemetery in Yazoo; Old Skip behind the house.

Only I remain, and on Christmases now far away from home, I remember them.

When you drive through the main entrance of the Yazoo cemetery, make a right at the water fountain near the witch's grave and then a left at the next curve and proceed down this road almost to the end, you will come upon an angel. It will be on your right, only a few feet from the road; you can hardly miss it. It adorns the grave of a little girl. Her name was Maud, and she was five years old when she died in 1921.

I had driven down alone from Oxford the night before. Most of my comrades there are taking the holidays elsewhere, in Florida, or Vermont, or, God forbid, Dallas. It is Christmas morning of 1985, the first Christmas I will spend in the town in almost thirty years; I am to go to a party that night among old friends. When I awakened on Christmas Eve I said to myself, *audibly* as those of us who live more or less by our own devices will understand: "Either Long Island or Yazoo, but decide quick."

The cemetery at this hour is deserted. A pair of elderly ladies had been dallying at a grave near the entrance, one of them carrying a Christmas wreath, but they have just departed. A solitary man, middle-aged, in a dark suit and tie, had been kneeling before a fresh plot among old stones with the Gregory Funeral Home tent covering it, but he too was gone. Although I am driving to my parents' graves, I am drawn almost as an act of the most fragile subconscious to Maud's angel. I do not quite know why. Perhaps it is because of the photograph I remember, taken by my mother on our ancient fold-out Kodak which my father had given her for Christmas. The picture is now in one of many boxes in my basement at Ole Miss containing the paraphernalia of one's past, and it is of me when I was a child Maud's age, sprawled in the summer's grass in front of the angel. I came across it not too long ago, faded and yellowing at the edges, and it brought back for me the dew of that late summer's day and the crickets chirping from the bayou beyond. Was that forty-five years ago? One faraway afternoon in the rain my young friends and I paused here and saw raindrops like tears dripping from the angel's eyes. "Look!" one of them said. "She's alive! Why is she so sad?" All around me now are the familiar grey tombstones of that childhood time, receding in every direction in the diaphanous mist, and I lean down and touch the angel's wings to remind myself I am the little boy who was there.

I have brought with me a half-dozen red roses, which I bought in the store just off the Oxford Square at closing time on Christmas Eve: "For your girlfriend?" the clerk had asked in a whiskey breath. "No," I replied. "I think for the dead." "Well," he said, "they can use them too." Now I put one of the roses on the grave beneath the angel. I hoped Santa Claus had once been good to Maud.

The new section is straight up the hill, separated from the old by a deep, precipitous ravine, as if a tortuous no-man's land was chosen to divide the two irrevocably, a chasm at once tangible and peremptory between the generations. They began using this vast green hill when I was a boy, and it is almost filled now, the stones stretching away as far as the eye could see. Where will they go from here?

My mother and father are here, under identical stones next to a treacherous side road. Much of a nearby slope has been eroded by the rains, and this adjacent terrain is heavy with desolation and ruin. I walk toward them among the graves of those their age I knew, some of them decorated with holiday flowers—the parents of my contemporaries, the American Legionnaires who sponsored our baseball teams, the grammar school teachers of my day. The whole hill is populated with people I once knew. I try hard to summon their faces. I pause before my parents, thinking of them when I was a child, when they were younger—so hard to conceive—than I am now. On each grave I place a rose, loathing to leave them here on this cheerless morning of the Yuletide.

Then I get into the car, driving down the hill past the untouched woods where I once played echo to the Taps for the military funerals of the Korean dead, and on into town.

The streets on the Delta side are preternaturally quiet. Earlier the children had been playing outdoors with their new toys, but it has begun to rain, a cold, impenetrable rain that has driven them inside. Christmas lights glitter in the gloom.

And here, on Grand Avenue, is the house—*my* house. I park surreptitiously across the street to take a look. I do not even know who lives in it now. But I knew every inch of the house; my sweetest dreams and bleakest nightmares are filled with it. It exists in my deepest blood. At this very hour four decades ago we would have been getting ready to go to Jackson.

There are no cars in the driveway, and no lights in the house. I make a U-turn, stop in front, and gaze about me. There are sounds of activity in the Graeber and Norquist and North houses along the street, but not a soul is in sight. I take another rose and get out of the car.

I look into the windows. The parlor seems empty and bereft without my mother's baby grand. My father's easy chair and his short-wave radio are gone from the side room, filled now with alien furniture. There are no college pennants on the walls of my own room, no battered oak desk, no Corona portable typewriter. The back yard where I had my basketball goal, the grass around it forever dead from our strenuous footfalls, is strangely neat and manicured. Do no boys live in this house?

It is my heart which tells me where Old Skip is. There is no stone, but no one need show me the patch of earth at the edge of the porch where we wrapped him in my baseball jacket and laid him into the ground. I stand over him in the misty rain. A rose too for the mischievous, affectionate comrade of my boyhood. The residents of our house will return to find it lying incongruously in the winter grass and wonder what interloper might have been here.

I will not be late for the rendezvous in Jackson. I drive up Broadway Hill past the houses which still go by their family names, to the intersection of 49E and W, south through Little Yazoo, Bentonia, Flora, Pocahontas. The road is four-lane now and skirts the little villages, but the countryside is unchanged— the seared kudzu on the tossing hills, the rolling plains beyond the Big Black River, the deep-green pastureland bordering the dark woods. And then Jackson, larger, more sprawling and *metropolitan* than any of us ever dreamed or feared it might become.

I retrace the Christmas journey—down Woodrow Wilson, right on North State past Millsaps, left on Fortification to Jefferson, a whole neighborhood ripped raw of the old places, the service stations and convenience stores mocking me in strict impunity.

My grandparents' house is no longer there, long since a parking lot for the Jitney Jungle across the street. The magnolia is still in front, but where the house was is grim, bare asphalt, cold and wet now from the rain. A stone ledge along the side still remains. It once formed a secret pathway with the house, and I would hide there in the verdant shadows. Just north of the ledge, where Mrs. Dixon's house once stood, they are now building what seems to be a high-rise.

Mamie and Percy, Maggie and Susie would be greeting us now, just beyond the magnolia where the front porch was. I close my eyes and hear their happy welcomes. Old Skip has raced beneath their feet into the house in search of turkey livers, and my great-aunts follow in their flowing black dresses.

I stand alone in the parking lot where the parlor was. I feel the ripple of the lost voices. I drift back into the kitchen. Get away from the oven, Skip! Time as one ages is a continuum. Past and present consume themselves into the ashes. Am I Emily, brought back from the grave in *Our Town*? "I can't bear it," she is reminding me. "Why did they ever have to get old? Mama, I'm here. I'm grown up."

There is no good place for the last two roses. I put them on the asphalt where the dining room table was. Tomorrow someone will run over them in the parking lot. But who would disturb them today?

Contributors

MARION BARNWELL, a resident of Jackson, grew up in Indianola, Mississippi. She received a B.A. degree from Newcomb College of Tulane University and a master's degree from Mississippi State University. She is an assistant professor of English at Delta State University, where she is an editor for *Tapestry*, a literary faculty journal. She is also editor, publisher, and contributor to a collection of short stories entitled *On the Way Home*, published in 1996 by Ruby Shoes Press. In 1997, her collection *A Place Called Mississippi* was published by University Press of Mississippi. Currently, she is working on a literary tour guide to Mississippi with Patti Carr Black, to be published by University Press of Mississippi.

JERRY L. BUSTIN, a graduate of Mississippi College and Jackson School of Law, has practiced law for thirty-two years and has served as municipal judge for the city of Forest, Mississippi, for twenty-eight years. He has published poetry in various anthologies and has won writing awards from the Mississippi Writers Association, the Gum Tree Festival, and Gulf Coast Writers. In 1996, Bustin submitted his fiction to Emerson College in Boston, Massachusetts, and won the privilege of attending a two-week course taught in the Netherlands at Castile Wells where John Updike was guest lecturer.

EDWARD COHEN, who grew up in Jackson, Mississippi, is a writer and filmmaker living in Venice, California. His documentaries for PBS have received numerous international film festival awards. His memoir, *The Peddler's Grandson: Growing Up Jewish in Mississippi,* won both the Mississippi Institute of Arts and Letters Award and the Mississippi Library Association Award for best nonfiction of 2000.

WILLIAM FAULKNER was born in 1897 in New Albany, Mississippi. He attended the University of Mississippi, lived briefly in Paris in 1925, and six years later settled in Oxford, Mississippi, where he lived for the rest of his life. In 1950, he was awarded the

Nobel Prize for literature. He is considered one of the greatest American writers of the twentieth century. Faulkner died in 1962.

ELLEN GILCHRIST, a native of Vicksburg, Mississippi, and a graduate of Millsaps College, has published poetry, short stories, novels, and journals. Her second volume of short stories, *Victory Over Japan*, won the National Book Award in 1984. Other awards include Mississippi Arts Festival poetry award, New York Quarterly award for poetry, National Endowment for the Arts grant, *Prairie Schooner* award, Mississippi Academy award, Saxifrage Award, American Book Award, University of Arkansas Fulbright Award, and a Mississippi Institute of Arts and Letters award for literature. Her most recent work is *The Cabal and Other Stories*. Gilchrist currently lives in Fayetteville, Arkansas and Ocean Springs, Mississippi.

CHRIS GILMER was born in Forest, Mississippi, and earned a Ph.D. in English with emphasis in creative writing from the University of Southern Mississippi's Center for Writers. He is a member of the faculty at Tougaloo College in Jackson, Mississippi, where he also serves as acting chairman of the Department of English. Dr. Gilmer has served as principal editor for a series of children's books and as principal author of one volume. He is also a published journalist and poet.

CAROLYN HAINES, a native of Lucedale, Mississippi, is currently finishing a three-book contract with Bantam for a mystery series set in the Mississippi Delta. *Them Bones* was published in 1999, *Buried Bones* in 2000, and *Splintered Bones* (working title) will be published in 2001. She is the author of *Touched* and *Summer of the Redeemers*, also set in Mississippi.

BARRY HANNAH was born in Meridian, Mississippi, and grew up in Clinton. He earned a Bachelor of Arts from Mississippi College, and a Master of Arts and Master of Fine Arts in Creative Writing from the University of Arkansas. Hannah has taught creative writing at numerous colleges and universities and is currently writer-in-residence at the University of Mississippi. He has been the recipient of the Bellamann Award for Creative Writing, the Arnold Gingrich Award in short fiction, a special award for literature from the American Institute of Arts and Letters, and a Guggenheim Fellowship. He has also served as judge for the Nelson Algren Award and the American Book Award. Hannah's works have been nominated for both the National Book Award (*Geronimo Rex*, 1972) and the Pulitzer Prize (*High Lonesome*, 1996).

NANCY ISONHOOD, a native of Duck Hill and currently a resident of Canton, Mississippi, served as Madison County judge for fifteen years, and vice president of the Mississippi Justice Court Association for three years.

CAROLINE LANGSTON, a native of Yazoo City, has had stories anthologized in the 1997 Pushcart Prize XXI volume, and in *New Stories from the South: The Year's Best 1995*. She has published fiction and essays in several journals, including *Ploughshares, The Oxford American, Mars Hill Review, The Women's Review of Books,* and *Arts and Letters*. She is currently a development assistant at National Public Radio in Washington, D.C.

CHARLINE R. MCCORD, a resident of Clinton, Mississippi, was born in Hattiesburg and grew up in Laurel, Mississippi, and Jackson, Tennessee. She holds a B.A. and an M.A. in English from Mississippi College, where she won the Bellamann Award for Creative Writing and edited the literary magazine. She is completing doctoral work at the University of Southern Mississippi on contemporary Southern women writers. McCord is Vice-President of Publishing for DREAM, Inc., and a part-time instructor of English at Mississippi College. She has published poetry, short fiction, interviews, book reviews, and feature articles.

WILLIE MORRIS, a native of Yazoo City, Mississippi, graduated from the University of Texas and studied at Oxford University as a Rhodes Scholar. He was editor of *The Texas Observer*, and served as editor-in-chief of *Harper's Magazine* from 1967 to 1971. He authored sixteen books, including *The Courtship of Marcus Dupree*, winner of the Christopher Medal, and *North Toward Home*, winner of the Houghton Mifflin Literary Fellowship. Morris died in August, 1999.

ELIZABETH SPENCER, acknowledged as one of America's outstanding writers of fiction, was born in Carrollton, Mississippi, and graduated from Belhaven College and Vanderbilt University. She received O. Henry Awards in 1960 and 1966, the Rosenthal Award of the National Institute of Arts and Letters, and the *Kenyon Review* Fiction Fellowship.

CLIFTON L. TAULBERT was born in Glen Allan, Mississippi, grew up in the Mississippi Delta, and graduated valedictorian of O'Bannon High School in Greenville. He is a nationally acclaimed speaker, writer, and businessman. In 1996, his memoir *When We Were Colored* was made into the film *Once Upon A Time When We Were Colored* by BET Pictures. Taulbert holds a B.A. degree from Oral Roberts University and a graduate degree from the Southwest Graduate School of Banking at Southern Methodist University. His sequel memoir, *The Last Train North*, won the Mississippi Library Association Award. He is president of the Freemount Marketing Company in Tulsa, Oklahoma, where he also serves on numerous civic boards.

JUDY H. TUCKER, a native of Hopoca in Leake County, Mississippi, is a sixth-generation Mississippian. A freelance writer, she researched and wrote the texts for Wyatt Waters' best-selling books *Another Coat of Paint* and *Painting Home*. Her one-act play "The Brooch" was produced at Late Nite at New Stage Theater in Jackson.

WYATT WATERS was born in Wesson, Mississippi, grew up in Florence, and moved to Clinton in the tenth grade. He holds both a B.A. and an M.A. in Art from Mississippi College, where he won the Bellamann Award for Art and Creative Writing. Waters frequently teaches art classes in the Jackson area, has had solo shows at the Mississippi Museum of Art and the Lauren Rogers Museum of Art in Laurel, has published two books of his paintings (*Another Coat of Paint* and *Painting Home*), and was commissioned to do commemorative posters for Jackson's *Jubilee Jam* and Washington, D.C.'s *Mississippi on the Mall*. His work has been featured in numerous magazine articles including *American Artists Special Watercolor Issues, Art and Antiques,* and *Mississippi Magazine*. wyattwaters.com

EUDORA WELTY was born in 1909 in Jackson, Mississippi. She attended Mississippi State College for Women, graduated from the University of Wisconsin, and went on to attend Columbia University Graduate School of Business. Her many honors include the Pulitzer Prize (*The Optimist's Daughter*), the American Book Award for fiction, the Gold Medal for the Novel given by the American Academy and Institute of Arts and Letters for her entire work in fiction, and the French Legion of Honor medal. Welty died in July 2001.

JACQUELINE WHEELOCK, born and reared on the Mississippi Gulf Coast, received the Bachelor of Science and Master of Education degrees in English from Southern University in Baton Rouge and a master's degree in library science from the University of Southern Mississippi. After teaching for twenty-five years, she retired to pursue a career in writing. In October 2000, she received the Zora Neale Hurston/Bessie Head Fiction Award, presented in conjunction with the Tenth Annual Gwendolyn Brooks Writers' Conference at Chicago State University. She and husband Donald are residents of Madison, Mississippi.